MURDER IN BEL-AIR

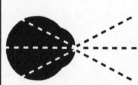

This Large Print Book carries the
Seal of Approval of N.A.V.H.

Murder in Bel-Air

Cara Black

THORNDIKE PRESS
A part of Gale, a Cengage Company

Farmington Hills, Mich • San Francisco • New York • Waterville, Maine
Meriden, Conn • Mason, Ohio • Chicago

LIBRARY OF CONGRESS CIP DATA ON FILE.
CATALOGUING IN PUBLICATION FOR THIS BOOK
IS AVAILABLE FROM THE LIBRARY OF CONGRESS

ISBN-13: 978-1-4328-6549-8 (hardcover alk. paper)

Published in 2019 by arrangement with Soho Press, Inc.

Printed in Mexico
1 2 3 4 5 6 7 23 22 21 20 19

In memory of Laurence Peltier,
who loved Côte d'Ivoire;
for Roy; and for the ghosts

Two hippopotamuses cannot share the same hole.

— a proverb from the Côte d'Ivoire

To live well is to live hidden.

— French saying

Dear Reader,

It's been twenty years — hard to believe, *non?* — since Aimée Leduc, my half-American, half-French private detective with a penchant for bad boys, scootered her Vespa onto the page. Aimée lives in vintage haute couture in her apartment on the Île Saint-Louis in Paris, a place I know well and certainly wouldn't mind living one day. *Murder in Bel-Air* is a twenty-year birthday of sorts, though between *Murder in the Marais* and this, Aimée's nineteenth foray, only six years have passed in her life.

Murder in Bel-Air takes place in 1999. Aimée's mother, Sydney Leduc — an American and former terrorist on Interpol's most wanted list — never makes it easy for Aimée. Is Sydney still a CIA operative with one foot in the shadow world, though she denies it? Why has she disappeared from her granddaughter, Chloé's, posh tot playgroup in its quiet *quartier* of Paris? How might this tie in with an impending coup d'état in Africa's Côte d'Ivoire in Africa, as it appears to, and why does Aimée feel compelled to find the mother who abandoned her when she was only eight years old?

This story was inspired by many — my friend Laurence, a French journalist who lived in the Côte d'Ivoire, Madame Gerbault, who lives in the Bel-Air quartier and always takes me to her favourite *fromagerie,* and finally, my own mother, though I worry that readers might presume Sydney Leduc is based on her. My mother would be shocked at the thought. Turn in her grave.

When I was growing up, my mother always told us stories about her own childhood in Chicago; about her best friend; about Mrs. Potowski, the baker's wife next door; about my grandmother's first boyfriend, a married man. I grew up hearing about every person on my mother's block on the south side of Chicago. I loved that I knew her neighbors in such an intimate way, and this was how I came to cherish a good story.

My mother raised four children and three generations of dogs, and stayed at home until my father lost his job and she became the breadwinner, running an employment agency. They were married more than fifty years, during which they went through so many ups and downs, addictions, the loss of a child, and yet they carried on.

My mother loved gruesome forensic TV shows. She always said, in her mild-mannered way, that if life had turned out differently, she would have gotten a job at a morgue or medical examiner's office because the work there was like a puzzle. Piecing together the empirical evidence. She loved puzzles and was an acute observer of little details. Once, after we'd met a wealthy businessman, she asked me, "Did you notice the hole in his shoe?" She always came out with these little takes, indirectly teaching me to observe, to listen and look for stories.

Aimée's mother does share a few characteristics with my own: low-maintenance but resilient, with a wicked sense of humor, always doing what needs to be done. My mother told all her children to look inside ourselves for answers. To "dress to the nines," no matter the occasion, and for the girls, to never reveal our age, because women don't. She was so French in that way. Twice, she visited Paris. She loved it so much. I wish I'd been able to go there with her.

I remember when I published my first

book and was terrified to speak about it in front of people. They would know I wasn't French; would they doubt the authenticity of my novel? My love for Paris? My mother waved aside these fears with a single piece of advice: *Be yourself.* That's all you can be.

Murder in Bel-Air is fiction, though anchored around real events. I borrowed a few of my mother's acute observational skills, but the novel isn't about her. Or perhaps it's all about her, since without her influence, her stories, the way she looked at the world, I may not have written this or anything else at all.

Cara Black, 2019

Paris · Late October 1999 · Monday, Midafternoon

The young woman stumbled on the cobblestones in her worn shoes, fist in her pocket, clutching the steak knife she'd nicked from the café. She'd felt eyes watching — fear had charged up her back, impossible to ignore. Her gut had screamed at her to get out of there.

Now.

Why hadn't her contact showed?

A car engine revved up, gears scraping. She glanced back and saw a black Renault slide onto Boulevard de Picpus. Her heart pounded.

Walk faster. Keep going. Past the boule players and around the bandstand. The sky was oyster grey. She could make it to the Métro station at Picpus.

At École Saint Michel, parents and small children waiting for school dismissal clogged her path until they took in her homeless appearance, which made them scatter. The

13

swollen clouds opened in a downpour.

She heard the car's clutch grind.

She broke into a run, lungs heaving, shoelaces flying. Turned the corner onto Avenue de Saint-Mandé. She could hear the car gaining on her. Any moment it could jump the median, ram her against the stone wall. Dripping wet, she sprinted toward the Métro steps ahead of her. She could make it. Get the documents to the only person she trusted and prevent a disaster.

A car door slammed. Footsteps slapped the wet pavement behind her. What if she got stuck on a platform — caught in the Métro? She reconsidered.

The double-grilled gate to a nearby building's courtyard was standing open as a car pulled out. In the pelting rain, she ducked inside, ran through the courtyard, scrambling past the parked cars and through an open portion in the fence to the empty adjoining lot, which was being paved. Its old gate opened onto a convent's grounds.

She skidded on the wet grass, perspiring in her oversized jacket, and ran along the stone wall. Past the cemetery, through the brown wood door to the tree-lined convent grounds. No one would find her there, at the Petites Soeurs des Pauvres homeless shelter. Through the grey haze of rain and

14

the branches of the fig trees, she could make out the white habit of the intake nun.

And then she was caught from behind. She gripped the steak knife in her pocket and whirled around — she recognized the man. "Don't touch me —"

"Running your mouth, *salope*?"

She struggled as he pushed her against the wall. Kicked at him desperately.

"Where's the — ?"

She tried to scream, but he covered her mouth with his hand. His sour breath in her face. She fought to aim the knife at him.

But he caught her fist in a grip like an iron vise and twisted, turning her own force against her. *Trained reflexes,* she thought — her last thought, as the steak knife plunged into her neck so deeply it hit the wall behind her. Blood pumped out of her carotid artery, staining the raindrops on the rhododendron blossoms. Her eyes glazed and the grey went black.

Paris · Late October 1999 ·
Monday, Midafternoon

Aimée Leduc smoothed down her little black Chanel dress in the dining room of le Train Bleu, the belle-epoque resto above the Gare de Lyon. In need of courage, she reached for a champagne flute of Kir Royal. All of a sudden, the faces around her blurred, and the room spun. She gripped the tablecloth, bunched it in her fists, and closed her eyes. Took a deep breath. Then another. The dizziness passed, quickly as it had come.

She could do this.

Determined, Aimée found her balance in her reheeled Louboutin ankle boots. Managed a wide smile and mounted the stage, heading toward the speaker's podium, where the host was waiting to introduce her. This tech conference, whose attendees were select and mostly men, had invited her to give the keynote address. An honor and a challenge on her first week back at work after a concussion that had kept her on bed rest for a month. But she'd recovered, hadn't she?

She eyed the players — the CEOs hungry for an edge in the world of *la start-up.* She had a mission: to network and pull in new clients for Leduc Detective's computer security services. Already, she felt the sweet tingle of new contracts. She'd thought up a great hook for her speech and was braced for industrial flirting over *apéros.* All week she'd rehearsed her speech, the talking points, memorized each pause for emphasis.

Now she nodded as she was introduced. She caught the glare of her rival in the audience. Marc Fabre, the tech entrepreneur with a shaved head that glinted in the chandelier's light — he'd tried to lock down this keynote for himself, she knew.

As she waited for the host to summon her to the podium, Aimée grew aware of a disturbance. She watched as a man rushed out to whisper in the host's ear and shot Aimée a look before crossing the platform to her.

"Your phone's off," the man said.

Mais bien sûr, she'd muted it for the presentation.

"There's an emergency — it's your daughter's playgroup. They've been trying to reach

17

you, so they called the restaurant."

Her heart dropped. "Has something happened to Chloé?"

"I don't know. You need to pick up your daughter. Immediately."

She felt a jolt of panic. "Was there an accident?"

"I don't know. Apparently, your mother was nowhere to be found."

Of all times. The playgroup was so far away, in Square Courteline — Sydney had insisted on it; Aimée had no idea why. But where was her mother? And who could she call to pick Chloé up? Her nanny, a university student, was in class; all her other go-tos were at work.

Whatever was going on, it had to be an emergency for them to have tracked her down at this conference.

She felt like a helpless child. She needed to maintain her composure. She tried not to let her feelings show — her fear and anger and the sinking in her stomach.

Marc Fabre stood and approached the podium, his face radiating concern. "Don't worry, Aimée. I'll pinch-hit for you." Of course he would. He tried to mask the delight in his eyes. "I hope everything's okay."

With her mother? Never. What stunt was

18

she pulling now?

With hurried excuses, Aimée grabbed her bag and the disk with the now-useless PowerPoint presentation she'd prepared. She scurried out of the restaurant, past the gilt arches and murals framed by pastry-like moldings. All those hours of work and rehearsal down the drain.

She tried her mother's phone. No answer. Voice-mail box was full.

Sydney Leduc, Aimée's American mother, a woman on Interpol's most-wanted list, always had an excuse for disrupting Aimée's life. But involving Chloé was another matter. Aimée was so angry she wanted to scream.

Her mother had enthused about this fancy playgroup, a mom and tot "art enrichment" experience. She'd insisted on signing Chloé up for it. And now she'd left her granddaughter alone with a bunch of strangers at a playgroup out in Bel-Air?

Worry creased Aimée's brow as she ran down the stairs and across the lobby by the train platforms. Passengers clustered, the departure and arrival board clicked above her, and the odd pigeon cooed from the art nouveau metal pillars supporting the glass ceiling.

Thank God only one person stood ahead

19

of her in the taxi line in front of the station. A first. She kept punching in her mother's number. Again it went to a recorded message: "This mailbox is full."

Sydney hadn't even left Aimée a message. She flipped hurriedly through her Moleskine, looking for the number of the center that ran the playgroup. Hadn't she written it down?

Rain pattered on the taxi's windshield as it sped alongside the *viaduc,* the old train line. Its planted walkway, the Promenade Plantée, crowned the rose brick arches, inside each of which nestled an artisanal gallery of one of the quartier's master craftsmen — a woodworker, a gilder, an upholsterer. If only the playgroup weren't so far. Who came all the way out to Bel-Air in the twelfth arrondissement except to visit the zoo and Bois de Vincennes? Well, René, her business partner, did sometimes visit the computer shops around Montgallet.

Aimée searched her trench coat pocket for her Nicorette gum. Popped a piece in her mouth. She didn't miss smoking. Not at all, hadn't craved a cigarette once in the thirty-one days and ten hours since she'd quit. Again.

The playgroup's main number went to voice mail, and she left a message. Her mind was racing.

Why had she trusted her mother? The woman had reappeared in her life out of the blue, as usual, with a determination to know her granddaughter. Sydney had taken advantage of Aimée's condition — bedridden for a month while she waited for the blood clot from her concussion to dissolve — to shoehorn herself into Aimée and Chloé's life. As if Sydney could forge some sort of relationship with Aimée after all these years. It had been a bumpy ride so far.

Could she say she even knew this woman? Her mother was a foreign presence with an American accent and all her secrets. All through her childhood, Aimée'd yearned for her mother, and now, as the proverb went, she realized she should've been careful what she wished for.

The taxi passed the *commissariat,* a modern behemoth whose architecture gave an incongruous nod to the past with its sculptured caryatids. Beyond were Haussmann buildings overlooking nonphotogenic rail lines. After the roundabout at Place Félix Eboué with the lion fountain Chloé loved, it was just another block to Boulevard de Picpus, which took the taxi through the quartier Bel-Air toward Square Courteline. Near the old bandstand and sandy *boules*

21

pit, she spotted the playgroup's shop front. The usual marmalade-striped cat sat in the blue-curtained window.

The rain halted. Clouds broke and sunlight slanted down over the puddles, peacock hued from car oil. Drops glistened from the red café awning next door. Aimée overtipped the young taxi driver, *comme toujours,* for late-night taxi karma, and stepped onto the slick pavement.

Chloé, her almost toddler, pounded clay with her chubby fists. She beamed when she saw her mother, and Aimée's heart warmed. That precious rosy-cheeked bundle was almost one year old.

"Bonjour, ma puce." Aimée swooped Chloé up, clayey hands and all. Kissed her warm pink cheeks and inhaled her baby scent.

The teacher, in a clay-smeared smock, took in Aimée's little black dress. Vuitton bag. Gave a strained smile. "We're a parent participation program, *mademoiselle.* Children can't be left here without an adult."

"Excusez-moi. I just got the message, but it wasn't clear . . . Did my mother have an accident?"

"Not here, *certainement.* Pouf, she was gone, just like that," the teacher said. "We have rules. This is not a day care. *C'est fini, mademoiselle.*"

Great. Aimée's mother had just gotten Chloé kicked out of playgroup.

At the café next door, Aimée ordered *un lait chaud* for Chloé's bottle and, for herself, *an expresso double.* Checked the conference schedule, wondering how she could salvage some *apéritif* networking time.

"So, *ma puce,* how's *Maman* going to get her job done and butter our baguette if your *grand-mère* flakes out?"

Chloé puffed her cheeks.

"That's what I thought," Aimée said.

The white-aproned, pencil-mustached man with an equally thin frame served them at a marble table by the window. *"Ah, mais ma petite,* where's your *grand-mère?"*

Good question. Aimée wanted to know, too.

"Malheureusement, my mother's not answering her phone," she said.

"Mais si charmante," he said, "now I've met three generations. All I can say is, good genes."

She smiled in spite of her anger. "Do you remember seeing my mother today?"

"Non, c'est bizarre. After playgroup she meets her friend here; they always *prennent un café. La petite* here always takes a —"

23

"Friend?" Aimée's antennae went up.

"Ben ouais," said the waiter as he wiped the tabletop, lapsing into slangy colloquialism. "The homeless woman from the shelter at the convent. So generous, eh, your mother, helping her out. *Une bonne paroissienne* in action."

Aimée's jaw dropped. "How do you mean, *monsieur?*"

The waiter leaned lower, exposing a gold cross on a chain below his collar. "She buys her a *café,* treats her like an equal. *Et alors,* those Sisters of the Poor appreciate volunteers like your mother. The nuns are always trying to involve the community in the soup kitchen."

Sydney Leduc, a former rogue CIA operative who had been imprisoned for radicalism — now a do-gooder? Aimée's mother had depths she hadn't known about.

Or had Chloé's entire playgroup attendance been a front?

"Ah, you didn't know?" said the waiter, noticing Aimée's shock.

"My mother" — it still felt odd to use those words — "keeps things close to her chest."

"The good ones do," he said, and crossed himself. A real Holy Roller, this waiter.

Time to get Chloé home. She glanced at

24

the clock. Too late for conference *apéritif* hour.

As Aimée felt Chloé's diaper — still dry — she grew aware of a knot of people gathering on the pavement in front of the café. Excited voices were raised: "But it's her." "Wore that same dirty blue . . ." "You know her, Jacques."

Aimée ignored the hubbub and settled Chloé in her stroller, looped the Armani baby bag over the handle. Forget a taxi. The sun shone; pigeons hopped in the puddles. They'd walk to the Métro.

The cashier was deep in a conversation with a young woman wearing an apron tied over her skirt. Her face was red, her eyes tear swollen.

"Knifed," she said, her voice trembling. "Right in the convent garden."

The cashier dropped a roll of franc coins. They pinged and danced on the zinc counter. "You saw her, Louise?"

"I wish I hadn't."

A nervous tingle went up Aimée's spine. *Mon Dieu.* It couldn't be . . . her mother? She set the brake on Chloé's stroller. "Who are you talking about?"

"Calme-toi, Louise." The waiter, Jacques, had put his arm around the young woman. Looked at Aimée. *"C'est la pauvresse,* that

friend of your mother, the homeless one."

Aimée blinked. "But I don't understand. Is my mother there?"

Louise wiped her eyes with the back of her hand. "I know who you mean. Served her the other day. Didn't see her."

Sydney Leduc had done her disappearing act, and now her "friend" was dead — could it be a coincidence?

Out on the street, Aimée dialed her mother yet again. No answer. On Avenue de Saint-Mandé, she pushed the stroller past the police cars and made her way toward the Picpus Métro. Chloé had fallen asleep with her bottle in her hands.

Nuns in white habits clustered at the double-doored carriage entrance of a Haussmannian building, its balconies spilling with red geraniums. The sisters folded their hands in prayer as a gurney clattered over uneven pavers. Aimée's throat caught. With a jerk, the gurney wheels stuck in a crack; the mound of a body under the foil blanket shuddered.

Aimée's gaze caught something falling from the gurney onto the pavement. A worn, mud-spattered tennis shoe with untied laces. Sticking out from under the blanket was a bare foot, its red-lacquered pedicured toes glinting in the sun. A nun made the sign of the cross, then quickly covered the exposed foot with the foil blanket.

"*Attention.* Move along, *s'il vous plaît,*" said the medic.

Instead of moving, Aimée caught the nun's eye. As discreetly as possible, she motioned to the nun. "Sister, I think my mother knew her, that poor woman . . ."

"Tragic."

"Can we talk, please?"

Aimée read hesitation in the nun's eyes. Suspicion? Fear?

"My duties can't wait. I'm sorry," the nun said.

The ambulance doors clanged shut. Church bells sounded.

Chloé's stuffed rabbit fell to the pavement. Aimée scooped up the rabbit and dried its tail off. By the time she looked up again, the nuns were heading toward a gate in the wall, beyond which Aimée saw grass and a garden. The convent. She couldn't let the nun get away.

Aimée reached out to catch the woman's sleeve. "Sister, I'm worried. My mother abandoned my daughter at her playgroup," said Aimée. "Just around the corner. Now she isn't answering her phone."

"I'm sorry, *mademoiselle;* I don't understand what that has to do with —"

"Well, normally she'd meet this homeless woman —"

"We prefer SDF, *sans domicile fixe.*"

"*Bien sûr.* But the waiter next door just told me they usually met for coffee at this exact time. Now my mother is missing, and that poor woman is dead. I hope it's just a terrible coincidence, but . . ."

The nun glanced behind her. One of the sisters was closing the gate.

"Please, Sister," said Aimée. "I'm worried something's happened to my mother. Do you know anything about where she might be?"

The nun glanced at her watch. "Come back later. Help serve."

A flyer for *soupe populaire,* served by *bénévoles,* an early-evening soup kitchen service, was thrust in Aimée's hands, and the sister disappeared behind the gate.

Volunteering at a soup kitchen — had Sydney ever been involved in this kind of charity work? Aimée didn't know the first thing about her mother, but if Sydney had been helping out, had it really just been out of charitable motivations?

Forget the Métro. Aimée hailed a taxi.

MONDAY, LATE AFTERNOON

"I thought you were giving a speech," said Babette, Chloé's nanny.

"So did I," Aimée said, setting Chloé in the kitchen high chair next to Gabrielle, the baby whose family lived across the courtyard — tawny haired like Chloé, but a month younger.

Aimée kicked off her ankle boots, glancing out the window at the quai, speckled with the light of a fading blood-orange sunset. The bubbling pot of something wonderful-smelling helped drive away thoughts of the approaching autumn darkness.

"Heard from Sydney?" Aimée asked.

A shake of Babette's ponytail.

"Makes two of us. I'm worried."

Aimée filled Babette in while she spooned *haricots verts* into Gabrielle's mouth. Aimée split childcare expenses with Gabrielle's parents, but it was sometimes Gabrielle's

29

uncle Benoît who came to pick her up. He taught at the Sorbonne and called his infrequent nights with Aimée as much of a relationship he'd ever had. A month had passed since she'd last seen him.

Benoît was great in the kitchen and under the duvet. And convenient — when he was around. Thinking of him, she felt a stab of guilt. Was she too lazy to move on? Or to be honest with him?

"Leaving Chloé! That's not like Sydney," Babette said. "Or is it?"

Back to her old tricks? Aimée had fallen for them again. Trusted her. Anger and worry were at war in her mind. Nothing involving Sydney Leduc was ever simple.

Aimée changed into black denims, red high-tops, an old cashmere Jean Paul Gaultier sweater, and her black leather jacket. Suitable soup-kitchen attire, she hoped. Packed her mini tool set in her makeup kit and an extra scarf.

"Going out?" Babette asked.

Aimée nodded. "Feeding the hungry. Can you put Chloé to bed if I'm not home after bath time?"

"Pas de problème."

"And call me if you hear from Sydney."

Babette nodded. "If I don't give her a piece of my mind first."

Aimée hugged Chloé, who was absorbed in smearing her *haricots verts* onto the table, and kissed both girls *bonne nuit.*

An unseasonably mild October evening suffused her building's courtyard. The rain had freshened the air, which held a lingering warmth. Sitting on her scooter under the pear tree branches, Aimée applied Chanel red, double knotted her scarf, pulled on her helmet, and zipped up her leather jacket. Turning the key, she revved up the engine, maneuvered the wheels over the cobbles and out the massive open double doors. She gunned down the tree-lined quai over the fallen leaves toward Pont Marie and sped into the night.

Aimée parked her scooter by the modernistic building of the National Forests Office. According to the soup kitchen flyer, Petites Soeurs des Pauvres ran a soup kitchen, a shelter, and student lodging, as well as maintaining herb and medicinal gardens. She skimmed the rest of the history and the request for donations for their continued work.

The usual.

Once through the open convent door, she searched for a directory, only to find a list on the mailboxes: Foyer Picpus, Maison Saint Augustin, Communauté Pierre Coudrin Pères des Sacrés-Coeurs, Soeurs de l'Enfant Jésus, Religieuses du Sacré-Coeur de l'Adoration. They all fit in this space?

Finally she spotted a line of people snaking from another wing of the convent and followed arrows for *"la soupe."* Instinctively scanned for her mother. Foolish — why would she be standing in line at a soup kitchen?

She wasn't there, of course.

The nineteenth-century building, one of several on the grounds, was a redbrick hulk at the very center of the convent's walled-off greenery, like the core of an apple. Scents of wet foliage and damp earth wafted through the garden. Deep bells rang from the nearby chapel Notre-Dame de Paix de Picpus, echoed by the croak of a bullfrog. Beyond, signs said, lay the Picpus Cemetery.

Inside the soup-kitchen area, bright lights illuminated the cart where nuns and volunteers ladled out soup and distributed chunks of baguette. Steam rose in the night air. Women and men, young and old, shuffled from foot to foot in line. Some were well dressed, people who had clearly fallen on hard times; some smelled not so fragrant. There was little conversation.

"I'm here to volunteer," Aimée said to the tall nun who seemed to be in charge. She looked around for the nun she'd spoken to earlier. She needed to get the woman alone to ask her what she knew about Sydney. Aimée described her to the one in charge.

"Sister Agnès," the tall nun said.

"She wanted to explain the duties to me."

"*Désolée*, she's busy."

Great. "But she told me it's important to understand the mission."

"No rocket science here. Talk to her later. We're full up with volunteers tonight anyway."

True. But she'd come all this way. Made Babette stay late.

Aimée glanced at her Tintin watch. Almost two hours had passed since her mother had disappeared. An hour and a half since she'd seen a woman's body wheeled into the morgue van. She needed at least a hint as to her mother's whereabouts.

"*S'il vous plaît,* I'm here," Aimée said. "Please let me help."

"Fine. Grab an apron in the kitchen. You can chop vegetables."

In the cellar-like stone kitchen, she took an apron from the hook. The warm, vaulted room felt medieval; she imagined hungry peasants storming a castle if not fed. A small nun with thick-lensed glasses stirred a pot at the large warm AGA stove.

"Sister Agnès said to find her here," Aimée said.

"*Vraiment?*" asked the small nun. "She's busy with the officials."

About the murder? Was she at the crime scene? Aimée had to find her.

"Let me get that," Aimée said as the little

34

nun struggled with a bulging burlap sack of potatoes.

"Merci." The nun wiped her brow under her wimple. "It goes in the back pantry."

Damn heavy, too.

After dumping the potatoes, Aimée ducked into the corridor and followed it around to an outdoor courtyard. A fuzzed greenish light filtered through the trees. There were a few cars, and a crime-scene tech in white overalls stood by a police van door. He walked as he spoke on a cell phone he held between his neck and shoulder as he wound up a roll of yellow crime-scene tape. "Crime scene in Bel-Air. I'm picking up my kit . . ."

Keeping to the tree shadows and treading on the grass instead of the gravel path, Aimée followed him at a distance as he continued his conversation. The long expanse of green stretched half a block at least, past fruit trees, a statue of Christ, an old outbuilding that looked like a washhouse. Pinpricks of light flickered like fireflies through the trees on her left. The place felt like a maze in the near darkness. She tried to orient herself, to place where she was in relation to the gate the nuns had disappeared through — the gate the body had come out of.

Hard to tell.

The crime-scene tech's bootie-clad feet crunched on the gravel path. All of a sudden, from behind the trees appeared a nineteenth-century building that reminded her of a small country house. Maybe once it had been.

The tech tapped his knuckles on a lit ground-floor window. His reflected face was distorted by the bubbled old glass. The window creaked open.

"We're finished, sir," he said.

A moment later, two people emerged from a wooden door.

Aimée recognized the nun, Sister Agnès, who was clutching a pink Tati shopping bag and speaking to a man in a dark suit. Aimée hunched down under the nearest hedgerow and crept closer to hear.

"Her things," Sister Agnès said. "I thought she would have had more, as I said, but I don't recall . . ."

The man in the suit snapped on his latex gloves and rifled through the bag. Pulled out a hairbrush, washcloth, pack of Gauloises. Sniffed. "Not much."

He returned the contents to the pink Tati bag and handed it to the tech. "Have the lab prioritize this. I want the analysis tonight." He spoke as one accustomed to

36

giving orders. The tech returned the way he'd come.

"More . . . did you mean other belongings, Sister?" the man in the suit asked. "Maybe I can help you look for them."

"*Trop tard.* The police detective, I told him and *la Procureure* the same thing. He already helped me look. We searched the dormitory, everywhere. Didn't find anything else."

Aimée's pulse jumped. This suit was not the *brigade criminelle* investigator — who was he? And *la Proc,* the magistrate, who assigned the investigative force, had been here earlier. That could mean several things. None good.

"But now that we know the victim's true identity . . ." he was saying as they walked.

Aimée followed, crawling behind the hedge, racing to keep up and listen.

"What do you mean, her true identity?" Sister Agnès asked. "She's Genelle Tournon; her papers said so. I gave them to . . ."

Perspiration snaked down Aimée's spine as she tried to catch the whole conversation. The apron dragged in the damp soil.

"*Brigade criminelle* wasn't aware, Sister . . . We've identified the victim's fingerprints. A foreign national, a Germaine Tillion."

The suit was foreign intelligence — DGSE

37

or whatever the latest spy-world acronym was.

The people who'd been interested in her mother.

Who the hell was this dead woman? This Genelle, or Germaine, who had taken coffee with Aimée's mother and Chloé?

Part of the conversation drifted away. "If you can tell us more about her behavior . . ."

Merde. They'd turned a corner.

For a crazy moment, Aimée wondered if her mother had killed this woman. Set up a hit. That memory surfacing from childhood, a heated argument between her father and grandfather: *She's poison, une terroriste.* The lapse into an uncomfortable silence when Aimée had walked into the kitchen for warm milk.

Aimée hurried, keeping her head down, until she saw light streaming over worn stone. The open door revealed a dormitory-style room with three-tiered bunk beds, piles of blankets, and a basket with hotel-sized soaps and shampoos. An old oak wood storage cupboard with coat hooks. Spartan, clean.

She listened at the door.

The suit was riffling through the cupboard.

"We don't believe in locks here," said the nun.

He proceeded to check under the bunk beds, in the trash bins. "What else can you tell me?"

Sister Agnès tented her fingers. "She came several weeks ago, a month maybe. I'll need to consult the intake log."

"Already done, Sister," he said. "Can you clarify why the Little Sisters of the Poor are registered at a different address on rue de Picpus?"

"Confusing, I know," she said. "Our mother house suffered extensive water damage this spring. It's falling apart, *monsieur.* By the grace of God and this convent's generosity, we're able to continue our work, the program for those like Genelle, here in temporary quarters."

"We need your full cooperation in finding any trace she might have left behind. It's time sensitive due to the victim's identity . . ."

"*Monsieur,* this convent is private and belongs to the Saint Augustin order. I don't know who you're with —"

"My branch isn't important, Sister." His voice rose in officiousness. "I answer to the republic."

"Well, we answer to God."

Aimée almost cheered.

Footsteps approached. She ducked into one of the several recessed archways in an arcade. A rumbling vibrated the stone pavers below her high-tops. From the fresh-linen smells, she figured she was standing above the laundry.

When would this suit leave?

She heard a cell phone ring, then his terse *"oui."* A moment later, he hung up. *"Merci* for your help, Sister. We'll keep you in-formed. And we expect the same from you."

His footsteps exited the dorm room and trailed off down the hallway. Aimée held her breath, waiting until she heard Sister Agnès come out, then hurried after the nun.

Monday, Early Evening

When Aimée caught up with the nun, she had questions ready. But Sister Agnès looked Aimée over, noticed the dirty apron, put her finger to her lips, and jerked her thumb toward a small side chapel lit only by votive candles.

Inside, the nun looked around, checking the confessional before she spoke. Cautious. Had she done this before?

"We can't get involved," said Sister Agnès in a whisper.

Involved in what? But Aimée nodded. Leaned in to listen.

"We offer sanctuary to those in need, regardless of their situation. Everyone can find a haven here. We're a lifeline to those in need."

Aimée's damp sweater stuck to her shoulder blades. "I understand."

"Do you? Our mission's important; nothing can jeopardize the people we help here."

41

"D'accord," Aimée agreed. "I wouldn't dream of putting your work at risk, Sister. But my mother's involved in this somehow. I need to know about her relationship with this woman."

The nun glanced at her watch. Whispered quickly, "When I saw you, I knew who you were. You look just like your mother. And I recognized your baby. Such a sweet one."

"Can you tell me what you know about the dead woman? Genelle, did you say her name was? That man told you that wasn't her real name, *non?*"

"You were eavesdropping."

Aimée shifted in her high-tops. Felt like a schoolgirl. "Forgive me; I overheard some of your conversation."

Sister Agnès was still holding the man's business card. When she looked away to nod to another nun coming down the chapel aisle, Aimée peered at it, trying to make out its contents in the low light. *Daniel Lacenaire,* some government logo . . .

"I have to go," Sister Agnès said. "I'm late for the soup kitchen."

"Please, can't you tell me anything about her? Genelle or Germaine?"

Sister Agnès looked behind her. "She worked in the laundry room. Everyone has chores in our program. She kept to herself."

42

"How often did you see her with my mother?"

The nun hesitated. "Genelle introduced us once in the garden. They sat together on a bench to talk. Seems your mother was helping her find a job. It's why I remembered her. That's all I know."

"Didn't Genelle associate with anyone else?"

"Not that I saw." The nun clutched her rosary. She was holding something back.

Votive candles flickered. The smell of melted wax made Aimée want to sneeze. "But there must be something. Please, Sister. My mother isn't answering her phone. She left my baby at playgroup. She just disappeared. Not like her at all." A lie, though it had been some time since she'd last done this. "I'm worried."

"I don't think your mother has anything to do with us. Our community is a safe refuge."

Until one of their charges was murdered on their grounds.

"Genelle was supposed to meet my mother today, but now she's dead, and my mother is missing," Aimée said. "If there's anything that can lead me to her, I need to know."

"I don't know. *Desolée.*" The nun turned

43

to leave.

"What if she's in danger? Or hurt?"

Sister Agnès turned back, fingering her rosary, and seemed to come to a decision. "Let me talk to the sisters after prayer tonight."

Aimée met the nun's knowing gaze. "You don't believe my mother hurt Genelle. That's why you're talking to me in the first place."

"Your mother wanted to help her; of that I'm sure."

Aimée followed her past the chapel pews. "Please, let me talk to the nuns."

"Our order is semicloistered, so that could take time." The nun opened the chapel door. "We feed and shelter everyone. *Alors*, it's not for me to judge."

Judge?

"I'm late. Must go now. Call me tomorrow."

The nun's white hem brushed the damp grass, and she disappeared, ghostlike, into the shadows.

Flicking on her penlight, Aimée set out for the crime scene, following the gravel path to a small door in the wall. A little shove and she'd stepped into a lane of fig trees in another grassy enclosure. Something soft squished underfoot — the seedy purple

44

skin of burst figs. She crossed yet another expanse of grass. Yellow crime scene tape looped around a cedar tree and a hedge by a high stone wall. She shone her penlight. Disturbed gravel, mud, and trampled grass. A struggle? Hard to tell from the mash of footprints.

Below a shadowed lintel dated 1794, she read: THE BLOODY VICTIMS FROM THE GUILLOTINE AT THE PLACE DU TRÔNE WERE CARTED INTO THESE GARDENS OF THE DAMES CHANOINESSES DE ST. AUGUSTIN DE PICPUS THROUGH THIS DOOR. HERE RESTED THE 1,306 MUTILATED BODIES IN MASS GRAVES.

She shivered. By the yellow tape, her penlight caught on reddish-brown smears on the aged stone wall. More blood added to this violent history.

Not ten yards away, she noticed the gate that led to the parking area behind the building on Avenue de Saint-Mandé. So close to where she'd been standing earlier that day.

She backtracked to the dormitory, passing a bench under willow branches.

Had her mother sat on this bench when Genelle introduced her to Sister Agnès?

What had their connection been? Could it really have been as simple as Sydney trying to help the homeless woman find a job?

Aimée didn't buy it. What homeless woman in a shelter sported a pedicure with fresh nail polish? Or had her identity uncovered by the intelligence services in under two hours?

Homelessness was a perfect cover for a clandestine mission by an intelligence operative. Or maybe the woman was an amateur, an unwitting accomplice in some affair Sydney Leduc had been embroiled in?

Whoever the woman was, if she had a pedicure *comme ça,* she must have had a stash. A place to hide her other clothes and some cash, like Aimée had read in that article about the working homeless — women who slept in their cars, in train stations, and rotated through shelters.

Assuming she had another life, where would Genelle/Germaine hide it apart from the plastic Tati bag? Aimée remembered the rumbling from the laundry room, where Sister Agnès said Genelle had worked.

Theories remained theories until you tested them, Aimée's detective father used to say. Shoe leather got answers.

Better check it out.

Down in the cellar, a strip of fluorescent lights illuminated the industrial-sized washers. Between them sheets hung on clotheslines among old, chipped porcelain basins and wood drying racks. The fresh smell of laundry hung over the whitewashed concrete floor.

Judging by the rifled piles of laundry and telltale wet footprints, the DGSE suit's team and *brigade criminelle* had already searched. What could she hope to find that they hadn't?

Yet they had missed things before. Where should she start looking? Her father would have said, *Think like the victim* — desperate, with something to lose. Aimée opened the built-in, old-fashioned airing-out cupboards, as her *grand-mère* had called them. Bed linen, mismatched fancy towels with monograms. Donated, it seemed, by the Ritz and Hôtel Plaza Athénée.

She prowled in the space behind the washing machines and the drying racks, felt the wet slap of sheets against her neck. Humid air and condensation fogged the few windows. Where could one hide something?

She ran her hands under the worn wood tables and around their backs. She penlight checked every damp corner. Her skin was clammy; fatigue knotted her shoulders. Her hunch had proven wrong.

Late. She needed to get home.

As she was about to leave, it hit her. Where did men never look?

One by one, she opened the large washing machine lids, felt around for the filters. Released the slimy filter tabs. On her third attempt, when she pulled out the filter with a wet mess of lint, threads, and hair, she found a large folded plastic baggie, clouded with moisture.

She listened for anyone coming. Only the spin and rumbling of another washer's last cycle. *Better hurry.* She emptied everything but the baggie into the trash. Set the baggie on a wicker hamper; it wasn't smelling too fresh. Dried it off with a rag. Her forehead was damp from exertion.

She tried opening the baggie, but the damn thing's air-tight seal was melted, so it took her several yanks to rip it open.

She lost her balance, slipping on the wet concrete and falling into the hamper, which spilled dirty clothes everywhere. At least she hadn't made much noise. Looking around, she saw papers floating in the air, landing on her sprawled legs. *Dollar bills.*

She blinked. *Wrong. Hundred-dollar bills.*

A baggie worth of them.

Inside the ripped baggie, rubber banded to a stack of bills, was a damp envelope emblazoned with the return address of the Grand Hôtel d'Abidjan. Curious, Aimée opened it. Inside was a piece of paper with a key taped to it. It was a yellowed, torn-edged page from a book. Aimée unfolded it and picked out the words that had been circled: *Use gifts for good, not evil, or suffer their curse.*

Along the paper's edge, written in black ink, was a series of letters and numbers: *GBH*120gdel.*

A proverb, a code, a stack of cash, and a key.

To what?

Did this involve her mother or something else? She decided to show it to Sister Agnès to find out; the woman definitely knew something. She stuffed the items back inside and wrapped the rubber band around the whole bundle to keep it closed.

Back in the soup kitchen, the volunteers were cleaning up, lugging empty pots to the sink. Sister Agnès was speaking to a tall man wearing a blue duffle coat and wool cap. His muscles bulged under the coat as he leaned threateningly over the nun. "Don't you understand? She left me something . . ." he was saying. Aimée couldn't place his accent over the kitchen noise.

Who was he? Why had he shown up? She balled her fists in worry. Could this be about Genelle, or the baggie Aimée had found? Even her mother?

"We're a shelter, not a baggage claim, *monsieur,*" Sister Agnès said. "I've never seen you before. You don't even know her name . . ."

Aimée couldn't hear his reply. But the nun had moved to the side of a pillar and caught Aimée's gaze. Sister Agnès shook her head, pulled her hand from the pocket of her apron, and motioned subtly for Aimée to keep moving, her hand close to her side just out of the man's view.

Aimée took the gestured advice.

Not a taxi in sight. She wasn't eager to drive her scooter across Paris with this kind of money on her. Still, she needed to get away from there, away from the cruising police car.

50

She called René, her partner, at the office, but the call went to the answering machine. Next she tried his cell number.

"I want to hear all about your speech, Aimée," he said.

"Meet me at the office, René. As fast as you can."

She hung up, keyed her scooter's ignition, and scanned the street. Heading in the direction opposite the police car's, she stopped at the first garbage bin she saw and rooted around. With some pulling and shoving, she extracted some torn birthday wrapping paper and used it to cover the damp baggie. Felt a little better.

She stuck it back into her bag and slung the bag across her chest. Alert, she kept to the speed limit in the narrow lanes winding through the Bastille area. Checked behind her often to see if anyone was following. Only dog walkers or couples arm in arm on the dark side streets as she entered the Marais. Images filled her mind — the wall smeared with dried blood, the suit from the intelligence unit, Sister Agnès's deep-set eyes hinting at institutional secrets. That damned fresh laundry scent clung to her leather jacket.

Stupid. Why hadn't she left the package with the nun? But Aimée already knew why.

She thought of the torn book page, the saying that had been circled. Was it a threat? A woman had been murdered.

Abidjan . . . The word was familiar. Someplace in Africa, though she couldn't remember where.

Money — even blood money, which this no doubt was — would feed many of the convent's clients. But . . .

Her mind spun. *Concentrate, Aimée.*

So hard these days, especially when she got tired at night. Her doctor had cleared her for work but warned of postconcussive symptoms: headaches and memory loss, residual effects of the dissolved blood clot. Nothing she could afford to suffer, not with her job or with a baby.

A biting chill came up from the river. Goosebumps pimpled her neck. She wove through the back lanes and narrow streets, worried and angry over her mother's disappearance. Could this be some kind of payoff or payment? For what, Aimée didn't know.

Ten minutes later, she'd parked off rue du Louvre. She took the birdcage of an elevator to the third floor. All the lights were off on her landing. She punched in Leduc Detective's door code and stumbled into the empty office.

Did a quick count of the hundred-dollar

bills, which were bound in currency wrappers . . . *Mon Dieu.*

Panic hit her. What if the baggie held a sensor or tracker somewhere in it? Could she expect a special forces raid any minute? An elite Kalashnikov-toting, balaclavaed team pounding up the building stairs?

Stupid. If there were something like that, whoever had planted it would have been the ones to find the money, not Aimée. *Stay calm; stash it for now.*

She hadn't turned the chandelier on, and she pulled the shade down. Sitting on the floor, she swiveled the swing arm lamp to focus its beam on the baggie's contents.

She counted the money again, then ran her hand along the inside of the baggie.

Her fingers came back beige and gritty.

She sniffed. Rubbed her fingers together. Sand.

The office door clicked open. *René.*

"So how many contracts did you snag in that new Chanel? Paid for itself, eh?" he was saying. "It's my birthday next month, but you're giving me my present early. *Alors, dis-moi.*"

Her smiling partner, René Friant, a dwarf in a tweed jacket, had turned on the chandelier, filling the office with light.

"Turn that off, René," she said. "Come look."

René's jaw dropped. "Did you rob a bank?"

"Not quite."

"You're sitting in the dark with money on the floor — dollars?" René's calfskin briefcase fell to the floor. "Thousand . . . *non,* hundred-dollar bills?" His voice came out in a squeak.

"Shhh . . . René, it's *compliqué.*"

He choked. "*Compliqué,* that's all you can say? You're serious? Have you lost your mind, Aimée? Where'd this money come from?"

Her stomach clenched. "Quick, René, if anyone comes in —"

Her phone vibrated in her jacket pocket.

Rigid with fear, she forced herself to look at the caller ID. Babette. News about her mother?

"Heard anything, Babette?" Aimée asked.

"Not a peep. Chloé's ready for bed. Should I put her to sleep?"

"*Merci, mais non,*" she said, shooting René a look. "I'll be home in fifteen minutes. René will give me a ride."

She hung up.

"I will?" All four feet of him bristled with fury. "Not on your life. You owe me an

54

explanation. More than that, *même* — you brought illicit money into our place of business? I won't have any part of this."

She lifted the loose floorboard under her desk and stuck the baggie underneath. Shoved the board back in place and covered it with a trash bin. "René, it's not what you think."

"And what do I think, Aimée?"

She stood, checked the answering machine. No messages.

"Some payoff, grand theft, a drug deal gone wrong?" His voice was rising.

"I'll tell you in the car."

"No way in hell will I aid and abet another crime. Not this time."

She'd pulled him into trouble before. Understood his fury. But she had to get him out of the office.

"Suit yourself," she said. "If the SWAT team arrives, you're on your own."

"What?"

She packed up and hit the lights. Checked the door alarm.

And with much clearing of his throat, he followed behind her down the winding staircase.

MONDAY, LATE EVENING

René downshifted in his prized Citroën DS, a classic armadillo of a car customized for his height, on the Pont Marie. Streetlamps cast shafts of smoky topaz light on the Seine's black glass surface. Ahead lay the butterscotch stone façade of Aimée's seventeenth-century Ile Saint-Louis apartment. René pulled over. "How could you blow off the keynote? The networking *apéritifs*? I can't believe how important —"

"Babette's waiting, René. And I tried calling you."

A little white lie. In her panic over Chloé, she'd totally forgotten.

"If I'd gotten your message in time, I could have done damage control."

"It's my mother."

He parked and put on the parking brake. Shook his head. "I should have known."

After Aimée'd pulled the covers over Chloé,

she checked the window hasps. All locked tight. But nothing felt right.

With Chloé asleep and the baby monitor on, Aimée set down a bottle of Pernod, whose taste and licorice aroma René loved. Poured a splash, added water from a carafe. She needed his help, and based on the way he was tapping his handmade Lobb shoes on the herringbone floor, it was going to take her more than a Pernod to get back into his good graces.

Tired, she was so tired. The adrenalin that had been coursing through her since she'd found the money had drained away. After all those hours of conference prep — and for nothing.

René swirled the milky mixture, sipped as he opened his laptop. "Whose money did you steal?"

Aimée went to the window, parted the shutter slats, and looked out on the quai below. "Impossible to steal from a corpse, René."

René choked on his drink.

She took a breath. "I got an emergency message right when I was about to deliver the keynote. It sounded like Sydney'd had an accident."

She told him about everything: the playgroup, the waiter in the café, seeing the homeless woman's perfectly pedicured foot, no word from her mother, overhearing the suit from foreign intelligence, her conversation with the nun.

"Tant pis," René said. "How do you know this belongs to the dead woman?"

She didn't. Yet a feeling in her bones told her it did.

"Why not give it to the police?"

"There was a message inside."

"Telling you to take it?" René shook his head. "What is this, some kind of setup?"

"Too complicated, René. I was going to give it to Sister Agnès, but a man showed up and started arguing with her. She motioned for me to get out of there."

"So she knows you have it."

Aimée nodded, although she wasn't actually sure. "But if a woman was killed for this . . ."

"How much is there?"

Her shoulders sagged. She curled up on the recamier. "Three hundred thousand US dollars. And a key."

René spilled his drink. "So you think the homeless woman might have acted as a courier, stolen this money instead of delivering it, then hidden out in the convent?"

"I didn't say any of that!" But it made her think. "This key means something."

"How's your mother involved?"

"Like I'd know. But what if she's in danger from the same people who killed this Genelle?"

Where *was* her mother? The litany of her childhood. Some things never changed.

"Don't get mixed up in this." René sat next to her on the recamier, his short legs dangling. His brows knit in worry. "Look at you; you're exhausted. Go see the neurologist tomorrow."

Did she look that bad? The dull thud of a headache, which she'd tried to ignore, intensified. Right then, all she wanted to do was take a Doliprane and sleep.

"Didn't the neurologist insist you take it slow, ease back in? *Après tout,* you're just back in the office," said René. "Return the money. Let them deal with it."

"Mais bien sûr," she said. "I can't keep it. I don't want one franc. But I need to do the right thing. Figure it out, give it to the right people. And then there's this."

She handed him the envelope.

"Grand Hôtel d'Abidjan," he said, reading. "What is this, a code?"

She thought of the stacks of bills, banded neatly. It felt like a pro job. She recalled how quickly DGSE had uncovered the

59

victim's identity. "What if she wasn't killed for the money, but for something else?"

TUESDAY, EARLY MORNING

"You're up early, Leduc." On the other end of the phone, Morbier, her godfather, cleared his throat.

"Early's relative when you have a *bébé*." She leaned over the crib, phone between cheek and shoulder, and picked up Chloé, who was sopping wet after a major diaper leak.

"Is Chloé all right?" Morbier called himself Chloé's great-god-father, as if that were a real thing.

"Fine." Aimée tickled her daughter's toes amidst wiping her down and changing her diaper. A squeal of laughter. "Hear that? If only she didn't wake up every day at dawn."

Aimée had hardly slept. Nightmares about her mother and that money had kept waking her. What did the key open?

She stifled a yawn. "We need to talk."

"I'm listening, Leduc."

"Not on the phone," she said. "Where do

you live now?"

He gave her his new address. From the hallway, she heard Babette's cheery *'bonjour.'*

"Twenty minutes," Aimée said. "Please have a coffee waiting for me."

She pulled the previous day's little black Chanel from the armoire and reworked it — the beauty of a classic — adding pearls and a vintage pink-and-charcoal-nubbed wool jacket. Threw tights, makeup, and extra heels in her bag, grabbed her laptop and tech conference materials.

Minutes later, after kissing Chloé, ruffling her bichon frise Miles Davis's ears, and issuing Babette last-minute instructions for zoo tickets, Aimée was gunning her scooter over the Pont Sully, just making the traffic light.

"Is she back to her old tricks, Morbier?"

She searched her godfather's sharp gaze, those dark, droopy eyes that reminded her of a basset hound's. A retired police *commissaire,* Morbier never missed a thing.

"Who, Leduc? You need to spell it out for an old invalid like me."

Morbier sat under a wool blanket in his wheelchair. The wheelchair she'd put him in when she'd gotten him shot. But she couldn't think about that.

62

"My mother, who else?" she said. "She promised me she'd walked away from her old life."

Morbier snorted. "I can't keep up with my rehab appointments, much less Sydney Leduc."

Like she believed that. "You were always in 'discreet' contact with her. Why wouldn't you be now?"

"Why would we be in discreet contact when we can just talk in the open? No more need for secrecy."

Right.

The morning light settled over the twelfth-century courtyard, penetrating the crooks and corners of old stone. Morbier's new digs in an old metalsmith's atelier had a lot going for them: it was an easy-access *rez-de-chaussée* on the ground floor with good lighting and a glass ceiling and lively artisan neighbors in the three-courtyard-deep *cour d'industrie.* Ideal, considering the working-class roots he boasted about.

"I needed that," she said, after downing the steaming espresso from the demitasse he'd handed her. She looked around. A tousled duvet over a daybed, a galley-style kitchen. On a desk, thick files that looked suspiciously like old cases.

"How about another?" she said, handing

him back the demitasse. "So my head can function properly. You know, I'd call this place *très charmant.*"

"*Vraiment?* You like it, Leduc?"

What did it matter what she liked?

It mattered that he was finally able to function on his own in his wheelchair.

"*Parfait* for you, Morbier," she said. "A café around the corner, the market a few blocks away, and your rehab at Hôpital Saint-Antoine practically across the *rue.*" She paused, guilt washing over her. "What's wrong, Morbier?"

He shook his head. His hair was stone white, his thick brows salt and pepper. "Call yourself a detective, Leduc?" Morbier sipped his coffee, noticed her look. His sagging jowls stretched in a grin. "*Tout va bien.* The carpenter next door's installing a walkway for me. But that's not why you came."

She took a breath. "Sydney's missing, Morbier."

Those basset-hound eyes studied her. "Since when?"

"She left Chloé at playgroup yesterday. Disappeared. They called me out of the conference; I thought there'd been an accident."

Morbier's white-stubbled jaw clenched.

64

"Very unlike her. She'd never leave Chloé."

Like she left me?

She opened her mouth but knew she would sound like a child and bit her tongue. Hated feeling that way again, as she always did with Morbier. Always reverting to tantrums.

All the feelings of abandonment she'd wrestled with for years resurfaced, with that familiar shame of not being enough. She'd almost put it behind her, until her mother walked back into her life. Only to leave again.

As if he'd read her mind, Morbier said, "*C'est différent, Leduc.* All those years ago, she left to protect you." He hit the button on the coffee grinder.

When the machine was off again, she said, "I don't know about that, Morbier."

She gave him an edited version of what had happened the day before, leaving out the baggie and what she'd done with it.

"Sydney, volunteering at a convent?" he said. "She never struck me as the Christian type."

"I need to find her, Morbier." And he could help. He was retired but had maintained his contacts and remained very plugged into the police force, as was hinted by those files piled on his desk.

"You think she tells me her agenda? She could be anywhere. Got more lives than a cat."

He had that right.

"Something's wrong, Morbier," she said. "Help me find out who this Germaine Tillion is and how foreign intelligence identified her within two hours."

His eyes were unreadable. "That's persimmons and onions."

Thinking about the combination made her wince. "What does that mean? Two things that have nothing to do with each other?"

"*Exactement.* I served with the police, not with spooks."

She tried to put it together. "My mother's ex-CIA."

"Wouldn't surprise me," he said.

Of course he knew. He would never talk about it.

"You still know people who know people," she said.

"A long shot, Leduc."

She took the second demitasse he proffered to her. Dropped in brown sugar cubes. He never had white ones — too bourgeois.

Aimée downed the espresso. "Please, Morbier, she's in danger. There's an intelligence agent, Daniel Lacenaire" — she hoped she'd read the name right on the card he'd

66

given Sister Agnès — "sniffing around. I can't track her down without . . ." She paused. Her mother was still a suspected spy, a former terrorist. "Without bringing attention to her."

A shake of his white-haired head. "Better you don't look, Leduc. She'd tell you if she wanted you to know where she was."

Had her mother known about the money? It wasn't chump change. But Aimée didn't trust Morbier enough to tell him about the cash.

"What if she can't?" she asked.

"You're between a rock and a hard spot, eh?" He reached for a shopping bag. Released the handbrake on his wheelchair. "Push me over the cobbles, Leduc," he said, "and hand me my jacket."

It wasn't like him to acknowledge his limitations.

As she complied, she asked, "You'll help me, ask around? Get details on Daniel Lacenaire?"

"With the DGSE?"

So he did know him.

She nodded.

"Only on the condition you prioritize your child and stay out of your mother's business. Oh, and bring my great-goddaughter over for madeleines. Keep to that bargain,

67

and stay out of it."

That was his price? Like she could keep that promise. But she nodded. She hefted her bag onto her shoulder.

"You're just back at work and look like hell, Leduc."

Complimentary, as always. But that was the second time she'd heard that in so many days. Noticed something in his eyes.

"You know more than you're letting on, Morbier."

His return gaze read, *So do you.*

Stay out of it? Not Aimée. She was wired differently.

All the way to her scooter, her mind spun. Sydney Leduc had given up all her old work. Hadn't she?

TUESDAY, EARLY MORNING

On the second day of the tech conference, the theme was "Tech in the New Millennium." The first event was coffee-and-brioche schmoozing at nine. She still had plenty of time. She would stop by Square Courteline to revisit the playgroup. Question the waiter who knew her mother.

Already fortified by caffeine, she made it to the café in five minutes. Yellow leaves fluttered over the bandstand, gauze clouds drifted in the sky, and the sun warmed the brisk air. The last gasp of mild autumn before the November chill.

The day before, she hadn't paid any attention to the café's vintage movie posters or the fifties pinball machine that blinked as it lit up. On the gleaming zinc counter were a basket of croissants, a wire holder full of hard-boiled eggs, and a saltshaker.

The young waitress who had been so distraught the previous day was slapping orange halves into a juicer. The trickle of pulpy juice gave off a tangy citrus aroma, reminding Aimée of visiting her grandmother down south, the orange groves and raspberry bushes of her childhood.

"Bonjour," Aimée said. "I'll have a *jus d'orange, s'il vous plaît."*

No recognition flickered in the waitress's eyes. Aimée had heard her name the previous afternoon — what was it?

"That's five francs," the waitress said listlessly, setting down the tall glass of juice in a mechanical motion.

This woman had seen the victim's body. If Aimée could warm her up, she might be able to get some information.

"Merci." Aimée set down a ten-franc note that glimmered in the sunlight. Finally the name came to her. "Keep the change, Louise. Have one for yourself. Feeling better today?"

"What do you mean?"

"That was quite a shock yesterday," said Aimée, desperate to draw her out. "I mean seeing that poor woman. I'm surprised you're at work."

"I open for Jacques," said Louise. "He attends daily mass."

One of the devout. Louise swiped the counter with a damp blue-checked cloth.

70

Arcs of moisture trailed on the counter.

"You told me you remembered serving my mother and Genelle," Aimée said.

"Did I?" Louise thought. "Genelle's the one who . . . ?" Her voice trailed off. "Now I remember." She looked away.

"Tragic," said Aimée, deciding to plunge in. "What did they talk about?"

"Your mother takes the *bébé* to the play-group, right? Ask her yourself."

"I would, Louise. But she hasn't returned my calls; no one's seen or heard from her since yesterday."

There, she'd blurted it out.

Louise froze.

"Louise, what if my mother . . . saw something, or the killer's after her? I just don't know."

"You think I do?" Louise shook her head. Her cheek muscles twitched. "*Bon sang,* had enough nightmares last night."

Poor Louise seemed traumatized by what she'd seen. She'd probably been trying to put it out of her mind.

But Aimée couldn't give up.

"Me, too, Louise. I'm worried. Can you remember anything at all about their meetings here? What did they drink?"

"*Café crème,* and warm milk for *la bébé.*" She said it by rote. "They always sat at station three."

"See, you remember," said Aimée. "What would they talk about?"

"I don't listen in on customers. It's unprofessional."

Too bad.

"Bien sûr," Aimée said. "Did anything strike you as unusual?"

"For a homeless woman, she smelled okay. A lot of them don't."

Aimée thought about the woman's pedicure and sipped the juice. Thick, the way she liked it. The pulp stuck in her teeth. "The nun at the convent said my mother was trying to help Genelle find a job. Did you see them here yesterday?"

Louise stacked demitasse cups. Shrugged. "Don't think so."

But something in Louise's tone told Aimée to probe further. "You remember something, don't you?"

"I thought I saw her outside . . . there, waiting on the pavement; I can't remember when . . . but I'm not sure. If she came in, I didn't see."

Had Genelle come to meet her mother and Sydney not shown up?

"Anything else?" Aimée asked.

Louise thought. "Nice tan — that's what I thought at first. Not the spray-on kind. But then I realized she was a *noisette* . . ."

The term for an espresso with a dollop of foamed milk. "What do you mean?"

"You know, half-and-half." Louise shrugged. "Part *africaine.*"

Aimée thought back to the envelope with the Grand Hôtel d'Abidjan address. "Remember anything about her outfit?"

"What she wore?" Louise thought for a moment. "Old blue tracksuit, too big for her. Scruffy hair." She turned back to the counter. "I don't want to remember, okay?"

Great.

"*Desolée,* I know it's hard, but one last question," Aimée said. "Has anyone else been asking about her?"

"Talk to Jacques."

Louise turned away to serve another client.

Aimée left her card on the counter.

Next door at the playgroup, the teacher frowned at Aimée while toddlers clamored and smeared finger paint on easels. A smell of spilled apple juice pervaded the space.

"If this is about your daughter returning —"

"Non, madame," said Aimée. "I'll make it quick. One question — what did my mother say to you before she left?"

The teacher gave a disgusted shrug. "That's just it, *mademoiselle.* Nothing. We found a note with the phone number to call for you. That's unacceptable."

Aimée needed to placate this woman and try to get some useful information. "I understand. You have rules. I'm sorry to keep asking, but I'm desperate. Did you see her leave?"

"My job is to work with the children, not babysit the adults. One of the mothers found the note on the bench and handed it to me."

"Is that mother here today?"

"I'm busy, *mademoiselle.*"

"Just one last question. What time was this?"

"Before clay time."

"Which is?"

The teacher threw her a look as if she were slow. "A little before three."

Aimée caught the gaze of a mother sitting on the bench between two toddlers hammering wooden nails. Was she the right woman? *Only one way to find out.*

Aimée sat down on the bench. The woman had a swanlike neck and a noticeable drooping shoulder. "If I could take just one moment — did you see my mother, Chloé's grandmother, yesterday?"

The teacher shot them a dark look.

"Briefly." The woman shifted on the bench, looked uncomfortable. "*Regardez,* I'm here with my son; this isn't a good time."

Was she afraid of the teacher or of what she'd seen?

"Understood," Aimée said. "Can I call you? Please, my mother's missing."

The woman hesitated. "Florence Triquet. I do upholstery. I'm in the book."

TUESDAY MORNING

Aimée checked her phone. No messages.

She shelved the worry for her mother for later. Almost show time, and Aimée hadn't even done her makeup.

As Aimée mounted her scooter, she sensed someone was watching her. When she turned, she caught sight of a lurking figure across the boulevard, partially hidden behind a plane tree, but it was gone as soon as she spotted it.

TUESDAY MORNING, 8:45 A.M.

Le Train Bleu's nineteenth-century *salle de toilette* was straight out of another *époque,* when the restaurant's namesake had departed from a platform below: all polished wood cubicles, brass fixtures, and porcelain sinks large enough to give Chloé a bath in, plus a *dame de pipi* who counted towels.

Aimée got to work, applying primer and Dior under-eye concealer and lightly brushing on foundation. With quick strokes she lined her eyes with kohl, smudging it for a smoky effect, and wanded mascara through her eyelashes. Ran Chanel red over her lips and dotted her cheeks for color.

Much better. She looked human. Time to earn Leduc Detective's rent.

Six hours later, Aimée gave a mental sigh of relief as she stuck the business cards she'd collected into her red Moleskine. Jotted stars next to the new appointments she'd made to discuss custom services. Thank God she'd worn the Chanel. She'd gotten serious interest in their computer security maintenance package, René's brainchild.

At least that would make him happy.

She could still taste the fresh Brittany oysters from the CEOs' lunch. She really had to get out more often.

As she was putting her bag in her scooter compartment outside the Gare de Lyon, a large hand gripped her shoulder. She'd been followed.

In attack mode, she gripped her pen, ready to jab it into what she imagined would be a big meaty thigh, and turned.

"You're a difficult woman to catch, Aimée." It was Marc Fabre, from Securadex. His grin faded to surprise, and he released his grip, then stepped back. "Didn't mean to startle you."

Don't ever sneak up on me, she almost snapped at him. Instead, she managed a smile. Marc had come to gloat, no doubt, over having given the keynote or about his new contracts. His shaved head was shiny but his chin stubble dark, his black-rimmed glasses *très courant.*

"Everything okay? I mean, is your mother all right? That's what I meant to ask."

She wanted to brush him off with a flippant reply. But she heard concern in his voice. Who knew if it was real?

She shrugged. Above them, the granite sky promised rain. She had to hurry. Looped her scarf around her neck and reached for her helmet.

"*Desolé,* forgive me for prying," he said. "It's not my business."

"*Non,* Marc, it's just that . . ." She tried to think of what to say. She never revealed anything about her personal life in her business dealings. "You know how it goes, I'm sure." *Keep it vague.* "A crisis here, a crisis there, putting out fires at the office . . ."

"Must be daunting, worrying about your mother when you're running a business," he said. "Family issues — I've got them, too."

She nodded, wondering what he was after. Aiming for her sympathy?

"Marc, what do you want?"

His head shone like a cue ball. Kind of sexy, but . . . *non,* not her bad-boy type.

"A truce — let's call off the rivalry," he said. "There's a huge project coming up, and if we pooled resources, made a bid together, *allez,* you know we'd stand a better chance."

Now the snake was offering her a piece of the tart?

"You mean for the ministry?" she said. "I've heard the rumors, too."

"Interested?"

It could work. Or not.

"I'll get back to you."

TUESDAY, LATE AFTERNOON

The sky was pigeon grey and full of fat rain clouds. Before going home, Aimée needed to figure out how she was going to return Genelle's baggie to Sister Agnès and see if the nun had learned anything from her sisters. Aimée had left a phone message but hadn't heard back.

The convent was ten minutes away. If she left right then, she could catch Sister Agnès before soup kitchen prep. And she just might avoid the rain.

She hadn't bargained on the traffic behind a stalled bus on Avenue Daumesnil. So she wound through the narrow passages near Montgallet. *Some shortcut. Just as clogged as everywhere else.*

The sky opened. She gunned the scooter toward a passage and sheltered under a glass marquise overhang in a metalworker's narrow courtyard. Left the engine running.

Where had her cell phone gone? Busy

searching her damp pockets, she heard the car door shut only when it was too late. The man approaching her under the dripping eves wore the same dark blue duffle coat and wool cap he'd had on the night before when she'd seen him arguing with the nun.

His large figure blocked her way. His stance exuded training — special forces training.

Her damp hands froze. Stuck in the rain wearing Chanel and her grandmother's pearls.

"You have something for me, don't you?" he said. "Hand it over and I'll take it from here."

His sentence structure and accent were foreign . . . Dutch, German, maybe South African?

Aimée's heart thudded so loud in her chest she thought he'd hear it. She knew he meant Genelle or Germaine's stash. But how much did he know about the victim? Or her?

"What are you talking about? Who are you?" she asked.

"I could ask the same."

She felt an alert stillness about him. That of a hunter surveying his prey.

Play dumb. Not hard. He'd been following her since who knew when — yesterday?

— and she hadn't noticed. She wanted to kick herself.

"I don't understand," she said.

"Don't play me, *chérie.*" He'd noticed her grip the handlebar of the still-purring scooter. Probably clocked every escape route that her eyes had found.

"Come any closer and you'll be feeling my Taser," she lied. "This isn't the first time a type like you has followed me somewhere."

He laughed. "I'm just looking for the package Genelle left me. Tell me where it is."

The night before he hadn't known Genelle's name.

"Who?" Aimée asked.

His hands came out of his pockets. Her eyes caught on the tattoos on his clenched knuckles. "I said, don't play me."

He was big and had a tactical advantage. *Alors,* she needed to find a way out and move quick. Meanwhile, she needed to keep him talking.

"*Quoi,* you're a stranger coming up to me, demanding something," she said. "I don't even know what you're on about."

He moved closer. Raindrops trickled from his cap like tears. "Give me Genelle's package."

"I don't know a Genelle or anything about

a package."

"You've been asking around at the café."

"Café? Oh, you mean where I lost my phone?" she said. "What a pain, and it was in my other purse the whole time." She gave him a look. *"Monsieur,* whoever you are, I'd say you're disappointed in love, *n'est-ce pas?"* Desperate, white knuckles clenching on the handlebars, she kept up the charade. "I know your type. She drops you, and you want the ring back. You think she confided in me?"

"Quit stalling."

"You don't know much about women, do you?" she said, smiling.

Pause. "What's that to do with anything?"

She'd struck a chord. Thrown him off-balance.

"Where are you from?" she asked.

"Arles." His answer came too quick. And she'd never heard a Provençal accent like his. Not even close to that musical patois.

She saw him tense, and his lips moved — he was whispering something.

Merde. Was he wired?

With no more of a plan than to get the hell out, she accelerated, veering left as she kicked straight out with her right foot. Counted on the element of surprise. Her stiletto heel got him in the thigh. Wobbling

84

over the cobblestones in the rain, the scooter shot forward and out of the courtyard.

Right into traffic. Her handlebars scraped a van, and she almost lost her balance. But somehow she kept going, weaving in the downpour with a cacophony of horns blaring behind her.

TUESDAY, LATE AFTERNOON

She left her Vespa in the Ile Saint-Louis mechanic's garage where the temperamental Italian scooter lived most of the time anyway. No more pink scooter for now. She ran, drenched, to her apartment, going in the rear entrance via the backstreet.

As she peeled off her wet clothes, she thought about what she knew. The duffle coat wasn't French, and he was working for someone.

Big trouble.

Where was her mother?

And how soon could Aimée get rid of the money she'd stashed under the floorboards in her office?

She called the convent. Only the answering machine. She left another message for Sister Agnès.

She called Morbier. Voice mail. Tried again.

This time he answered.

"What now, Leduc?"

"Any info on Lacenaire?"

"Didn't I tell you to stay out of it?"

"Hard to when I've been followed, Morbier."

"Stuck your nose where it shouldn't go? Again?"

Merde. Her and her big mouth. If she confessed to following up, he wouldn't help her.

"I've got a bad feeling, Morbier."

That sounded weak.

"Do as we agreed, Leduc. Focus on your daughter and your job. Got to go."

He hung up.

Helpful, as usual.

But he knew something. She wouldn't let up until he came through.

The sky matched the *grisaille* tin rooftops as the rain stopped. After she'd jumped in a hot bath and climbed into dry jeans, she had a couple hours before she had to fetch Chloé from across the courtyard.

In her grandfather's library, she scanned the shelves and pulled out a book on tattoos. She flipped the pages. Aboriginal, Maori, Hells Angels . . . Not what she was looking for. On the next shelf, she found a volume on naval and sailor tattoos through the centuries. Another on military and

87

paramilitary tattoos.

She licked her finger, paging through the photos of designs, insignias, Latin phrases, mottoes. Then she found it. The tattoo she'd seen on the man's knuckles.

Legio Patria Nostra

The motto of the *Légion étrangère,* the Foreign Legion, a special branch of the French Armed Forces composed of foreign recruits. Didn't ex-legionnaires become mercenaries, hired guns?

She pushed aside thoughts of what could have happened if she hadn't gotten away.

Her grandfather's library contained three shelves just on l'Afrique. Research would settle her nerves, still jittery after the encounter. An hour's reading acquainted her with Abidjan, the capital of Côte d'Ivoire, a French colony until 1960. Once the brightest jewel in de Gaulle's necklace of *Françafrique.* After independence, Côte d'Ivoire had boasted a uniquely stable government, relative prosperity, a French-educated elite, and mineral and oil resources. Not to mention the cocoa beans responsible for her favorite *chocolat chaud.*

Miles Davis curled up on the floor by her feet, warming her toes while she sat on the brocade Napoleon III chaise and made notes in her red Moleskine.

She heard the metallic clicking of a key turned in the lock. Bolted upright. Her mother, back and with an explanation?

Aimée's heart skipped. The Moleskine fell from her lap.

Melac, Chloé's biological father, stepped into the salon, tall, thin hipped, and with those grey-blue eyes his daughter had inherited.

"Taking it easy. Good," said Melac, setting down a market bag. Leeks peeked from the top. "Glad you're following doctor's orders."

Little did he know.

He'd been with *brigade criminelle* until a bus accident that killed his older daughter, at which point he'd quit and moved to Brittany. Now he was back in Paris, working high-profile private security. A sought-after former *brigade criminelle* officer, his experience guaranteed him plum jobs and his own schedule.

"I'm making Chloé's favorite, *potage de légumes,*" he said. "Yours too. And *casse-croûte au fromage.*"

Quite the chef these days. After going AWOL to be with his dying daughter, Melac had reappeared at Chloé's christening with a new wife, wanting in on life with his baby. The last thing Aimée would have asked for.

Still, somehow they'd reached an agreement.

Or at least a truce.

Miles Davis sprang toward Melac's shopping bag, sniffing and wagging his tail.

"Even got *monsieur*'s horsemeat," Melac said.

Melac had been helping out since her concussion a month before, sharing Chloé's care with Sydney in between his security shifts. For some reason the new wife stayed in Brittany.

"Have you talked to Sydney?" she asked.

"She's not answering. *Alors,* I need to change tomorrow's pickup time for Chloé. Wasn't she supposed to babysit tonight?"

He didn't know.

"Look, Melac —"

He'd pulled out his ringing phone, checked it. *"Attends."* His eyes shuttered. "Must take this."

No doubt Donatine, his provincial, organic-everything wife who spun wool from their sheep and milked their goats. Aimée hated how her own green-devil jealousy erupted every time Donatine intruded on her life, every time she was reminded of Melac's rose-gold serpent wedding ring.

And yet, why was he camping out in

Aimée's salon? When he wasn't staying with her, he was at his friends'; from time to time, he even slept in a bunk in the firemen's *caserne.*

Long ago, she'd realized Melac would never change. She wished it didn't still bother her.

Her phone rumbled somewhere beneath the chaise's cushions. A number she didn't know. Her mother?

"Allô?" Aimée said, almost dropping the phone.

Several clicks. The line buzzed. Dead.

What in the —

The phone rang again. Once.

Had her mother called and hung up, suspecting her line was bugged?

Aimée hit REDIAL.

Ringing. Ringing. No answer.

Was it a signal? Signal for what?

Restless, she stood. Paced. *Think.* Her blood fizzed. She had to do something. Couldn't stand the waiting, feeling helpless.

Better to harness the nervous energy. She'd follow up with the woman from the playgroup, the last person to have seen her mother, as far as Aimée knew. In *les pages jaunes,* her finger scanned the twelfth arrondissement for upholsterers. Found the name she was looking for near the Bel-Air

91

quartier.

"Bonsoir," she said when the woman answered her phone. "I'm Chloé's mother; we spoke briefly at the playgroup. You said I could ring you."

"Now? I'm busy." Florence Triquet sounded annoyed.

Like Aimée cared.

"Please, I'll keep it brief," she said. "Can you remember if my mother said anything before she disappeared from the playgroup? Was she acting differently? Did she get a phone call?"

"My clients —"

"Won't like a policeman appearing, will they?" interrupted Aimée. "It's a murder investigation now."

"What?"

"Please think back. Try to recall whatever you can."

"Un moment." A hand muffled the receiver.

Aimée paced. A frying-garlic aroma came from the kitchen. She realized several hours had passed since the oysters at lunch.

"Tell me what happened," said Florence Triquet.

"You first."

A sigh. *"D'accord.* But I don't remember much."

Helpful, this woman. Aimée thought back

92

to the setup in the storefront for a detail to help prompt the woman's memory. "Did she sit near the window?"

"Must have. That's where I found the paper with a phone number to call her daughter — you."

"You were the one who found it?"

"*Oui,* left on the bench. I remember, now, seeing her go outside."

"Did she get into a car, a taxi?"

"No idea. But . . . That's right. I remember one strange thing. Chloé's balloon was gone. The children get balloons on their chairs at the beginning of class, and they take them home at the end. But I noticed Chloé's was missing. Maybe your mother took it with her?" Aimée heard voices in the background. "I handed the paper with the phone number to the teacher. That's it. Is your mother all right?"

"She's disappeared."

"Look, I'm really sorry, but I do have a client waiting."

Hung up.

Aimée went to the tall window. An old habit, staring out at the Seine, at Pont Marie, looking for her mother — she'd done it ever since she was eight years old. Since the day her mother had left a note on the apartment door after school telling Aimée to stay

93

with the neighbors.

Trees cast filigreed shadows over the cobbled quai. On the dark, gel-like Seine, streetlights cast reflections — quivers of bronze. Like always.

A cold hollowness filled her.

Until she noticed something bobbing in the air, silhouetted against the Seine. A car's passing headlight beam illuminated a red balloon tied to the bench across from her window.

In the brief streak of light, she saw a chalk mark on the wall behind it.

TUESDAY, EARLY EVENING

"Back in a minute!" she yelled to Melac from the hallway, grabbing her penlight. She slid into ballet flats and ran down the flights of worn steps, across the courtyard, and out the heavy door.

She almost ran into her downstairs neighbor, Monsieur Bonnet. He had a copy of *Le Monde* tucked under his arm and was clutching a white patisserie box tied with ribbon. Courtesy demanded she hold the door for this gentleman in his eighties who complained about his château's leaking roof whenever building dues came up. Her other neighbors included a countess, an actor, a bigwig at Printemps, and assorted nobility who'd inherited their flats.

"*Merci,*" Monsieur Bonnet said. "You're in a hurry as usual."

The breeze off the Seine chilled her bare ankles. She scanned the quai. No one.

The balloon bobbed in the wind. She

shone her penlight on the damp wall, which was spotted with lichen — bursts of acid green, mustard yellow, and white. Behind the bench she recognized a chalked arrow. The arrow led to a postcard tied to the balloon. On the front a photo of the Ile Saint-Louis, on the back a simple drawing. Her breath caught. The figure she recognized — Emil, the mouse who lived in the Louvre, the hero of a cartoon Aimée's mother used to draw for her when she was small. Aimée had loved those Emil stories, her mother's pictures, and time they'd spent together.

Emil and the balloon hadn't been there a few hours ago.

Aimée stared at the drawing — Emil was carrying a baby bag she recognized as Chloé's. She noticed Emil's wink.

Using her sleeve, she wiped the chalk arrow into a pale white cloud. Untied the balloon and let it float away over the Seine.

Message received.

TUESDAY, EARLY EVENING

Aimée picked up Chloé from across the courtyard and settled her with apple slices in the highchair where she could watch Melac cook. In her bedroom, Aimée emptied Chloé's baby bag and spread everything over the wood floor — diaper rash creme, baby wipes, extra empty bottle, diapers, bib, teething biscuits, gummed Peter Rabbit book. The usual.

There had to be something there.

Next she turned the bag inside out, checking each pocket, running her fingers over the seams, the strap. No holes, false seams. Nothing.

She went through everything again. Then again.

Finally, she squeezed some diaper rash creme onto a wipe. Out with it came a narrow glass cylinder, the kind in which perfume samples were given out at Printemps. She wiped it off, uncapped the cylinder, and

97

tweezered out the contents.

With her fingertips she unrolled a grid-lined page she recognized from the to-do notepad she kept in the baby bag. On it, in Sydney's slanted writing: *Please, if you're reading this, locate Germaine's code and take it to GBH. Hate involving you, but you're the only one I trust. Only you. Don't worry; I'll be in touch.*

Aimée took a deep breath. Sydney had signaled to make sure Aimée got the message. But why not come herself and ask?

Relief mingled with worry.

If her mother had gone into hiding and left Aimée with a task . . . why? Already a Foreign Legionnaire was stalking and threatening her.

Did she have a choice? How was her mother mixed up in this? So many questions.

A gurgle heralded a crawling Chloé at the door. She wore a food-stained bib but squealed when she saw her bottle on the floor. "It's empty, *ma puce.*"

Chloé crawled toward the diaper rash lotion tube quick as lightning. Aimée scooped her up.

"That's right; *Grand-mère*'s gone off the grid."

Chloé's big grey-blue eyes widened.

"You think I should help her?"

Chloé squeezed Aimée's thumb.

"I'll take that as a yes."

"Yes to what?" said Melac, taking in the disarray on the floor.

A not-so-fragrant aroma drifted from Chloé's diaper. "Quit the beans for now, Melac. No wonder she got a terrible diaper rash."

"Tell Sydney —"

She made a decision. "Look, could you help me out? Get in touch with your intelligence contact?"

"Why?" He'd reached for his leather jacket. *Merde*, she'd forgotten he was working tonight.

"It's complicated."

"So's my relationship with intelligence." Melac's eyes narrowed. "I don't ask favors unless . . . *Alors*, in my world one doesn't bother the higher levels without good reason. Not my nature to owe those types." He glanced at his buzzing phone. "What's going on?"

"Sydney's gone." The words burst out.

"Typical." His brow furrowed. "And now, of all times. She didn't even tell you that she couldn't babysit?" His eyes searched hers. "What?"

Before she could give him an edited version, he answered his ringing phone. Held up his hand. Mouthed, *Work.*

The front door shut behind him.

After Chloé's bath and good-night songs, Aimée pulled out the message she'd found in the baggie. Tried to make sense of the code in light of her mother's message. Couldn't.

Hadn't René been enthusing over a new decoding program the week before?

She called him at home. No answer. She tried his cell. She heard Radio Classique playing in the background when he picked up. Imagined him behind his desk.

"Don't tell me you're still at work, René."

"All your tech-conference schmoozing spiked interest," he said, excited. "Tomorrow I'll join you for some of your meetings before our presentation. It's a lot for you, just back on the job. How do you feel?"

"Fine." Apart from the burning headache she had from worrying — about hiding a murder victim's cache, about her missing mother, and about being threatened by a legionnaire. She popped two Doliprane.

"That's the good news."

From the way René said it, she knew there was more. She felt it in the pit of her stomach.

"And the bad?" she asked.

"We'll get it under control."

"Tell me, René."

"That's the problem, Aimée," he said. Pause. "Don't know if it's related or not, but there's been a lot of backdoor action."

Not good. "Knocking on our firewall?" She reached for her laptop. Powered it on.

"I'm running diagnostics," said René. "Called Saj in the meantime."

It had to be serious if he was calling in Saj, their permanent part-time hacker. "I'll update you within the hour," René said.

She networked into their mainframe. Delved into admin maintenance. Saw the numerous attempts to breach their firewall.

"Think I see what you're talking about," she said. "Good spotting."

If René was already running diagnostics, there was nothing to do but wait.

"Look, what's that program on coded encryption you were raving about?" she asked.

"Baksheesh?" She could hear his fingers clicking over the keys. "Already ran that code from the woman's paper through it — 120gdel." René loved puzzles. "Not so interesting."

"Not interesting as in . . . ?"

"No doubt an address. You know . . . say it's for a locker at a station: number one

101

twenty at the Gare de Lyon. There's a key, right?"

Simple.

Her thoughts went to the baggage lockers at the Gare de Lyon. She'd passed them that day. Anonymous and accessible. Yet notorious as the first place *flics* thought to surveil.

She reached for her bag and took out the key. Turned the small brass head around, feeling the smooth worn edges, and noticed part of a grooved number. Key to a safe, a deposit box? Or . . . what did it remind her of? A locker key from a gym, a *bain douche*? Not a station locker key.

"What if it's from a swimming pool locker or public bath?" she asked. "She was SDF, right? Or playing the persona, anyway."

"Aimée, you should return the money. Let the nuns deal with it."

But her mother's message was burning in her mind — *take it to GBH,* whoever that was.

First things first. To find GBH, she'd need to know about the slain Germaine Tillion. If Aimée could figure out who the woman was . . .

"Call you later, René."

Time to make another call.

TUESDAY EVENING

Aimée blew on the thick, scalding soup in her bowl. The kitchen windows fogged with condensation, and the *casse-croûte*'s melting cheese dripped on her fingers. Miles Davis nestled by her bare feet on the warm floor.

On her laptop screen, Germaine Tillion's smiling face stared back at Aimée, a photo accompanying an article in the Abidjan newspaper *Ivoir'soir*. Crinkly hair bundled up in a knot with ringlets falling to her light cocoa shoulders, Germaine stood arm in arm with a grinning twin brother, Armand, at a party at Club Madou. The caption read *Happier times for Germaine, well-known DJ, and Armand, home from Paris studies.* The headline read, SOCIETY FAMILY'S REBEL SON GUNNED DOWN IN BOUAKÉ AMBUSH.

Details were few, ongoing reports to follow. But no other reports had followed this month-old article.

103

On her phone Aimée reached Pablo, her graveyard contact at *Le Monde* archives. "This all you could find?" she asked.

"Like I've got nothing else to do, Aimée?"

She rubbed her eyes, tiredness catching up with her.

"Do they have you writing obituaries again?" Pablo, a Catalan poet, published beautiful slim tomes that René called genius. "You're too good for that, Pablo."

"If I want to survive a round of layoffs, it's better to act useful." Pause. "Manuela's pregnant."

"Congratulations." Aimée left out the *I guess.*

"I've scanned what's in our archived database," he said. "Just sent you one more."

She opened a second email, which contained a funeral notice for Edouard Tillion, French businessman, and his Ivoirian wife, Cécile. The notice had been posted five years earlier. Private services were to be held at the family cacao plantation; survivors, their children, Germaine and Armand.

The parents dead, and now both children — it struck Aimée as more than bad luck.

"Why couldn't you find anything else on such a prominent family?" she asked.

"Simple. The government controls the press."

"Don't you have contacts at reporting desks in Africa for AFP's wire service?"

"Liberia's hot now . . . an arms embargo, civil war. That's where the news is, not in the so-called stable Côte d'Ivoire."

Pablo promised to keep digging. As she hung up, she got thinking. She remembered seeing an Ivoirian resto somewhere . . . Where had it been? She could picture it — dark wood storefront, tribal carvings in the window, a yellow and green sign down a narrow passage. Then she remembered: she'd seen it while she'd been taking her "shortcut" toward the convent before she'd been threatened by the Foreign Legionnaire. Somewhere off rue du Faubourg Saint-Antoine.

By the time she located the address and number, it was after business hours. She took a chance and dialed.

"Allô?" she said.

"We're closed. Come tomorrow," said a tired, accented voice.

"Bien sûr, I will, but here's a crazy question," she said. "In Abidjan I went to Club Madou and loved the music. The DJ was a woman, and I'm dying to buy her mixes."

"That's another language to me. Ask my son," the man said.

The phone got passed. In the background

105

she heard the scraping of chairs.

"You want to know about what?" said a young man's voice.

It was late; they were closing up. She'd be direct.

"Sorry, but I want to find mixes by the female DJ who plays at Club Madou in Abidjan. I think her name's Germaine . . ."

"GT's the only one I've heard of . . . no clue where you'd find mixtapes."

DJ GT — was that Germaine Tillion? "You wouldn't know if she's got a website or email, would you?"

"There's not much on the Internet. It's hit and miss. With all the power outages and blackouts in Côte d'Ivoire, few people rely on the web. But you could try joining those LISTSERVs."

"Which LISTSERVs?"

"My friends follow an Ivoirian LISTSERV via Dakar in Senegal. Look under *zouglou* music."

Zouglou?

"Merci," she said.

Ten minutes searching on a Parisian DJ site revealed *zouglou*'s popularity. Lyrics were written in Ivoirian dialects and French street slang, paralleling the evolution of Western rap. From what she gathered, *zouglou* coupled political satire with an infectious beat. A few *zouglou* performers had lived in exile to avoid government censorship since the Mapouka, a traditional woman's dance from Dabou, had been banned the year before.

Music a threat?

Tired, she crawled under the duvet, propped the laptop on a down pillow. Miles Davis curled in a white fluff ball beside her. Heaven. If only Chloé would sleep through the night.

A blue glow from the *bateaux-mouches* flickered on her high ceiling. Not a minute after she'd joined the LISTSERV Zouglou, posted her introduction and DJ question, the LISTSERV went down. There went that idea.

Bon, nothing to do until it came back online. No update from René. Her father's words replayed in her head: *Peel back the onion, layer by layer. Know the victim, and you'll know the scenario.*

In her red Moleskine, she wrote out tomorrow's to-do list — *LISTSERV, Gare de Lyon lockers, gym at Piscine Reuilly.* She unrolled her mother's message again, releasing a scent of Chanel No. 5 and diaper cream.

Her mother had known Aimée would search for her. Had counted on Aimée finding the money and this code, getting them to the right person.

Was it because her mother couldn't? The note from Chloé's baby bag was a day old. Was Sydney even still alive?

Yet the message and balloon were recent.

A knock sounded on her door.

Could it be her? she wondered. Even though she knew her mother would never have knocked.

MIDNIGHT

Benoît, the Sorbonne academic who lived with his sister across the courtyard, stood beside a suitcase on her landing with ruffled hair and a sleepy-eyed half grin.

"So, stranger, locked out?" she asked.

He nodded. "And I've missed you."

A month had passed without a word from him.

"More like any port in a storm," she said.

"I just came in from Phnom Penh. We need to talk."

"Not a good time." She wasn't about to listen to him rationalize whatever life he'd hidden from her. Another woman? A family? "No explanations needed. Use my phone, and call your sister."

"I just heard about your injury. I'm sorry."

She felt his arms enfolding her. His breath hot in her hair. That fragrance of his, muskiness scented by wool and a long flight.

"Are you all right?"

If only she didn't want to stay in the warm cocoon of him. If only her fingers hadn't reached up to search the soft velvet skin behind his ears. "I'm okay."

"Liar."

He'd lifted her up and carried her to the duvet.

Swept aside her laptop and notebook, nuzzled her neck.

Why didn't she want him to stop? It had been more than a month since he'd cooked for her and spent the night. Then her legs wrapped around his hips, and she didn't care.

Pale sunlight filtered through the windows. She felt the cold empty space beside her. No Benoît.

Why didn't she ever learn?

Next time the academic came back from Cambodia stranded, he could find a hotel room. Still, her skin tingled, and her head felt clearer than it had in days.

From the kitchen she could hear Babette's voice, Chloé's squeals, and the sound of Miles Davis's Limoges bowl scraping the floor. Time to jump in the shower, wash off Benoît's musky smell, and dress for work.

Toweling her hair dry, she heard a beeping from her computer. A new-message alert she'd set for the LISTSERV. No time to read the message. René would pick her up in five minutes for the last day of the tech conference.

Her *depot-vents* consignment-shop finds were standing ready: a Yves Saint Laurent

111

silk blouse, an Armani jacket, and a black pencil skirt that paired nicely with ankle boots. She tousled her hair, smudged her eyes with kohl, and ran mascara through her lashes. Stuck the paper with the code in her bag's secret liner pocket and slid the key into her Agent Provocateur bra. Dashing through her apartment to say goodbye to Chloé, Aimée skidded to a halt at the door to the crowded kitchen, facing an interesting scene.

Benoît, wearing a T-shirt with an Angkor Beer logo, was eyeing Melac, who crouched by Chloé's high chair. A red bruise was swelling on Benoît's arm. Babette stood frozen with a wooden spoon clutched in her hand like a weapon. Miles Davis growled. Palpable tension sparked in the air like oil dancing on a white-hot pan.

"What are you doing here, Melac?" Aimée asked.

"We've already been introduced," said Benoît, his eyes narrowed.

"I can see that," she said, flustered. "What happened?"

An awkward silence filled the kitchen.

Melac wiped Chloé's mouth with her bib. Stood. "Next time, inform me you've got someone here before I —"

"Take things into your own hands?" she

interrupted.

Was he jealous? As if he had the right.

She wouldn't apologize. This was her home, her space, her rules. She wouldn't fight with Melac in front of her baby and nanny.

"I'm late." Aimée bent down, kissed Chloé, and winked at Babette. "Open the windows. It's a little hot in here."

WEDNESDAY, MIDMORNING

Aimée slipped away from le Train Bleu during the coffee break and headed downstairs to the station hall. Under the soot-clouded glass roof, travelers hurried to catch their trains, mingling with arrivals on the platforms. The arrival/departure board clicked above her.

She hurried toward the lockers. All she had to do was check whether the key fit and, if it did, take whatever was in the locker and figure things out from there. Two minutes, tops.

She kept an eye out for *flics* or a security camera, even though René had told her the train station's video surveillance had stopped running due to budget cuts — his friend's company had previously held that contract.

So far, so good. No one even looked like a plainclothes police officer.

But where she remembered the lockers

being, she instead found a kiosk with a notice: DUE TO THE INSTALLATION OF NEW FACILITIES, VISIT OUR TEMPORARY STORAGE LOCKERS. LEFT LUGGAGE, LEVEL 1.

Where were the old lockers? Would it be wise to inquire?

She wound through crowds and down the stairs, then through a vast corridor leading to the Métro lines. On the left lay a long open counter with racks of tagged suitcases and a line of travelers waiting to access a wall of station lockers that had been moved from upstairs.

Two *flics* were surveying the crowd. Not good.

The woman ahead of her in line was fuming. "I'll miss my train. Why don't they hurry up?"

Good question.

"Does it always take this long?" Aimée asked. "I've got a locker key; can't we just —"

"I do, too," the woman said, fingering a locker key. "I heard on the news there was a bomb scare."

Bomb scare? Aimée compared the key clutched in her moist palm to the woman's.

Not the same at all.

The two *flics* stood closer, watching.

115

Aimée noticed another pair stood by the lockers.

With tiny steps she backed up, almost bumping into a rushing family.

Melted into the crowd.

WEDNESDAY, 5 P.M.

René's face was still shining after the applause at the conference as he packed up their presentation. He even grinned at Marc by accident — Aimée knew René distrusted their rival, too.

Marc shook René's hand. Turned to Aimée. "Join us for *apéros* later?"

The last thing Aimée wanted.

"We'd love to, wouldn't we, René?" she said.

René caught her signal. "Tomorrow's perfect," he said. "We'll have time to talk about your idea."

Marc shrugged. "Too late, it's a done deal. I hadn't heard back from you, so I submitted the proposal myself."

Of course he had. He'd been testing the waters. Best of luck to him.

"I have something else," he said. "Something much better."

Fat chance.

The calculating *salaud* wanted something from them.

René released the parking brake in his Citroën DS, shifted, and eased the car into Boulevard Diderot. He'd updated her on the firewall status — Saj was monitoring their systems.

"You think Marc's behind this?" René asked.

"Wouldn't put it past him," she said, her mind on the addresses she'd written down on her to-do list. "Make a right. We're going to the Gare de Bercy."

"Where you load your car on the train? Why?"

She explained her plan.

"Do you really think you'll find a locker where the key fits?"

"Won't know until I try," she said.

"Another wild-goose chase?" René sighed. "*Allez,* Aimée, weren't you going to return the money to the nun?"

"First I've got to locate whatever this key opens."

She'd come up with a story for whoever needed to know: She'd found the key in her aunt's belongings, wondered if it fit their lockers; would they be so kind as to help? Aimée and René didn't spend long at the

Gare de Bercy before she saw the key she had didn't match the ones for the lockers there. An hour later, she'd checked lockers at two *bains-douches,* the Reuilly swimming pool, and two public gymnasiums. She'd gotten nowhere.

"Satisfied now?" René's eyebrows rose in irritation.

"I'm missing something." She pulled out her Paris map and thumbed to the twelfth arrondissement. "I've checked all the public access places with lockers I can think of."

"What about hospitals? There are three hospitals around Bel-Air, and Saint-Antoine, which isn't far, is huge."

"You mean a staff locker?" Thought for a moment. "If Genelle was masquerading as an SDF, how would she get into a hospital?" Aimée set the map on the dashboard. "Let's say it's some place close, here in Bel-Air. Accessible."

She stuck her finger on the convent, then used her kohl eye pencil to draw a circle around it with a several-block radius.

"See, Hôpital Rothschild," said René.

She still didn't buy a hospital — too many eyes.

"And a Catholic school, another convent adjoining it, apartment buildings, the National Forests Office, the Métro, the Picpus

Cemetery . . ." She flicked a dead leaf off her heel.

The victim, this Genelle, had hidden something valuable that had cost her her life. Where?

René pointed. "Next door's the chapel where the Sisters of the Adoration pray nonstop for the victims of the guillotine in the Terror."

People were still doing that for the Terror today? "Even now?"

René rolled down his window. Nodded. "The whole place creeped me out," he said. "There's a mass grave there, the pit where they threw in the commoners outside the private cemetery. Even the name is creepy, 'Picpus,' fleabite. There's a bizarre sixteenth-century legend about villagers suffering a plague of red and white blisters until a monk cured them with an ointment for fleas. Some miracle. Picpus — who'd want to keep a name like that?"

Aimée remembered the sign under the lintel. "And you know all this how?"

René averted his eyes. "The *comte*."

Curious, she looked up from the map. René rarely spoke of his childhood growing up in the *comte* d'Amboise's château, where René's mother had curated the *comte*'s mechanical toy collection — among other

120

things. Aimée often suspected René was the fruit of their liaison. She knew so little about his upbringing. "How's that, René?"

"He took me when I was young."

"The *comte* brought you there?"

"He's a descendant, so a branch of his family got the blade. After the Revolution, noble families bought the land secretly and reburied their guillotined with headstones, in family crypts . . . Even today, aristocratic descendants have the right to burial in those crypts." He shrugged. "*Bien sûr,* they left the commoners in the mass pit. The Marquis de Lafayette's buried there under an American flag."

"Go back."

René switched on the ignition.

"Good idea," he said. "Let's go home and get takeout."

She grabbed René's arm. "*Non, non,* I mean the part about crypts. You mean like mausoleums?"

René shrugged again. "Little locked houses of the dead. Creepy."

"That's it."

Why hadn't she noticed it two nights before?

"What do you mean?" he asked.

"Look, there's only a wall between the convent and Cimetière de Picpus."

"Et alors?"

"Hurry, René, before it closes."

The sign on the tall ancient doors read, TEMPORARY CLOSURE DUE TO CHAPEL MAINTENANCE. Taped beside it was a layout of the chapel and grounds accompanied by detailed instructions for donations to the *tronc,* the offering box.

More bureaucratic than the tax office.

"Forget that," said René.

Next door she saw the line for the Sisters of the Poor soup kitchen forming. Couldn't risk the legionnaire watching. Or putting the nun in danger.

She'd called and left two messages for Sister Agnès the day before. Still hadn't heard back. Tried again.

"*Oui, mademoiselle,* I took down your messages," said the receptionist at the convent. "*C'est dommage,* but Sister Agnès already left on retreat."

Great.

"When does she return?" Aimée asked.

"Ah, it's her order's yearly retreat at Mont-Saint-Michel. They'll be cloistered until next month."

There went that idea. "Sister, do you have a list of names of volunteers who help out at the soup kitchen?"

"No, we don't keep records."

A dead end.

"Merci," Aimée said.

She remembered the street where the ambulance had picked up Genelle/Germaine's body. Thought back to the layout of the dark convent grounds she'd trailed the crime-scene tech through. The warren of old arcades, the corridors, paths, the chapel and the soup kitchen.

"These grounds communicate, René. Go around the block and park on Avenue de Saint-Mandé."

"I'm not breaking into a cemetery. Forget it."

"We don't have to," she said. *Not really.* "Go along with me, René."

"When hasn't that gotten me in trouble?"

As if her mother wasn't already in trouble?

"One last stop, okay?" she said.

He shifted into first. On the avenue she pointed to a row of Haussmannian buildings across the street from a *salon de thé.* Cars were wedged in nose to fender.

"I can't park," he said. "It's jammed."

"Pull in where that camionette's coming out. See? Turn in there."

"You're sure?"

"There's parking behind."

René eased the fat Citroën inside, barely avoiding scraping his pride and joy on the blue grilled gates. No way in hell could the ambulance have made it through this old carriageway — this was why the nuns had been watching the body be loaded into the ambulance out on the street.

"Keep going, René."

"But it's private parking here. I'll get a ticket or even towed away."

Nervous as always about his car.

"We won't stay here that long. Keep going around to the back. There. See the wall?"

A few cars and a small backhoe were parked on a lot, half of which was newly paved and giving off the tang of fresh tar. Chestnut trees topped the old wall, the stucco flaking, exposing stone.

René stared at the notice on the gate, a smaller version of what Aimée had seen on the other side, while Aimée studied the lock-pick set she kept in her compact. Useless with a big ancient lock like this.

"No way in hell will I climb that wall," said René.

A red-faced, stout man wearing a blue work coat strode toward them. His footsteps spit gravel. He wiped a smear of something white off his chin. They'd interrupted him either shaving or eating a cream puff.

"This isn't public parking," he said. "It's private property."

"That's right, *monsieur,*" she said, reaching into her alias card case. "We appreciate your vigilance. And cooperation."

She flashed her father's old police ID, doctored with new seals and her own photo. Not the most attractive photo, with her mouth puckered as if she'd tasted a lemon.

"My colleague, the doctor here, and I need to revisit the crime scene," she said.

René blinked. The hovering smell of tar layered the air; crisp orange leaves crackled and swirled in the rising wind.

"No one told me," the man said.

"The investigation's incomplete, *monsieur.* The doctor, a forensic biologist, needs samples."

René pursed his lips.

"I'm not supposed to provide access without notice," the man said. "You'll need to arrange another time."

No doubt they'd disturbed his dessert.

"No one values rules more than I, *monsieur.* However, we both know murder

126

respects no regulation or timetable." She shrugged. "I'd appreciate your assistance. I assume you saw the victim. This could provide insight, a vital detail."

"But I told the police already; I heard — I mean I just found her."

He'd stumbled, caught himself. He knew more than he'd said in his statement. She shot René a look.

"Correct," she said. "You'll show us where, so my colleague can verify the flora evidence in the surrounding area."

René coughed.

"You mean —"

"Exactement, monsieur," she interrupted the man, overwhelming him with officiousness, "foliage samples from the grass and trees on the crime site. Please, open the gate while the doctor gets his kit."

She heard the keys jangle in the man's pocket. "I don't want to get in trouble. The tenants were already disturbed enough."

"You won't, *monsieur.* You're helping the police, doing your civic duty."

While René gathered his briefcase, she slipped him her eyebrow tweezers, a random toothpick, and glassine envelopes that had once held crumbled teething biscuits, which she had smoothed out quickly. Licked the crumbs off her fingers.

"Keep him busy," she whispered.

"How can I pretend I'm a forensic biologist, whatever that is?" he asked.

"I just made that up. You'll think of something." She winked. "Dr. Friant."

WEDNESDAY, 7 P.M.

The guard led them through the gate to the cedar tree hanging with the rippling crime scene tape. René dutifully crawled and picked with the tweezers. The guard held René's car flashlight, pointing locations out. With the guard occupied, Aimée hurried under another double row of chestnut trees and found the walled cemetery beyond the site of the mass graves.

Stupid. She'd passed this wall the other night and hadn't thought to look inside.

Inside, she found a tumble of tilted headstones tattooed with lichen, as well as rows of mausoleums and crypts. Some were maintained, others cracked and sunken with age. In the distance several American flags proclaimed the tomb of Lafayette.

Consulting the legend, she looked for plot 120 and searched among the numbers engraved on the backs of the mausoleums. Little locked houses of the dead all right.

She passed row after row. Often numbers had worn off. Her boots slipped on the mossed stone ledges.

Number 120. A rusted metal fence surrounded the limestone mausoleum; dusty plastic flowers were wedged in the door. IN MEMORY OF GEORGES DE LARRIGUE AND *la famille* LARRIGUE.

Plot 120 . . . gdel.

She looked around. No one. The rising wind made her shiver.

Or was it the fact that she was breaking into a crypt?

She took the key, warm from her skin, out of her bra. Slid it into the large keyhole. A perfect fit.

Twisted it and pushed the door open.

The metal door scraped, and she paused. Looked around again. Only the long shadows from the trees.

She had to hurry. Poor René could pick up only so much with her tweezers.

Her penlight beam shone on dirty cobwebs and a dead spider that hung over Georges de Larrigue's coffin. More cobwebs curtained the ceiling and veiled a leaded stained-glass window.

She stuck the penlight in her mouth and ran her fingers around the sides of the stone-encased coffin. Then behind. Felt something.

Yanked.

A manila envelope tumbled to the ground near her feet.

She took one look at the letters printed on it — *GBH* — and stuck it in her bag. In a flash, she'd relocked the mausoleum and was running, forgetting the penlight in her mouth until she realized she couldn't breathe.

"I hope you've collected enough samples, Doctor," she said, trying not to pant. "We've been called to the *commissariat.* Now."

The guard, now talkative, continued to expound on his theories about the murder all the way to the car. He opened the doors to the street and guided René out, stood waving goodbye on the curb.

"You've got a new best friend, René," Aimée said.

"Tell me about it," he said. "I thought he'd never stop being helpful. Upshot, he heard a car pull out before the victim was found but saw nothing." René shifted into second. "Hope it was worth it; did you find something?"

"Hungry?"

"Starving."

"Let's go where we won't get disturbed."

A filmy haze floated across her vision.

When this happened, the doctor had warned her, it was important to stay calm. To close her eyes, breathe.

Calm?

When she opened her eyes again, the film had disappeared and been replaced by a dull, creeping ache behind her temple.

She popped two Doliprane and swallowed them dry.

WEDNESDAY EVENING

Wednesday evenings, Aimée usually had Babette stay late so she could schedule meetings or catch up on work at the office. When Aimée had checked in, Babette had reported that Chloé had loved her yogurt, played with bubbles in the bath, and gone to sleep, *mais non,* no word from Sydney.

Aimée sat across from René in the closet-sized back room of la Liberté, the anarchist café. It had a seasonal prix-fixe menu, all ingredients fresh from the local market, the Marché d'Aligre, and, as regulars knew, a select wine list. Farouk, the chef, concocted one superb daily special in the tiny kitchen. The owner worked on a crossword puzzle in *Le Parisien* with several clients at the counter.

"You think it's safe here, Aimée?" René asked.

"The cabinetmakers fomented the Revolution and marched up to Bastille from here,

133

René. Same spirit, hasn't changed." She looked around. Only one old woman reading *l'Humanité*, the Communist newspaper, over a glass of deep red. "Plus, we're early."

She was itching to open the envelope, but her phone was ringing. Babette again. Then a voice mail. A flash emergency — the washing machine had broken, flooding the kitchen. Aimée made a round of calls to plumbers, every number she tried busy, busy, busy. Ten minutes later, she'd secured a promise from her neighbor's Polish plumber to come first thing in the morning. Their food arrived just as Saj called with updates on the firewall. She was eating so distractedly she almost didn't notice the autumnal colors: orange-glazed turbot slivers topped by parsley, served on a bed of whipped beets with dollops of pureed *potiron.*

Finally off the phone, she caught René up. "All under control. But Saj wants us in early so he can explain the new maintenance and security protocol he's worked out."

Dirty diapers, a flooded kitchen, and problems with their firewall. *Another day at the office.*

Finally she had a chance to pull out the envelope and set it on the table.

René stared in surprise. "That's what you

found?"

"Hidden in a crypt. Meant for a GBH, I'd say. Whatever that stands for."

"GBH. Gamma benzene hexachloride?"

"What's that?"

"Treatment for lice."

Who knew?

"I found this in the mausoleum numbered one twenty behind the coffin of Georges de Larrigue."

"120gdel . . . Okay, I get that Genelle or Germaine hid this. Must be important. What's inside?"

She opened the flap. Pulled out a packet of papers. Spread them next to her ramekin of *mousse au chocolat.*

"René, it's part of a map. The names look African."

He nodded. "It's western Côte d'Ivoire. See the border and mountain range straddling Liberia?"

She shifted the papers around between them. A list of names, European and African. Official-looking documents — cargo manifests or maybe bills of lading.

René unfolded a much-thumbed rectangle. "This looks like a flight plan."

He lifted up a torn sheet from a newspaper dated three days earlier. Written in the white margin was *Gérard Bjedje Hlili* with an address, *34 rue de Pommard.*

"This your man, GBH?" René asked.

It was coming together. "We've got it, René! Germaine must have hidden the key in the washer as a double safe."

" 'Double safe' as in keeping the money and this information separate?"

"Maybe she was afraid she'd be murdered before she could deliver these documents to GBH."

"So she knew his whereabouts?"

"Who else could have written down his name and address here?"

Aimée's appetite vanished. She pushed aside the *mousse au chocolat* and threw down her serviette.

René licked his spoon. "What's the hurry?"

"What if we're too late, René? This information's already three days old."

René wiped chocolate from the corner of his mouth. Folded his serviette. "This is all kind of dodgy, don't you think, Aimée?"

"That's beside the point." *Was it?* " 'Dodgy' as in having to do with smuggling?" she said.

"I don't know," said René. "But there's no reason you should get involved."

And what was she supposed to do, with her absent mother at the root of it? "A little late for that."

"There you go, jumping off the deep end."

"Deep end? A woman's been murdered. She might have died for whatever this is, René. Sydney made it clear that this needs to get to GBH. Now we've got his name and this address —"

"Think, Aimée. Act rational for a moment."

"Fine." She set a wad of francs on the table. "I'm taking a taxi."

As she stood, a wave of dizziness hit her. She gripped the back of her chair. The doctor had warned her against stressing out. She closed her eyes, inhaled.

"You all right, Aimée?" René's voice sounded far away. Somewhere in space.

Breathe. Again.

Clarity seeped back in. She opened her eyes. The dizziness had passed.

"*Regardes,* it's your third day back at work." Rene'd scrambled down from his chair. "You need to rest."

She could do this, couldn't she?

"I'm fine." She smiled at the chef. "Espresso to go, please, Farouk."

137

"Feels familiar, these little houses." René downshifted on the dark, tree-lined street, which was illuminated by streetlamps. "But you're sure you want to do this?"

Despite mounting dread over the significance of these documents, the only thing she felt sure about was that this was the right way to offload them and the money. The whole thing smelled odd; everything had been upside down since she'd gotten the call from the playgroup. If delivering the documents to GBH was so simple, why had her mother not done it herself? Aimée pushed the thought aside — maybe Sydney hadn't been able to for some reason.

"That's it. Number thirty-four," she said.

Rue de Pommard was a line of three-story houses with mansard windows peeping from tile roofs. *Petites maisons* of *meulière* stone — the red-brown composite often found embedded with ancient shells quarried outside Paris. Twentieth-century bourgeois Parisians had embraced the look, embellishing the houses with art-nouveau details.

"Now I remember," said René. "I was here with my computer repairman friend from Montgallet once. He makes house calls out here — a lot of media types and journalists who are all clueless about tech. It's a trendy neighborhood."

No doubt. Each house had a garden. Chloé would have loved it.

Number thirty-four was set back from the street. By the time René had parked the car, Aimée couldn't get rid of the feeling that someone was watching her again. Fear prickled the back of her neck. Darkness shrouded the place.

Was Gérard Bjedje Hlili waiting for the drop-off?

Hedgerows towered, glistening with mist floating from the direction of the old Bercy wine depot. Orange-red leaves rustled in the gutter.

"I don't like this," said René, lowering his voice.

As if she did? But she shouldn't drag René into it. "Stay here. Wait."

"Not on your life," he hissed. "The side door's ajar."

"You see in the dark now?"

"Easy to tell from how the light glints off the door's glass at an angle."

She saw what René meant. "Ajar" as in *entrez*? One way to find out.

As a precaution, she stuck the envelope inside the waistband of her pencil skirt, which held it snug against the skin of her back.

Only a few lights on in this compound of small stone houses. Not a sound but the occasional rumble coming off the rail tracks from the switchyard of the Gare de Bercy.

She'd ignore her unease over what the documents suggested. Hand them over to GBH. Arrange to leave him the money the next day. Finish this and get her mother's whereabouts from this man.

Standing in the shadow by the half-open door, Aimée noticed a wide-open window facing the yard. Heard movement in the house. Debated whether to knock or walk in until she heard a man's voice from inside: "Flown the coop . . . Almost two hours and no sign of him . . . Your fault. I should have grabbed him when . . . What do you mean 'visitors'?"

She froze in the chill night air. Someone had seen them. René tugged her arm. She made her feet move and followed him behind the hedgerow. A figure slid out of the open door and shut it behind him without a sound.

He was coming right toward them. Stuffing down the urge to run, she motioned René not to move.

"That GBH?" René whispered.

She shook her head. "Bad news." She recognized his stealthy movements, felt that tremor of unease she'd had in the rainy courtyard, that animal presence. "That's the legionnaire who threatened me. See the tattoos on his knuckles?"

"And there's a watcher on the street."

The legionnaire's steel-toed boots stopped in front of the hedge where she and René were hiding. Had he smelled her perfume? Any moment he'd see them.

Aimée heard the unmistakable metallic click of a safety sliding off. *Gun,* she mouthed at René, *get down.* She grabbed her Swiss Army knife and dove at the *mec*'s ankles as René, thinking quickly, scooped up a handful of dirt and threw it at the legionnaire's face.

A thupt, thupt drilled into the stone wall behind them. Grit and powder sprinkled her hair, got in her ears. The *salaud* was using a suppressor.

Her knife ripped fabric and made contact with a sinewy muscle. A yell. She jammed the blade deeper, held on for dear life. She had to throw him off balance. "Drop the gun."

He staggered, rubbing his eyes, trying to kick her off. "Give it to me, you —"

René sprang at him while she wrestled with the *salaud*'s leg. He swung out, and René, a black belt, blocked his hand. The gun, safety off, flew free and discharged as it landed. A spit of glass as a window shattered. *Merde.* At least it hadn't hit them.

The legionnaire staggered and fell. René kicked him in the head, and he went quiet.

She grabbed his feet, ripping her skirt as she struggled to drag him. *Heavy, this big mec.* "Help me." Together they pulled him into the bushes. Blood trickled from his leg, the knife still stuck in it.

She put her fingers to her lips. Mouthed, *He's wired.*

René pulled out the man's earbud. "Not anymore."

She quickly rifled through his pockets, found his phone and a notebook, and shoveled everything into her bag. Winced as she pulled her knife from his calf.

"Let's go, Aimée," René said.

Not until she checked the house.

Before René could stop her, she ran to the unlocked door and let herself in, scarf over her head in case there was surveillance. With her penlight she scanned the rooms — IKEA furniture, binoculars on a kitchen table, a sleeping bag on the couch. A case of instant noodles and packs of instant Nestlé coffee. Like every safe house she'd ever accompanied her father to. It breathed transience, anonymous fear, and waiting. No trace of her mother. No one there at all.

Back out in the yard by the fence, rose-bush branches were broken, and there was a mash of footsteps in the dirt. GBH was gone.

WEDNESDAY NIGHT

René's hands trembled on the steering wheel.

"He got really quiet, Aimée."

"Don't worry about him, René. He pulled a gun, remember? Shot and tried to kill us." She turned around. Bit her lip. "We're being followed."

"You do know how to top off an evening, Aimée."

Perspiration beaded René's brow. He turned left into Place Lachambeaudie. Ahead stood the well-lit pillared church of Notre-Dame-de-la-Nativité de Bercy, an island in the stream of traffic on Place Lachambeaudie. Churchgoers congregated on the steps after a nighttime service.

A dark car with beaming headlights was closing in.

"Hold on," said René between clenched teeth.

"Go for it."

She braced her hands on the dashboard, planted her heeled boots on the floor. He cut a hard left behind the church and swerved into the opposite lane, throwing Aimée against the door handle. René looped around the church, past the fire station, and accelerated. But instead of heading toward the Seine, he looped again around the church and at the last moment took a hard right into the street threading through the old wine depot.

In the distance behind them, the headlights popped up.

"*Merde,* there aren't many ways out of here," he said.

She pulled out her map and located the quartier as quickly as she could in the dark bouncing car. "You don't have to get out. Just before the Bercy warehouse tunnels, take a hard left up into the freight yard."

The Citroën DS juddered, taking the curve and spitting gravel as René downshifted up the slope. He pulled behind a camion by the corrugated iron–roofed rail freight depot. Killed the lights. His hands were shaking.

"You all right?" René asked.

Aimée craned her neck to see if the car had followed. "I'll know in a minute."

A minute passed. Then another. Their

breath fogged the car's windows. A train passed on the network of rails below them. Switch points with red pinpricks of light connected to the black rails, looking like a realist painting.

"Think it's safe?" René reached for the key in the ignition.

"Not the way we came in. Ten to one the car's waiting." She looked at the map again. "We've got to walk over the bridge just there. Get a taxi."

"Along the rail lines? You're crazy." Then, in a plaintive whine, he added, "I can't leave my car here."

"We've been seen. Marked. Put a note on your windshield, say you had engine trouble; you'll pick it up first thing in the morning."

They followed a path to the old upper-level tracks of an abandoned rail spur toward la Petite Ceinture, disused and overgrown with weeds and wildflowers. Thank God she'd worn ankle boots. The area skirted les Maréchaux, the old ring road of Paris encircling the outskirts.

Every few minutes she turned back to see if they'd been followed. *Not yet.* René grumbled, "It's hell on my shoes." His Lobbs were handmade.

She knew walking took it out of René, as he suffered hip dysplasia, which was common in dwarves. She slowed her pace.

Her phone trilled, an eerie ringing in the night, as the wild flowers whipped her legs and the breeze carried the tang of oil and fir trees. They took a break on a crumbling cement outcrop on a spit of land where the rail lines forked.

"*Allô?*" she said.

No answer. A click.

Her mother? Another message?

"What's your poison?" said a crackling voice in the dark.

Startled, she almost dropped the phone.

René jumped from the outcrop with his arms braced in attack mode.

Laughter. "*Le petit*'s a kung fu fighter."

A lantern illuminated a man in stained overalls holding a bottle. He tapped the side of his red-veined nose, warning them about trouble.

"Keep your eye out for patrols," he said.

"The railway guards?" asked Aimée.

He took a gulp, then nodded.

"When?" René asked.

"Should walk this way any minute now," the man said.

Great.

"What about you?" she asked.

"*Moi?*" He laughed again. Pointed. "Patrols ignore our bunker, an old war shelter.

Plenty of *bon vin* and *mes camarades.*"

René shot Aimée a look. "It's got to be safer down there."

Aimée looked around. Safer with a bunch of winos? "I don't think so." She felt wet-ness on her neck. Swiped it and her fingers came back red and sticky.

"You're bleeding," said René, blinking in the light. "Were you hit? Didn't you feel it?"

Had her adrenalin been pumping so much she hadn't realized she'd been grazed by one of the legionnaire's bullets? Or shrap-nel? Blood drenched the collar of her silk YSL blouse — *merde.*

Idiot. She needed to stop the bleeding. "Okay, I hope they have water."

They entered a stucco half triangle pro-truding from the earth under a canopy of swaying fir branches, felt their way down the leaf-strewn stairs to a narrow candle-lit cavern. Two men sat passed out by a niche arranged like an altar, with candles and empty bottles. One snored. The other had a sleeping kitten resting on his lap.

"Party central, eh?" said René, looking around for a bottle of water. "Sit down; let me clean your head."

The shelter reeked of wine, candle wax, and mold. She wanted to turn around and leave. Impatient, she found a three-legged stool by the wine altar.

René probed her scalp, using his cloth handkerchief to part her hair.

A sharp pain bit into her scalp. She gritted her teeth.

"Don't move," he said.

René showed her a sliver of bloody metal shrapnel in his handkerchief. "Not deep — that's the good news."

Head wounds bled. She didn't want stitches. Going to a doctor for a shrapnel wound would raise questions.

She handed René a roll of adhesive tape from her bag.

"That's what we use for the calendar at the office," he said.

"Tape me up, René. Hurry."

WEDNESDAY, LATE NIGHT

While the man who'd led them down from the outcrop pulled out a guitar and strummed a Georges Brassens song between pulls on the bottle, she took out the legionnaire's phone. The war-era bomb shelter had the ambiance of a flophouse with an old-man-squat flavor. So damn thirsty, but she wouldn't have touched the offered bottle with a barge pole.

"Non, merci."

The phone was a grey military-grade clamshell model. She flipped it open.

It required a code. She handed it to René. "Time to work your magic."

He flicked four alphanumeric keys. Nothing. He squinted at the keypad. Tried again. On the third try, the small screen blipped and showed a call list.

A genius with code.

She wrote down the one phone number it contained in her Moleskine's to-do list.

150

"Trash it," said René. "Destroy it in case —"

"Hold on," said the drifter, his fingers paused on the guitar strings. "You're victims of a consumer society. A throwaway world. Give it to me."

"It's hot," said René. "No reception down here anyway."

On the wall behind him in the flickering candlelight, Aimée saw a peeling blackout notice dated 1942. The rank smell of mold in the corners was getting to her.

"You stole it?" the man asked.

"It could have a tracer installed," René said.

The man set his guitar down on the dirt floor. "Looks fine to me. Don't you owe me for the hospitality?" *A threat?*

The *mec* with the cat in his lap opened his eyes. He held a knife in his hand, the blade glinting. Hawked and spit. "Clément's right. *C'est obligatoire.*"

A threat all right. Had the drifter invited them into the bunker to rip them off?

Aimée stood and nudged René back toward the steps. The last thing they needed was a knife fight with winos.

"You don't want this phone," said Aimée. "Not very nice people could find you."

The knife wielder shoved the cat onto the

151

sleeping man's lap. He sprang up and moved fast across the shelter.

"So you're hiding? On the run, eh?" he said. "Might be worth something to somebody."

Time to get the hell out of here.

"*Bon,* it's yours." Aimée threw it. "Good luck."

"What's the code?" said the knife wielder.

"Two-seven-four-two!" René yelled over his shoulder as Aimée pushed him up the cobwebbed stairs.

They ran, keeping to the tree shadows along the tracks, on the lookout for a patrol, checking behind them to see if the men were following. Wild dandelion puffs fluttered in the rushes of air from the passing trains, the seed fuzz glowing in the distant light like tossed stars. Two round water towers, empty and graffitied, loomed over their path, which would take them beyond a series of smaller warehouses on the tracks. A three-quarter moon glowed above them like a sleepy-eyed pearl.

René panted. "How far?"

"Rue de Charenton's close. I'm calling a taxi now." She dialed as she ran, pressing the cell phone to her ear.

As they ran, a train passed like a slow-moving snake of lights. The sound carried across the field of tracks, a thwack thwack.

"Did you hear that?" said René.

Fear vibrated down to the soles of her feet. *Gunshots?* Close, they were so close to rue de Charenton.

"Keep going, René."

Climbing the stairs up to the street, she could see the taxi's green light. *Almost there.*

Then a dull thunk behind them, a flash of light over the tracks. An explosion.

"*Mon Dieu,* do you think . . . ?" René stood frozen on the steps. "Did those winos use the phone already?"

Her stomach wrenched — had whoever followed them traced the legionnaire's phone? "No time to find out. Move, René. Hurry."

Feeling sick to her stomach, she collapsed inside the taxi. As she gave the driver René's address, she furiously thought over what in the world these documents could mean.

She dropped a shaken René off first. All the way to Ile Saint-Louis, she wondered where GBH had escaped to.

No chalk marks on the quai wall.

After paying Babette and kissing a sleeping Chloé, Aimée peeled off her clothes and set the envelope on the duvet and curled up. The plumbing was now under control, but there had still been no word from Sydney.

Her legs ached; pain prickled her scalp. She reached for a Doliprane.

Tired, but she couldn't sleep. Her mind spun — the cemetery, the house on rue de Pommard, the legionnaire, the aggressive winos.

Her phone rang. René's number.

"Aimée, I was listening to my police scanner, and there are reports . . ."

"What reports, René?"

"Gunshots fired. Two separate incidents. Homicides." Pause. "You know what that means?"

"The legionnaire's cohort got to the winos and cleaned up?"

She shivered under the duvet.

"My car will stick out like a sore thumb," he said.

"You're going to report it stolen. Right now. Stolen three hours ago from rue du Louvre. You're only noticing it now because you worked late, left the office, and couldn't find your car."

She hung up and turned on the light. Spread out the contents of the legionnaire's pockets on her lap. Got to work.

"According to what I found in the legionnaire's pocket, his name was Hans Volker — if we believe his South African driver's license," said Aimée. "He also carried a checkbook from Banque d'Abidjan in the name of Jochim Wilmsdorf. Not to mention a gym card from Johannesburg in the name of Karl Duisberg."

Aimée wrote the names on the whiteboard using blue marker. Early-morning sunlight streamed into the Leduc Detective office from the window overlooking rue du Louvre.

"He used a pistol with a suppressor and carried a cell phone containing this number." She wrote that down, too.

"And he was wired," said René, from his ergonomic chair. Chloé crawled on the parquet floor, playing with her bunny.

Saj, cross-legged on his tatami mat, nodded as he typed on his laptop. He'd imprisoned his long blond dreadlocks in a bun and was wearing an aqua muslin shirt and a wristlet of prayer beads that clacked. Back from a meditation course in India, he exuded calm.

Aimée wished she could bottle it. Not that she wanted anything to do with the oils he'd brought back, insisting they were stress reducers. Or to join him in yoga and guided meditation.

"Hans also carried a diagram of this house on rue de Pommard," she said. "Along with a small photo of this man, who we can assume is Gérard Bjedje Hlili, since his name's written underneath."

She taped up an enlarged copy of the photo. It showed a young cocoa-complected man in shirtsleeves addressing a group of people from the back of a truck, which was parked under palm trees by what appeared to be a village well. Even in the photo he emanated an undefinable charisma.

"I'm searching the Interpol site," said Saj. "But since we know Hans's identity, what are we looking for?"

"Hans wasn't working alone." Aimée related how he'd been wired when he'd accosted her demanding Genelle's package. "I want to know who employed him."

René was studying what Aimée had taped

on the board. "Hans and the watcher — his accomplice, who we're assuming followed us — wanted these documents. Waybills, flight manifests, cargo lists of farm equipment, a map of Côte d'Ivoire. They must be important. Important enough to shoot winos for the legionnaire's phone."

Saj nodded. "Maybe the documents indicate some kind of sensitive cargo or something headed to, for example, Liberia right next door, a country that's restricted by a UN embargo." He pointed to the topographical map Aimée had taped up of the shared border. *"Attends."* Saj unclipped something from his man bun. A metal drawing compass. "I always keep this handy."

At the dry-erase board, Saj put the point of the compass at a spot on the map, extended the thin arm, made a mark with a mechanical pencil, and measured the distance. He wrote down some numbers, calculated, and checked the figures against the flight path information.

"Those coordinates should match the airport destination of Bouaké." Saj tapped the map. "However, they don't. They appear to be in a nature reserve in the Nimba mountain range of the Guinea Highlands on the border."

"Meaning?" she asked.

René stood. "According to the manifest, this flight originated in Belarus, had several stopovers and an end destination of Bouaké. Here." René grabbed a ruler and pointed to a spot on the map in northern Côte d'Ivoire. "But why, as Saj points out, would it land instead between Touba and Danané, here in a nature reserve, as the coordinates indicate?" He tapped the ruler again on a western region. "That's mountainous and without an airstrip."

"What if it crashed?" Aimée picked up a squirming Chloé, who needed a diaper change. "And it carried more than farm equipment?" For a moment, the office was silent apart from Chloé's gurgles and the printer spewing Saj's new security surveillance protocols.

Saj tugged his prayer beads. "Don't you wonder . . . ?"

"Why a South African legionnaire employed by a shadow firm would be hunting this information?" she finished for him.

"What's the bigger picture?" said René. "How was the homeless woman your mother knew involved in this? Who's Gérard Hlili, and why should you get these documents to him?"

A knock on Leduc Detective's door. Then the front door alarm sounded, startling

Chloé, who was lying mid–diaper change on Aimée's desk.

"That's Babette," said René. "Eight o'clock, right on time."

Aimée shot René a look. "Babette knows the code."

René pulled another dry-erase board showing current firewall projects over the Germaine Tillion murder board. Aimée shoved the legionnaire's pocket contents into her desk drawer. Saj sat back down on his tatami mat.

René switched off the alarm.

Babette walked in from the reception area, her eyes large with warning. "Sorry, I forgot the new code."

Two men followed her, one in a leather bomber jacket, one in a hoodie. "Mademoiselle Leduc," said the bomber jacket. It wasn't a question. The hoodie checked his phone.

Part of the legionnaire's rat pack, sent to finish business?

THURSDAY MORNING

"We're appointment only," said Aimée, fastening Chloé's diaper. Reached for her cell phone, willing her hands not to shake.

"Good. You've got an appointment right now," said the one in the bomber jacket.

"I'm booked, *messieurs.*"

"Monsieur Daniel Lacenaire says it's important. We've got a car waiting."

The suit who had questioned Sister Agnès at the convent. Wary after the previous night's encounter with the legionnaire, Aimée hesitated. Could she believe these men were undercover intelligence?

And why hadn't Morbier gotten back to her with info on Lacenaire?

Play dumb.

"That should mean something to me?" she asked.

Babette picked up Chloé, slid her feet into her onesie. "We need to hurry to make story time."

160

A code, which they'd worked out back in September after a thwarted kidnapping attempt. Babette would take Chloé to Martine, Aimée's best friend, until further notice.

"The country's security should mean something to you, *mademoiselle*. Monsieur Lacenaire said to mention the name Sydney Leduc," said bomber jacket.

Aimée felt her heart start pounding.

With a studied indifference, the man in the hoodie had turned to René, who was standing in attack stance. "*Restez tranquil, monsieur.* We're the good guys."

THURSDAY MORNING

Riding in the unmarked late-model Peugeot, Aimée took stock. These two weren't superspies, just everyday intelligence agents. The current breed resembled every young thirtysomething on the Métro, blending in and never drawing attention. Urban professionals.

Still, their eyes gave them away. Trained, like any *flics* undercover, their gazes never stopped moving. They saw things before they happened. As Melac did. As her father had when he'd been on a 'mission,' as he'd called them.

The passing buildings blurred, looking like a hazy old black-and-white film. A warning sign. She closed her eyes and rubbed her temples. Took deep breaths, per the doctor's instructions.

Terrified after the postconcussion tests had revealed a blood clot in her brain, she'd obeyed the doctor to the letter. Couldn't risk blindness or loss of taste, which René had repeatedly warned her a Parisian chef with her condition had suffered.

While she recovered, praying the clot would dissolve, the doctor had forbidden computer use and reading, to avoid strain and permanent damage. She'd suffered a month of blurry and double vision, balance problems, colors fading, and off-kilter depth perception.

Test after test. And damn it, her eyes hurt. So she'd listened to music and, when that bored her, old tapes of her grandfather's lectures to the officers' class at the police academy. Full of surveillance and interrogation techniques and the ABCs of undercover — bits he'd told her his pal in intelligence had shared with him. *We're all one family.* In the police captain's introduction to the lectures, he referred to Claude Leduc's talks as the gold standard, their in-house undercover manual. The academy had presented him with the recorded copies as a special gift on some anniversary. She loved listening in her darkened room, huddled under the duvet, hearing her grandfather's soothing, humor-filled voice, imagining him still with her. Claude Leduc, detective, chef, auction house frequenter, wine lover, and general bon vivant, who'd had a mistress she wasn't supposed to know about. He had encouraged her to follow her passion and what she was good at: detective work, not medicine.

Her subconscious was on overdrive thanks to him. Maybe his insight had rubbed off and helped her better read these *mecs,* how they operated. So far, textbook, according to *Grand-père.*

The car slowed down. From the back seat, Aimée opened her eyes to see an impasse, a narrow cul-de-sac resembling many in the southeastern twelfth arrondissement. Cobbled, dotted by small industrial spaces, windows sprinkled with geraniums. A building sported a fading sign for DUBONNET, the classic digestive of quinine and wine, with herbs and spices to cut the bitter flavor, once used to combat malaria. The impasse exuded old Paris. Two- and three-story buildings, some with a VENDRE sign in front — they'd get snapped up soon.

A worn wood gate slid open on a redbrick metalworks foundry bordered by a small warehouse. Or so it appeared from the exterior.

The hoodie parked and disappeared, and the black bomber jacket escorted her into a wheeled modular unit sprouting a forest of roof antennae — out of place in the cobbled courtyard of the foundry.

"Mind setting your jacket and shoes here and emptying your bag into the tray?" he said.

"If I did?" Of course she minded. Had a business to run. But it wasn't really a question.

"Then I'd have to insist." Businesslike, no smile.

Once through the metal detector and body scanner inside the wheeled unit, she collected her things, slipped into her heels and jacket. He led her up a rusted outdoor metal staircase to the upper floor of the factory.

Knowing she was out of her league, she determined to keep quiet. Play it smart for once. Let Lacenaire, Monsieur Big Shot, do the talking. She'd had a foretaste overhearing him in the convent garden. Knew he'd come up empty at the convent.

She hadn't. Score one for her.

But he'd used Sydney to hook her. Score Lacenaire.

Now she would find out how much he actually knew.

"Mademoiselle Leduc, you look familiar." Lacenaire was of average height, in his late thirties, with parted mouse-brown hair — little about him stood out. In his familiar

165

suit and tie, he looked exactly as he had the other night, apart from tired eyes. "Have we met?"

Her blood went cold, but she controlled her shiver. "*Moi?* I don't think so. But everyone says I've got a familiar-looking face."

"*Au contraire.* You're striking. Tall, big eyes — you stand out."

Great. A sexist. She put her shaking hands in her pockets, tried to read behind his lines.

"Sit down."

"You are . . . ?"

"Daniel Lacenaire, but you know that."

He was testing her.

She shook her head and shrugged. Sat down.

His pale complexion matched the bland, washed-out furniture in the glass-walled office, which overlooked what had been a factory. Now the work floor had been outfitted with long shared desks along the old metal machinery tracks. Ten or so people sat at computer terminals. A busy hive — another kind of factory.

Wasn't this pretty conspicuous for an intelligence site? The antennae, all the people going in and out?

"We're a secure facility," he said, as if he'd read her thoughts. "We own the block."

Of course they did. DGSE, the foreign

intelligence agency, probably had places like this all over. She knew their HQ compound near the Périphérique was referred to as *"la piscine"* since it was across from the Olympic-sized public pool. Not very original. They practically culled agent cover names from the Tintin books.

The hoodie appeared bearing a tray: two demitasses of espresso and a sugar bowl.

"As you like it, *non,* Mademoiselle Leduc?" Hoodie said, falsely obsequious.

He made her squirm. Were the thumbscrews next?

"Or do you prefer a *noisette?*"

Was that a shaded reference to Genelle/Germaine, per the term the café waitress had used to refer to her? If it wasn't, it was an odd suggestion, since, if he'd been spying on her and was familiar with her tastes, he must have known she drank only straight espresso.

"Non, merci." Her insides tightened into a hard ball.

Hoodie sat down in one of the hard-backed chairs at the door. On guard duty. He checked his phone.

She dropped in two white sugar cubes, like a typical bourgeois, and stirred. Sipped. All the while forcing herself to breathe.

Lacenaire's type was trained to smell fear.

And to instill it.

She glanced at her Tintin watch. "Lovely coffee." It was. "Monsieur Lacenaire, I've got a full day ahead of me, limited childcare —"

"Surely you're curious why you're here." Lacenaire paused, looking for a reaction. He wouldn't get one. "About Sydney Leduc. And you want me to do the talking."

"It's only polite, since I'm the guest, and you're the host."

He smiled. Threw up his hands as if in defeat. "Why did you kill Hans Volker?"

The espresso went down wrong. She stifled a choke. "Who?" There went acting cool and composed. She set down her demitasse.

"Oh, he had many names. Rolf Uiders, Peter Uhlsdorf, Fritz Lammers . . . a South African national, ex–Foreign Legion, mercenary, last seen in Abidjan, Côte d'Ivoire, on Sunday. That is, until last night, when he was found dead."

Merde. She smoothed back her hair, red streaked this month, making sure a spiky tuft covered her shrapnel wound. The hard wood chair pressed into her spine. The backs of her knees perspired.

"We're running tests on the knife in his breast pocket for possible links to a recent homicide. A young half-Ivoirian woman. Know anything about that?"

Fishing. But she cursed herself for not checking the dead man more thoroughly. She kept her face expressionless.

"We know you visited our safe house on rue de Pommard. There's video to prove it."

Hoodie stood and hit a key on the desk laptop. Turned the screen in her direction.

A smudged figure in the shadows, the distinctive silhouette of her ankle boots, captured by a camera trained on the safe house door. Her head down, scarf over it, disguising her features.

Lacenaire nodded to the video. "See? I knew I'd seen you somewhere."

Deny. *Non,* he'd expect that. Play dumb. "Who's that?"

He hit REWIND. She recognized the legionnaire coming out of the door, his lips moving . . . There was a glimpse of him pulling out his pistol, then his shoulders as he stopped. The thupt, thupt of shots muffled by the suppressor.

Then the action was out of camera range.

After a long pause, there she was again, going in the side door. Head down. Not great-quality footage. The hedgerow branches had grown since the camera was first installed, she figured.

"Let's try this again," he said. "Did you kill Hans Volker because he attacked you?"

Like she'd answer that.

He looked bored. "I doubt it myself."

Attack. Feint. Parry. Classic fencing moves. Exactly the interrogation techniques her grandfather had described in his lectures.

"Forensics concludes this idiot shot himself, so to speak. His pistol fired on ground impact. Plus, with his prints all over and gunshot residue on his hands . . . I couldn't prove anything else. A few kicks in the head weren't what killed him."

What did he want from her? How long would it be until she found a way in to ask about Sydney? But she kept quiet.

"Then there are the homicides that happened shortly afterward in an old bomb shelter by the national rail tracks. Not that they really matter — just a sad footnote, really."

The back of her neck was covered in sweat.

"You wouldn't know anything about that, would you?"

Like she'd admit it.

A sigh. "That's not my concern. Our asset, Gérard Bjedje Hlili, a foreign national under our protection, remains in danger.

170

This dead man, Hans Volker according to his latest alias, discovered the safe house, and our asset fled. Disappeared. But you know that."

She would have been stupid not to probe and get details.

"How did your asset get away?" she said. "When?"

"Unknown at this time."

She believed him. They didn't know where GBH was either — that was probably why she was really here.

"Why didn't this Hans Volker stop him?" she asked.

"A bit late to ask him, *non*?" Lacenaire said.

The man in the hoodie was taking notes, she realized.

"We were hoping you'd know that."

"Why's he so important, Lacenaire?"

"So full of questions all of a sudden." Pause. "Gérard Bjedje Hlili's the only politician popular with the under-thirty population in Côte d'Ivoire. An age group composing almost fifty percent of the country. This group's support is vital in the impending coup d'etat. Hlili's their big player. And we believe he's going to use certain documents to bolster his power." Lacenaire tented his fingers. "Sydney Leduc told you where to locate him."

She clenched her knuckles. Light slanted from the skylight, and she studied the pattern it made on the floor.

"Find him."

She bit her tongue before she could blurt out that this wasn't her problem, or at least it wouldn't be once she got Germaine's stash to GBH. "I don't understand."

"*Très simple.* We want you to locate this man who was under our protection."

"Why did you let him escape?" she said.

"It's complicated."

"I've got no clue who he is or where to find him."

"Friends across the pond joined the party," he said, parsing his words. "For political reasons, we need a contractor, an outsider such as yourself, to finish Sydney's task. Technically, we can't be involved."

Friends across the pond. Translation — the CIA. And Sydney had been working for them. She'd been lying again, telling Aimée her secret lives were all behind her.

The smell of the coffee was getting to Aimée. "Didn't you just say —"

"We can't be seen to be involved for political reasons of our own," he said. "Sydney Leduc told us you would find him. Our agreement with her is based on your as-

172

sistance. I can't tell you any more."

Aimée blinked. "First you accuse me of killing a legionnaire; then you turn around and ask me to find someone I don't know." She shook her head, expelled air from her mouth. *"C'est fou."*

"As I said, it's complicated."

"Isn't this your job?" She gestured to the hive working below. "Why don't you put *your* pack on the trail? Isn't that what an intelligence boss does?"

She caught a wince. She'd hit a nerve.

"Given the players, it's a delicate balance," he said. "We've had to improvise, call you in."

"Lacenaire, I don't see why I'd do any better than your crew."

"I'll keep Sydney safe until you find him."

She stiffened. "What do you mean keep her safe?"

He pulled a folded paper from his pocket. Torn edges, grid lined, like the note in Chloé's diaper rash creme. A drawing of the mouse with the words *Do the right thing.*

Angry, Aimée sucked in her breath. Slammed the demitasse down on the saucer. "I want to see her."

"She asked me to give you this. Said you'd understand."

"No deal unless I see her, *comprenez?*"

"*Desolé,* no contact or she'd be compromised."

"*Quoi?*" She stood. "You're holding her hostage?"

"Not us." A long silence. Lacenaire averted his eyes.

Now she was scared. Couldn't control the shaking in her hands. "You mean she's in danger? Who's holding her?"

"Cooperate as soon as possible, and she'll be safe."

But it was only his word on that. Yet she couldn't ignore the note if her mother was a hostage. "How am I supposed to believe you?"

"Try, or it will be too late."

Lacenaire had her where he'd wanted her all along — a patsy ready to go out on a limb.

Did she have a choice? Decided to play along. "All right."

He nodded to the hoodie, who pulled a file from inside his sweatshirt. Set it on the colorless desk.

"You didn't get this from us. *Compris?*" said the hoodie.

She opened it. GBH's photo stared at her, a whole dossier clipped to it.

Hoodie set down a burner phone. "You call when you find him. Only then."

174

THURSDAY MORNING

Twenty minutes later, another car, a dinged Renault, deposited her on rue Bailleul a block from Leduc Detective. During the ride, she'd read the thin file. It wasn't much.

As she walked, she tried to understand what she'd gleaned. For a moment, the pavement wavered. She felt a burning sensation behind her eyes. *Second time today.* She heeded the signs. Leaned against a damp wall and closed her eyes. Deep breaths.

How in the world could she find Gérard Hlili if the world's intelligence services couldn't or wouldn't? She was one person.

Their hands were tied for political reasons. Their friends across the pond were exerting pressure.

Damn the CIA. And her mother for working with them. Again.

"You trust these people, Aimée?"

She'd spread out GBH's dossier from the

175

DGSE on the office floor. "Not further than I can spit."

Right away, René noticed the redacted pages. "Missing pages, sloppy. How obvious, *non*? Page seven and then page ten? You'd expect spooks to know their stuff. We pay those James Bond salaries; shouldn't they find him?"

Saj nodded. "That's the truffle hounds' job."

"At least their espresso's *grand cru,*" Aimée said.

"And you bought Lacenaire's threat of international conspiracy?" said René. "My derriere."

"They need someone to do their dirty work, or they wouldn't have drafted me."

"Then what's their going consultant fee? Need I remind you we're a business, Aimée?" He snorted. "And don't tell me it's for the good of the republic."

She bit her lip. "My mother's life."

A silence settled on the office, broken only by the distant hum of traffic on rue du Louvre. Then René slammed his fist on the desk. "That's coercion."

Saj made a time-out signal. "Not if Aimée holds the aces." He pointed to the contents of Genelle's envelope taped to the dry-erase board. "Did the DGSE ask you about any

176

of this?"

She shook her head.

"*Bon.* I'd say you're one up on them. From what they told you, they're operating on the idea that GBH has Genelle's documents, *non?*"

Aimée nodded.

"Don't forget the dead legionnaire had GBH on his shopping list," said René. "He's got a trigger-happy accomplice."

True.

"We need to find out who he represents," René said. "Who else's trying to keep their finger in the tart."

Then she remembered Lacenaire's tidbit about the knife that had been found on the legionnaire's body. "What if his shopping list started with Genelle?"

"Killing her before he got the documents doesn't make sense," Saj said.

That had been her thought. Yet he hadn't exactly been a pro, from what she'd seen.

"Unless he screwed up, Saj," said René, "like he did last night."

René's phone trilled. He took the call. Before Aimée could dissect GBH's file and life any further, an alert came from her laptop. A reply to her query on the *zouglou* LISTSERV from Senegal.

Salut mon amie, Jinsti here. I love zouglou,

too. And I like your name and cool intro.

Some Internet sleaze trying to hit on her? But it could be a chance to wheedle out info on Germaine Tillion. *Better respond.*

Aimée typed a reply: *Génial. Can't find DJs like GT here. A music desert. Need her tape mix, thirsty too long.*

A few seconds' delay. Then a reply: *Know the feeling. She spins vinyl in Abidjan. Club Madou.*

Not for a while. Seems MIA . . .

Yeah, her brother got shot.

What happened?

Politics. You need to check out Fatima. She spins like you don't believe.

It went on like this until she tried: *Jinsti, help me out. I promised my friend a DJ GT tape. How can I find one? You don't think she's stopped spinning?*

I'll ask around. Got to go.

A probable dead end. Yet as her father had always said, you don't know what you'll find if you don't look. She thought of all the nights he'd worked, combing through his notes, hunched over reports, looking at the same details yet again. *Just one thing,* he'd say, *small as a speck of sand, and it can get you there.*

Sand. She'd felt sand in the envelope from

the Grand Hôtel d'Abidjan. What time was it there?

It took a few minutes to locate the number. She got through and the phone rang, a tinny faraway sound, until a recorded voice answered. She left a message.

René wrote *legionnaire* and *accomplice* on the dry-erase board. He circled *accomplice*. "I'll take this on."

"All yours," she said.

"Tell me what the DGSE said about the legionnaire and his aliases."

As she did, René jotted down the info.

"You think the accomplice found GBH, murdered him?" she asked.

René picked up a fax that had come in. Showed her a police vehicular report. Aimée winced. René's *classique* car, his pride and joy that he polished and waxed every week, destroyed.

"I'll find out if he did," said René, his jaw set. He grabbed his tailored Burberry trench coat. "No one blows up my car without payback."

"Got my present?" René smiled at Idris, a fellow gaming nerd, over the Air France information desk. René's feet dangled from the white plastic stool. Outside rain thrummed against the high coved windows in the cavernous terminal at Invalides. Created for the 1900 exposition, the symmetrical building, with its view of the grass-covered Esplanade des Invalides, reminded him of an orangerie.

"The things I do for you, René," Idris said, slipping a thick envelope into René's waiting, stubby fingers. "You owe me."

A Dungeons and Dragons addict like himself, Idris gamed at an old café near Châtelet. It had been Idris's haven since back when he'd travel in on the Réseau Express Régional from the *banlieue* or suburb where the neighbors burned cars in his housing project. For more than ten years, he and René had kept a monthly rendezvous while Idris worked his way up the Air France IT ladder.

"All the passenger manifests from Sunday through Tuesday, Idris?"

Idris nodded. "We run one flight a day from Abidjan. Nonstop, six and a half hours."

"What if he made a connection?"

"Then you're out of luck." Idris smiled, his bright white teeth perfect against a dark honey complexion. "Don't forget, you're my D&D partner tomorrow."

René shook his head.

Idris's eyes widened. "*Quoi?* You never miss —"

"I'm involved right now . . ."

"You mean in a relationship?" Then a huge grin. "*Sacré bleu,* about time, René."

Merde. At the bar the month before after their game was over, René had drunkenly opened his mouth about his feelings for Aimée.

"*Non,* Idris . . . it's complicated."

"*C'est l'amour,* René."

Only in his dreams. Aimée saw him as Chloé's godfather and her own best friend and business partner — all that he would ever amount to.

A taxi let René off at Bercy Village. The

181

insurance agent met him in the SNCF freight yard near the soot-stained metal carcass that had been his car. Total write-off.

René groaned. Nothing could ever replace this beauty, a limited edition with special features. The estimate the agent gave him for a replacement *classique* Citroën DS model — what a joke.

But shooting those idiotic winos — that was murder. Senseless. And it could have been him and Aimée instead.

Work would take his mind off the car. And the Bercy Café in the old wine depot was as good as the office. He took out the stapled passenger manifests. Fifteen hundred passengers. Groaned again — what a pain. Over a steaming cup of green tea, he got to work.

Pen in hand, he halved the list by gender, crossing off females. Dismissed another quarter by age — too young or too old. From among the 750 remaining male passengers who'd arrived within the three-day period he had manifests for, he narrowed it down to two who had arrived on Monday's early morning flight 03 from Abidjan.

Passenger number 139 fit the bill agewise and was a South African national, but given his handicapped status — he'd been wheelchair assisted, as noted by the cabin crew purser — René crossed him off. Passenger number 723, Andreas Devacour — this passenger ticked the boxes. Thirty-six years old, birthplace Arles, a replacement passport issued in Abidjan. René checked the list he'd made from the aliases Aimée had given him: Hans Volker, Jochim Wilmsdorf, Karl Duisberg, Rolf Uiders, Peter Uhlsdorf, and Fritz Lammers. No match. But no reason there shouldn't be one more alias. René knew that after a legionnaire's service, they were given a new identity and passport.

He found the place where Devacour was staying in France listed as Residence Crémieux on the embarkation card. Was this the *mec* with tattooed knuckles, now a corpse?

Well, what better time to find out?

René caught another taxi on the rain-slicked street. Close to the Gare de Lyon, he stopped at rue Crémieux, a rainbow of small houses on a pedestrian lane. Here? The rain abated, and he asked the taxi to wait.

No Devacour, Andreas registered now or in the last month. A family guesthouse, the middle-aged owner added, not a single man's idea of fun.

Now what?

183

Back in the taxi, René remembered seeing several two-star hotels, the kind that proliferated near train stations. Where you weren't asked a lot of questions at registration.

He asked the taxi driver, a young redheaded *mec* with a sparse matching beard, to take him back in the direction of the two-star hotels.

"So you're looking for someone?" the driver asked.

"A friend of someone."

"Book me for an hour, and I'll show you all the two-star hotels you want. If you find him in less than an hour, I'll prorate."

The kind of thing Aimée would do. This would be expensive, and there was no client paying expenses on this case. If only he had his own car.

"Deal."

At each hotel René asked for Andreas Devacour, Hans Volker, Joachim Wilmsdorf, and then the others on his alias list. Each time he slipped the receptionist some francs along with his card to sweeten the request, something he hated to do on principle. He also hated that his shoulders came up only to the reception counters and he had to crane his neck to look up at the receptionists.

"Désolé," came the reply at each of the

184

four two-star hotels he tried.

Thank God the rain had let up. But the damp got to his joints; his damn hip was acting up.

The legionnaire had covered his tracks.

"No luck?" asked the taxi driver, putting down his *jambon* tartine after the fifth hotel.

René shook his head. Weary, he sat back, his trench coat and good shoes sodden.

"There's only one more I can think of, *monsieur.*"

René hated facing an expensive defeat. He explained his search. Worth a try to get the taxi driver's thoughts.

"Ah, why didn't you say so?" The taxi driver wrapped up his sandwich in waxed paper. "My little brother imagines himself joining the legion one day. In his dreams. Doesn't stop him from hanging out with legionnaires, a ragtag lot — it's all drinking, *les femmes.*"

Interested, René leaned forward, careful to avoid hitting his chin on the back of the driver seat. "Hanging out where?"

"Cité Debergue, in a former garage, a billiard hall remodeled like an English pub.

My brother thinks it's *'classe.'* "

"Let's go."

As René got out, he remembered to ask the brother's name. Good thing, too.

A stocky bald man was polishing glasses behind a mahogany bar, which was well stocked and with Guinness on tap. In the dim light, René saw sea-green-baize tables, heard the click of pool balls. Apart from two players and the bartender, the bar was deserted.

"Members only," the bartender said.

A puff of white dust rose as a player rubbed chalk on his cue. René sneezed.

"Johnny Hervot recommended I drop by," René said. "Consider membership."

"Johnny?" A laugh. "That kid's not a member."

Great.

"Misinformed then," René said. "You know him and his pals?"

"Pals?"

Could this bartender answer only with questions? "Legionnaires. Devacour, Lammers, and Volker. Some others. Said to come here for a drink."

"Them?"

Another question.

René waited.

"We have standards here," the bartender said.

René hadn't expected that. "Good."

What else could he say? But he wouldn't leave without something. "So they're at the usual place?"

"Like I know."

There went this brilliant bit of investigation.

"*Regardez,* Johnny's okay." The bartender paused in the middle of toweling a wine glass. "A bit of advice — you don't want to drink with those *mecs.*"

René bristled at the condescending warning in the man's voice. *Comme d'habitude,* this man doubted a person his stature could defend himself. Nothing new. "Why's that?"

"Don't get me wrong; I like legionnaires. Happy to serve them, you know, but guys like Devacour give them a bad name."

One thing René already knew.

Outside on the narrow Cité Debergue, he explored his options: zero, unless he hung outside the billiards place at night until it heated up. Like he had more time to waste.

THURSDAY, MIDMORNING

René almost missed the sign for Hôtel Debergue, tucked back on the façade of one of Cité Debergue's low buildings, barely visible under a wall-mounted lantern. A blonde on her cell phone walked out of the hotel's lobby, her stilettos clicking a rhythm on the cobbles. A working lady.

Suddenly, he had a hunch he was in the right place.

He opened the door. From outside, the hotel appeared discreet; inside was another story. The lobby — dark woodwork and a faded red-velvet boudoir motif — spoke of an old neighborhood *hôtel de passe.* The pay-by-the-hour kind — thin walls, noisy lovemaking neighbors, and worn carpet. Hôtel Debergue had known better days. Not what one expected in this residential quartier.

"Has Andreas Devacour checked in?"

"Ça dépend." The young man at the recep-

tion, rail thin with slicked-back hair, shot a glance at a man smoking in the miniscule lobby.

"Depends on what?" asked René.

"You bring good news or not?" said the man in the lobby. He turned around. Muscled and wearing a hunting vest, he looked to be in his early forties, greying at the temples. He sat by a withered potted plant in a fug of smoke. No tattoos on his thick clenched knuckles.

"I'm looking for Monsieur Devacour," René said.

"Big things come in little packages, eh?" The man patted the frayed red-velvet seat beside him. "Sit down. Tell me, *petit,* what you want."

René wished this dollhouse-sized lobby wasn't full of the man's cigarette smoke. *"Non, merci.* You're the manager, *monsieur?"*

A grunt of laughter. "I like that. Pilou, he thinks I'm the manager."

The black-haired *mec* behind the reception gave a weak smile.

"I'm Nestor, Devacour's roommate." He smiled and stood.

Success. René brightened. Persistence paid off.

A second later Nestor's meaty hands grabbed René's lapels and lifted him up.

Nestor brought his face so close René could count the man's nose hairs. "What's a dwarf like you want with him?"

René choked. Smoke stung his eyes. His feet dangled.

He kicked Nestor's shins and, with a quick upward snap of both his elbows — he wished he had momentum for an optimal move — broke Nestor's grasp. Nestor grunted in pain, a surprised look on his face, and dropped René, who caught his balance on a chair.

"Who sent you?" Nestor asked.

René watched Nestor rub his shins. "I'm asking the questions, hothead. Prove you know who I'm talking about. What distinguishing characteristics does your roommate have?"

"You sound like a lawyer. What's it to you?"

"Answer my question, and you'll find out."

"What's it worth to me?"

Irritated, René wanted to aim another kick at him. "I'll ask a more helpful guest."

"No, you won't; you'll tell me." Nestor sat down, stabbing out his still-burning cigarette in a coral ashtray. "Did something happen?"

René heard a fringe of concern. "*Ça dépend.* Describe him."

He did, tattooed knuckles and all.

Andreas Devacour had checked out permanently.

"Tell me the last time you saw your roommate," René said.

"Not since yesterday."

"What about his friend?"

"Eh, that chauffeur?"

"Chauffeur" as in accomplice — the one at the other end of the wire. The one who'd chased them, shot the winos, and blown up René's Citroën.

"Go on," said René.

"Saw him once."

"Describe him."

"Sunglasses, dark hair . . ."

Nestor hadn't seen much, but he had paid attention to what he'd seen. He insisted the chauffeur was from a private firm; Andreas had laughed that Nestor couldn't afford him. The firm name was something beginning with an *R* — Nestor couldn't remember. Had driven a high-end Renault.

René remembered a high-end Renault in his rearview mirror the night before.

"Come on," Nestor said, expectant. "Don't you have something from Deauville?"

Deauville? René didn't need any more complications. And he sure didn't need the gag-inducing wave of perfume coming off of the woman in tottering heels who was standing at the reception desk with another muscled *mec.*

"*Allez,* little man, we're like brothers. You can tell me."

René glanced at the wall clock, a seventies chrome contraption. "Andreas, or whatever his real name is, has checked into the big hotel in the sky. What something from Deauville?"

Realization dawned in Nestor's eyes. He shook his head. "Once a loser, always a loser. Big talk, that's all he was."

"How do you mean?"

"Fifteen years in l'Afrique, earns a fortune, loses it. Comes back for the big win, he tells me. He'll be sitting pretty." A bark of laughter. Nestor lit another cigarette. "Even invites me to the Deauville casino. I figured you came with that casino ticket."

"Figure this, Nestor — if I can track your roommate here, so can the *flics.*"

René threw that out hoping that, if Nestor had trouble with the law, it might get him moving. *Et voilà.* Without a word, Nestor stood and beat it straight out of the lobby. René could practically see the trail of smoke in the man's wake.

René smiled as he approached the reception desk again. His chin reached the edge. On the wall behind it were framed military insignia and faded photos of men in fatigues.

"No trouble, no trouble," said the young *mec.*

"Then you'll hand me Nestor and Andreas's room key," René said. *"Comprenez?"*

A slap of metal as the key hit the counter. René took it. "What kind of two-star hotel are you, anyway?"

He scratched his neck. "Clubhouse, the *mecs* call it. My uncle owns this place. Bought it after he'd saved up in the Legion."

And then René understood. The clientele, such as Nestor and the muscled *mec* with the working girl, had been soldiers of fortune once — the type who became mercenaries after the Foreign Legion. This fleabag hotel was their stomping ground.

The door of room thirty-eight opened to a smell of vetiver aftershave and laundered sheets. Large enough for two twin beds and not much else except the *cache-misère* faded forties wallpaper and pasteboard armoire. A nineteenth-century print of a mustachioed man in a frock coat hung on the wall. The Spartan feel was enhanced by the beds, which had been made with military precision. On one bed lay a much-thumbed copy of *Oui* magazine, open to a naked woman.

René heard footsteps in the hall. Nervous, he scanned the room. Whatever evidence the *mec* might have left, René had to find it now.

In the armoire hung a white shirt and a pair of polished black shoes. He got down on his hands and knees and saw Air France luggage tags — a cheap roller bag under the far bed. What should he do — search it here and risk missing something or getting caught? Instinct told him to take it. Self-preservation told him to just walk away — robbing a dead man was more Aimée's style.

His phone vibrated. Aimée.

One minute later, he'd locked the hotel door behind him and was on his way, gripping the roller bag handle.

THURSDAY, LATE MORNING

Why wasn't René answering? Infuriating. She worried he'd gone to check out his ruined car in Bercy, where they'd had problems the night before, and stepped into danger.

"I'm concerned about René, Saj."

"He's a big boy." Saj looked up from his laptop. "You know what he's like when he's on a mission. He gets results, Aimée."

She hoped so.

"As you requested, I went back to the beginning," he said. "Ready?"

While she'd handheld a skittish client who had finally re-upped to a hefty security contract, Saj had taken over digging into the scanty, redacted file on Gérard Bjedje Hlili, twenty-four years old. Born in Abidjan, Côte d'Ivoire. Father in the sales force at the CIE, Ivorian clone of Electricité de France, until he rose in the managerial ranks. Mother from a fishing village in the

Comoé coastal region. The family had lived in Paris for several years when the father was transferred for top-tier managerial training; Gérard had been in school. Returned to Abidjan for *l'université* — Saj noted he had been in the same class as Germaine and Armand, the Tillion twins, well-off members of the Frenchified elite of Abidjan. Gérard and his mother had visited her village and come down with cholera in the 1995 epidemic. Gérard had survived, but his mother hadn't. Subsequently, his father lost everything backing a clean-water village development project run by a corrupt politician. Gérard grew disenchanted with the government. His father died of a heart attack, and Gérard had joined the FRP, a rebel group in his mother's birthplace.

A sad story. Aimée saw the roots of his activism.

"Say that rebel group's name again, Saj."

"Freedom Revolution Peace Party, the FRP."

Aimée typed the phrase and did a search. Several hits came up.

"Doesn't look like a fringe group or a marginal faction," she said. "Seems really popular among the younger voting crowd." She slipped her heels off. Rubbed her ankle.

197

"According to the DGSE, a coup d'etat will happen. Online chatter says the military has the edge and promises to end corruption."

"Where've we heard that before?"

"Saj, were the Tillion twins active in the FRP?"

"Not according to this file. But there's a lot missing."

"I read that Germaine's brother, Armand, died a month ago in a shooting."

"You think that's connected?"

"They all went to school together, but I don't know," she said. "Could the missing parts have anything to do with why Germaine, a hot DJ in Abidjan, was living in hiding as Genelle, a homeless woman taking shelter in a convent — or why she attempted to put information and cash in Hlili's hands before she got murdered?"

As Aimée pulled her heels back on, she wondered why Sydney had gotten involved.

"Everything's possible." Saj stood and stretched his long arms, emitting a puff of incense smell. His beads clacked. "Yet, I don't get why the DGSE put GBH in a safe house," said Saj. "Isn't it hands off in l'Afrique?"

"Côte d'Ivoire's the crown jewel of the *Françafrique* chain," said Aimée, pushing her chair back from the desk. "French business in Abidjan, the military connection . . . Doesn't it reek of a postcolonial lovefest?"

"More like an affair." Saj nodded. "The DGSE's job could be to keep Hlili, a popular young leader, in the wings. Safe and ready to motivate the masses. A leader who'd owe them favors."

Weak glints of sun reflected off the aged patinaed mirror.

"So the DGSE can't be seen being involved; that's why Sydney's the intermediary, right?"

"According to Lacenaire," said Aimée.

If she could trust him.

Saj clicked keys on his laptop. "You raised questions over those flight manifests and cargo lists, so I followed up. Things checked out until I delved deeper into the last cargo lists. Specifically the Tehran flight. Seems my poking around hit a snag."

" 'Snag' as in . . . ?"

"Superhack needed. They frontloaded security, beefed up the firewall."

Great.

"How long to penetrate it, Saj?"

"With René and me both on it full-time, maybe tonight or tomorrow morning."

She calculated the manpower away from real business such as their daily contracted security monitoring plus the client updates she needed for a round of meetings the next day. Was it worth it to spend energy on what could turn out to be a moot point? Would delving deeper help her figure out where Gérard Hlili was or whether she should still be trying to get him the documents? Would anything they could learn be relevant to finding her mother?

And where was Sydney? How could the DGSE claim to be keeping her safe?

All Aimée had were questions. And the clock was ticking.

"For now let's concentrate on finding GBH," she said.

Saj swiveled his neck one way, then the other.

"Neck problems, Saj?"

"My energy chakras are misaligned."

More head-swiveling, then a loud crack. A serene glow spread over Saj's face. "Maybe we've been wrong about the political opposition," he said, "or whoever hired the legionnaire."

"In what way?"

"Maybe they didn't want the documents. Maybe they just wanted these people, especially GBH, dead. Didn't GBH get the hell out before the legionnaire arrived?"

Saj had a point. "You're right," she said. "He's afraid, like Germaine was."

And maybe she needed her chakras aligned, too.

"So we know he attended school in Paris and lived here for five years. Knows the city, I'd say . . ." Saj paused. "At least, his quartier."

"Where's his old stomping grounds? Can we find his parents' old address?"

Gérard Bjedje Hlili had attended Sainte Clotilde, a private Catholic school on rue de Reuilly, not far from the convent, it turned out. But the old family address was redacted.

"Attends," said Aimée. "It shows GBH's father did his managerial training at EDF. The package included housing and children's school tuition."

That was all she needed. Within two minutes, she'd gotten through the EDF's back door into the company's employee site and found a list of EDF housing for staff. Most companies owned buildings, but she gasped at how many the government-run electricity company had. "Landlord" could have been its middle name.

"Voilà, 83 rue du Pensionnat." She knew that warren of streets off Place de la Nation.

She put a mark on the map, right off Avenue du Bel-Air — yet another mark in the twelfth arrondissement.

"Say he's hiding with old friends, maybe?" said Saj.

"Won't know until we ask."

In the back armoire, Aimée checked her disguises for something easy to pull over her agnès b. black cat jumpsuit. Found the perfect outfit. Stuck it in her bag. She looped her Hermès scarf around her neck and put her worry for René on hold. Rang Babette for her thrice-daily check-in on Chloé, who was down for a nap at Martine's.

"Everything okay, Aimée?" She heard the hesitation in Babette's voice.

"You've been great, Babette. To the letter. Just as we practiced."

"So Chloé should just stay with Martine?"

Aimée needed to find GBH. To know Sydney was safe. But a pang hit her. She missed Chloé's sweet baby smell, those apricot cheeks, and that drooling smile.

"Martine's good with that, *non*?" Aimée said. "Let's keep to that plan. I'll come later tonight."

THURSDAY, LATE MORNING

Aimée stopped at the concierge's loge. Chloé's diaper delivery should have arrived — Aimée had learned the hard way that she needed an office delivery as well as one at home.

"*Bonjour, madame,* has that package come?"

The office building's Portuguese concierge, usually all smiles, shrugged. "*Pas arrivé.* I'll keep a lookout."

Aimée peered at the bundle of mail the concierge was still sorting. An envelope addressed to Séverine Lafont, care of Leduc Detective.

"What's this?" Aimée asked.

A guilty look crossed the concierge's face.

"Who's Séverine Lafont?" Aimée demanded, her heartbeat speeding up. "Do you know anything about this?"

The concierge shook her head, her fingers picking at the buttons on her work smock.

"Has a letter arrived for this person before?"

Aimée had heard concierges used building addresses for scams to establish residency.

The concierge's eyebrows knit in worry. *"Mais non, mademoiselle."*

The poor woman was a terrible liar.

"But you will tell me the truth, *non?*" Aimée said. "And right now."

"I'm helping . . . Not supposed to tell . . ." She took a breath.

"Do you want to keep this job?"

The woman laid a hand on Aimée's arm. "But it's your mother, *mademoiselle.* Mail arrives for her here under that name."

Aimée's back stiffened. "Since when?"

"Last month or so. She asked me to hold letters for her."

Paid her well, too, no doubt, for a drop point for her alias.

"Told me she didn't want you to worry." A catch in her throat. "I wasn't supposed to tell you."

Although she shouldn't have been, Aimée was stunned — Sydney had been using her again. As the saying went, a tiger can't change its stripes. Aimée turned the envelope over. "Any more correspondence?"

"Not since she last picked up several days ago."

"*Merci.* And if you get another one" — she pressed her card into the calloused hands — "call me."

Out on rue du Louvre, she waved at Marcel, the one-armed Algerian vet, busy at his kiosk serving a line of newspaper buyers. While she tried to hail a taxi — all full — she opened the envelope.

Madame Lafont,

We regret to inform you that due to an instrument malfunction, the medical technicians were unable to read the results of your CT scan on October 6. Please call to schedule a new CT appointment as soon as possible. Contact . . .

Her mother needed a CT scan?

Right away, she called the contact number on the letter. Cloud wisps curled in the pale azure sky.

"I'm sorry, *mademoiselle,*" said a nurse. "Patient confidentiality forbids me from disclosing medical information."

"Let me talk to your supervisor."

"My supervisor's out."

As if she'd take no for an answer. "Connect me to the department head."

"He'll tell you the same thing. Hold on."

He did. Acknowledging only that, *oui,* with a medical release and affidavit signed by the patient and doctor, he could tell her more. Aimée hung up.

Fallen rust-colored leaves gusted around her ankles. The October late-morning light illuminated the outline of the Louvre's Cour Carrée and, beyond it, the banks of the Seine. Everything but her mother.

THURSDAY, MIDDAY

"I'm looking for a school for my daughter, and old family friends recommended that I visit you," said Aimée, adjusting her scarf in the Sainte Clotilde office. "Perhaps you remember the Hlilis and their son, Gérard Bjedje Hlili?"

The young woman behind the desk looked up from a file she was reading. "I started last month."

Great.

Aimée noticed a small girl waving goodbye to her teacher at a classroom door. Her father hefted her up onto his shoulders, and she laughed in delight. "Let's go fast, Papa."

Aimée's mind went back to Melac hefting Chloé onto his shoulders the week before. To that rare warm afternoon picnic, those pinpricks of light dancing on the pond's surface at the Jardin du Luxembourg. Watching them together, their matching eyes.

207

The young woman was saying, "*Desolée.* But I can schedule a tour for you."

Aimée caught herself, forcing herself to ignore the pang in her heart. Smiled.

"Of course, but I wanted to meet that teacher they rave about . . ." She thought back to the ages Gérard had been when he'd lived here, did a quick calculation to guess which grade's teacher would be most likely to remember him. "The fifth level."

"Monsieur Tardi? He's on sick leave."

"Anyone else on staff you can think of who's taught here for a while?"

She shrugged. "I don't know. Before my time."

Stall. Think of something. "What an architectural gem." Aimée gestured to a balconied seventeenth-century limestone pavilion fronting the garden at the entrance. An out-of-place jewel in this modern seventies-school maze.

The young woman smiled. "Everyone comments on the pavilion. It was the hunting lodge of the duc de Guise back when this was all royal hunting grounds. Our founder started the school there in 1809 because of the healthy air for children. A hundred years the school remained open and grew before it was closed down, but luckily it was restarted during the occupation."

The young woman wanted to be helpful, Aimée could tell. "Fascinating," she said.

"Baptiste, the caretaker, has been here forever. Lives in the pavilion." She pointed through the hallway to a man raking leaves — within earshot. Aimée had the distinct feeling he'd been listening the whole time. He dumped the leaves into an Eco-Emballages cart, the mayor's latest scheme to make Paris green. Even her own concierge raved over Eco-Emballages and its environmental advantages. "You can speak with him, but I don't know that he can help you."

"Merci."

Aimée smiled at the crooked-backed man in a *bleu de travail,* the timeless blue work coat men of her grandfather's generation and one generation younger still wore. He had muscular arms and looked fit aside from the crooked back for a man who appeared to be in his fifties.

"The receptionist said you've worked here a long time, *monsieur,*" she said. "That you might be able to help me."

Despite a flushed face and spider veins of a drinker, his brown-framed glasses gave him a bookish appearance. He continued

209

raking the curling leaves without looking up.

"I'm the caretaker, *mademoiselle*," he said. "Like my father before me."

He must have grown up here.

"Do you remember Gérard Bjedje Hlili and his family?" she asked. "He attended school here until 1993."

The damp leaves gave off the smell of autumn. Children's voices came from the schoolyard.

The man's hands tightened on the bamboo rake handle. So much his knuckles whitened. He knew something, and he was nervous. "Talk to reception, *mademoiselle*. I'm the caretaker."

"But she's new, *monsieur*. I think he came here looking for his friends —"

"No use asking me," he interrupted. "I've got work to do." A mask had come down over his face.

She stepped closer. "I don't know what you know" — she lowered her voice, looking around — "but I've got something for him from Germaine. I want to do the right thing."

He straightened and blinked.

She slipped her business card into his work-coat pocket and walked down the path. At the gate, she paused. Caught him looking up at the pavilion. He quickly looked away. A minute later, he'd disappeared.

Uneasy, she reached Avenue du Bel-Air four blocks away, turned right into rue du Pensionnat. She was scattering crumbs for Hlili, for her mother, but what if she was only attracting predators?

How well she remembered those low buildings on rue du Pensionnat. The long ivy-covered gate, the uneven cobbled courtyard of the old coaching inn that her grandfather used to point out to her after they'd spent a day at Foire du Trône in Bois de Vincennes — the huge carnival fair of medieval origins. She remembered holding her grandfather's hand in one of hers, in the other the traditional sticky gingerbread pig, *cochon aux épices.* She remembered him telling her the story of how, in the twelfth century, the king's son had died after falling off his horse, which had reared up, scared by a wild pig. How the sad king had banned pigs in Paris, the only exception being the pigs kept in the abbey of Saint-Antoine. How, thankful for the king's favor, the monks had baked pig gingerbread cookies for the fair and how the tradition had continued for eight hundred years.

She remembered how they'd always detour home via the bar owned by Tino, *Grand-père*'s old colleague, off Avenue du Bel-Air. Tino's bar was named Verse Toujours, an old phrase meaning, "Keep pouring, nonstop." The first time she'd heard the name as a little girl, she'd thought Tino's arm must have hurt from all the pouring and had offered him a Band-Aid. How her *grand-père* had laughed. The bar was still there, on rue du Pensionnat between Impasse des Arts and rue des Colonnes du Trône, the former wagon route that had once carried victims to the guillotine.

Drink in hand, Tino would sit her at the outdoor table by a bollard, and they'd play *jeu de 7 familles* with the same worn card set. Her *grand-père* was busy helping a friend, Tino would say — only years later had she realized *Grand-père* had been "helping" his mistress.

After cards, Tino would bring her another *limonade,* and they'd play the guessing game. Her favorite. He'd ask her how many streets radiated from Place du Trône, as he still called it. Or which dauphin the king had imprisoned at the Château de Vincennes. Or how many horses the stables in the old coaching inn across the *rue* held.

Tino, a retired beat *flic,* had grown up within the range of the bells of nearby Église de l'Immaculée Conception and seemed happy to stay there. He knew everyone in the quartier, their children, and their affairs, and he never forgot a face. She'd thought she'd stop by the bar and see what Tino knew about the EDF managerial enclave across the street, and about the Hlilis.

But now she stood in Bar Verse Toujours and barely recognized it. The old elaborately framed mirrors had disappeared, as had the zinc counter. The bar had been redecorated with American diner decor — the new rage — red tiles on the floor and the leather-seated banquettes replaced with stools and Formica tables. The thin middle-aged man behind the counter wore an apron that brushed his ankles and a perplexed expression when she inquired after Tino.

"The old owner?" he asked.

"A retired *flic.* Gave me treats when I was little, and we played cards."

A nod. "People ask after him, but he's

been in the Cimetière de Bercy a long time now."

Her heart fell. *How sad.* And there went that idea.

"How long have you run the bar, *monsieur?*"

It turned out he and his wife had taken it over a year before. It had been empty since Tino's demise.

"It's a struggle, I don't mind saying," the owner said.

"Do you know your neighbors across the street at the EDF?"

"Them? Think they'd spend a centime here?"

Aimée figured that was a rhetorical question.

"What about that concierge?" she asked. "I forget her name . . . She still there?"

"Madeleine, that old battle-ax? She'll leave in a box." He hiked his shoulders in a shrug. "Good luck."

Thinking she'd need it, she opened the small door in the ivy-covered wall onto the row of old stables — now garages. More upscale than she remembered from when she was a child.

If she'd met Madeleine, the concierge, before, her memories were faint. Childhood observations were veiled; a *limonade* had loomed most important at that time. She'd use Tino as an entrée to start the conversation.

"Tino, that old coot?" Madeleine wore a flowered work coat and a bun corkscrewed to her scalp. She slapped down the mail she was sorting and made a sign of the cross, her work-worn hands brushing her ample bosom. "Tino's with his maker now." A sigh. "Bless his soul and not to speak ill of the dead, but his family informed, you know."

Surprised, Aimée stepped back and her heel caught in the dirt of a flower bed. "He served in the police, *madame*. You mean he had informers?"

"I mean they squealed on *les bofs*." She rubbed her thumb and forefinger together to indicate money. "People knew. His father denounced our neighbor. *Buerre, oeufs,* and *fromage*." *Bofs* — the term for black marketers during the occupation. "Certain people made a lot of *fric* then. No one forgot."

She hadn't.

"Apple doesn't fall from the tree, eh? Tino was just like his father. During a demonstration at Place de la Nation, I saw him coming out of Printemps, smug as anything. 'Got a good deal?' I asked him. Got a bad deal for the unions full of *les communistes.* He'd been surveilling and taking photos of the demonstrators from the roof ledge of Printemps."

Determined not to get defensive or hear sad, horrific tales of the dark times, as her grandfather had called them, Aimée tried to get back on track. "I work for an insurance firm contracted by the EDF," she said, using a made-up story. "Actually, that's the reason I'm here, and I was hoping you could help."

"Why would I do that?"

Aimée gritted her teeth. Smiled. "Of course, you know all about your building tenants. The expert, *non?* We're investigating a claim by the Hlili family, who lived here for several years until 1993. Do you remember them?"

"What's this about?" The concierge's small eyes narrowed, and her crow's-feet radiated so they looked like a Himalayan relief map.

"Boring workman's compensation claims — wouldn't interest you," she said. "Routine inquiry. Can you recall the family?"

"Les Africains."

So she did.

"Apart from acting high and mighty, the Hlilis kept to themselves."

217

"Didn't their son attend Sainte Clotilde's?"

"Most of the tenants' children do. This to do with him?"

Madeleine was alert and interested now.

Aimée pretended to consult notes in her Moleskine. "We're not allowed to discuss ongoing claim issues. Have you seen him recently?"

"I might have," she said, self-importantly. Looked around the courtyard and back. "Then again, I might not."

Did this battle-ax want a bribe? For Aimée to cough up for a mean-spirited woman who'd badmouthed Tino — Aimée's grandfather's friend, who'd been good to her? Furious, Aimée didn't care whether the war stories were true or not.

"A mention of how helpful you've been in my investigation wouldn't go unnoticed in your pension, I'm sure," she said. Smiled again.

"You can do that?"

"Up to you."

Fat chance.

"Funny, I've never heard of that," Madeleine said.

"It's a new policy. They're sending notices this week in the mail."

And hell would freeze over.

"News to me."

Suspicious, she hadn't bought it yet.

Aimée checked a folder in her bag, pulling out a contract template she kept for prospective clients. Flashed it too quickly for the woman to read it. "This one . . . Ah, *non,* I forgot the updated version."

That did it. Madeleine opened her mouth, unleashing a fountain of information. Aimée filled two pages of her Moleskine with notes and even wrote over her to-do list.

"A funny teenager, I remember," Madeleine said.

"Funny in what way?"

"He had some strange friends. They played strange games," she said. "There was something about a local bully. Went by the name Crocodile. An African thing? I don't know. He pretended not to remember when I asked last week."

Aimée's pencil lead cracked in her Moleskine. "Last week? You're sure it's not more recent, maybe yesterday?"

"Like I'd forget when it's market day."

In theory, he had been staying at the DGSE safe house then.

"Was he here to look for his old friends?" Aimée asked.

"People do, you know," Madeleine said, thoughtful. "They look for home. Years after the war, in the sixties, the woodworker down the street came looking for his wife. He'd survived the camps." She shook her head. "Never found her."

Gérard had done the same. Searching at his old apartment, school. His quartier.

"Did Gérard find his friends?" Aimée asked.

"No one's here from that time."

"But it's only been what, six years? Not so long."

"They come and go. New batches of managerial trainers and pfft." She turned to wave at a couple coming across the court-yard and called, "I put your mail inside!"

There had to be a reason Gérard had come here. She sensed it. Grasping at straws, she said, "Do you remember his friends?"

Madeleine nodded.

"Do you have their addresses? I mean, to forward on mail."

"I might."

Of course she did. She knew everyone's business.

"Would some of his friends live in Paris, in the quartier?" Aimée asked.

Madeleine thought as she continued sorting the mail. "Not anymore. But there's Yvon Triquet. He's a master woodworker, a *compagnon du devoir.* He even received a *médaille* from the Louvre."

"This Yvon is a friend of Gérard?"

"Their fathers worked together; that's all I remember."

A connection or a dead end? But she had nothing else to go on. Gérard had escaped the legionnaire and the DGSE and gone under the radar. Hotels required ID. In his boots, she'd look for a short-term solution. What better place than with an old friend?

"His address, please, *madame.*"

THURSDAY, EARLY AFTERNOON

This stretch off rue du Faubourg Saint-Antoine was a series of courtyards, passages, and alleyways. Since the Middle Ages, it had housed guilds of woodworkers, artisans, and craftsmen employed by the powerful convents. *Les dames du faubourg,* the abbesses, often came from aristocratic families and were no strangers to court intrigues and alliances. An infamous fifteenth-century abbess had cornered the local meat market and dictated furniture styles to the woodworking guilds. One of the King Louises — Aimée couldn't remember which one — had become jealous of the nun and restricted her convent's power. The quartier still produced the classic furniture styles of Louis XIV and the Second Empire. Mazes of interconnecting yards and passages were still occupied by stainers, polishers, inlayers, gilders, and upholsterers.

Over the centuries the faubourg, the

working-class quartier, famous as the starting point of the Revolution, had evolved into a cradle of street fighters.

Morbier's home turf.

From the end of the block, Aimée walked until she saw 18 rue de Reuilly. Why would Gérard Hlili's friend Yvon, a Louvre-honored master artisan, work here, in this soot-stained, sagging building?

She tapped her heels until a man with a package entered the code and the door buzzed open. She slid in behind him. Waited until his footsteps drifted away.

She followed crème-colored walls past a private stairway, hooking left into a narrow courtyard of glass-windowed workshops. A world apart. Exquisite. Vines curtained the walls above, which had window boxes on every story, and tilted lemon trees grew in tubs on the cobbles. At the courtyard's end sat a three-sided, zinc-roofed building with a trompe-l'oeil painted clock tower topped by an iron rooster weather vane.

"You again?" came a voice from inside.

Florence Triquet, the mother from the playgroup, stuffed a handful of horsehair into the brocade seat of a Louis XV chair. Hammering came from the adjoining atelier — a clever open space containing two workshops.

Like a bad centime, I'll keep turning up, Aimée almost said. "We meet again."

"As you can see, I'm busy. I don't know anything else about your mother," Florence said, her cheeks flushed from exertion. A portable heater, perched on an old coal stove, emanated warmth.

Dumb. Aimée wished she'd put the names together before just showing up. "I'm here to speak with your husband, Yvon."

With that Aimée strode into the atelier, which was alive with the hissing from a slitting saw, the soft whistling of a broom, and the acrid scent of bubbling glue. "Yvon?"

"Un moment," a muffled voice said from the bowels of a weather-beaten walnut wood armoire. A man extricated himself. Wood shavings sprinkled his dark hair and shoulders. He put a hand broom in his work apron pocket and set down his saw. His dark brows, clouded with fine sawdust, crinkled in annoyance. It gave him a prematurely aged look, though he must have been roughly the same age as Gérard. "You are?"

She pulled out her card. "I'm trying to save your friend Gérard's life."

The annoyance spread to his tightening lips. Not a flicker of surprise. "*Et* what exactly is that to me?"

"He came to see you, *non?*" she said, test-

224

ing her hunch. "You're friends."

"We lived in the same place once, went to school together for a few years. But I wouldn't call him a friend."

"Close enough that he asked you for help."

"Politics aren't my thing."

Her antennae went up. "What do you mean?"

"I'll ask you the same thing. What do you mean when you say his life's in danger?"

Smart.

"A paid assassin tried to kill him last night," she said. "Gérard escaped. Now he's on the run."

"I don't know anything about that."

Sawdust powdered the concrete floor. Any minute, she'd start sneezing. "So what do you know?"

"Who are you again?"

Florence Triquet poked her head into the atelier. "I told you about her; she's the one from the playgroup, the one whose baby got left behind. She's obsessive. Irresponsible. A stalker."

Aimée's anger boiled. She wanted to punch Florence. Show her what real lack of responsibility looked like.

But a voice in Aimée's head said Florence wanted a confrontation. She took a long breath.

"Why can't you just leave us alone?" said Florence.

"I will," Aimée said. "Once I get answers."

Florence turned to her husband. "Did *l'Africain,* that radical, ask you for help?"

The woman had been eavesdropping on their conversation and apparently didn't think of Gérard as a friend.

Bells jingled as a door opened, sending in a gust of chill air. "Madame Triquet? I know I'm early, but . . ."

Florence sighed and left to greet her client.

Aimée stifled a sneeze. Waited.

Yvon shrugged. "Politics, like I said. The troubled situation in his country. Gérard's passionate about changing conditions for the poor — the polluted water, the substandard infrastructure. Raises good points, okay. He went on about change, how he was part of it."

"Go on."

"Not my thing, I told him. I'm a craftsman, worked hard for this. My clients include the ministry . . ."

"So you don't want to get involved. Kicked him out — that it?"

He hesitated. A shiver of guilt crossed his face.

"Look, that's not my concern," she said.

"I'm just trying to track him down so I can help him. He's hunted, on the run. What can you tell me?"

"You're a *flic?*"

"Like my card says, I'm a private detective."

Yvon snorted. "And I should trust you?"

"So you do know where Gérard is."

He clenched his fist. "That's just it — I don't. He was waiting for someone to make contact."

"I know," she said. "A woman named Genelle — or he might have known her as Germaine. She was found murdered in the Picpus convent grounds."

"*Quoi?* The murder they reported in *Le Parisien?*"

Aimée nodded. She'd seen the brief notice in the *fait divers* section the day before.

Yvon's jaw muscles quivered. "Gérard said he couldn't trust the situation. Didn't know who his friends were, who he could believe. Something about the Crocodile."

"Crocodile?" The concierge had mentioned a childhood bully by the same name. A coincidence?

"That's what he said." He jerked his eyes toward his wife, who was involved with her client. Lowered his voice. "Florence asked him to leave."

There was more; Aimée could tell. *"Et alors?"*

He leaned closer. "My brother's on vacation. His studio's by the Marché d'Aligre. I told Gérard my brother hides the keys under the flowerpot."

The first place a thief looked.

"When was that?" she asked.

"Last week. A few days ago I went to leave him money, but the key was there, nothing touched. I don't know if Gérard went there at all."

He might have, after last night.

Pause. "Don't tell my wife."

Aimée nodded again. Shoved her kohl eye pencil into his hand. "Write down the address and building entry code." She pointed to her wrist. "Hurry. I can help him."

After a moment's hesitation, he did. He looked at her card. "It's strange, but you remind me of a friend of my mother's. A very strong resemblance."

She didn't hear that often. She felt her heart speed up. "How's that?"

"Non, different family name. Never mind."

"Maybe we're related. What's her name?"

"Madame Lafont."

Aimée went still. "Séverine Lafont?"

"Think so."

Another gust of chill air filled the studio,

accompanied by a booming voice. "Yvon, please tell me you can save my aunt's armoire." A man strode in wearing a tailored camelhair coat and the kind of handmade shoes René wore.

Aimée slid out the door. Double knotted her scarf against the cold. *Séverine Lafont.* Good God, how was her mother mixed up in this?

But she would have to hunt down Yvon Triquet's mother another time to dig into that. First, she had to get to Gérard — before someone else did.

Thursday, Early Afternoon

Perspiration beaded René's brow as he looked up and down rue du Rendez-Vous. Where had the taxi driver gone? Abandoned him, and here he was, lugging a dead man's suitcase. What if Nestor, the legionnaire's crony, summoned reinforcements?

Time to get the hell out.

Legs pumping, he rounded the corner. His shirt stuck to his spine. There on the tree-lined avenue, the young taxi driver leaned against his hood, smoking.

"I thought you'd left." René panted.

"But you haven't paid the fare yet."

"Good point. Quick, let's go."

In the taxi, the driver adjusted his visor. "Found who or what you were looking for, I guess." His gaze caught the roller bag.

"In a way. Keep driving."

"What about our deal?"

René negotiated more time and opened the suitcase. A burner phone, low on bat-

230

tery, programmed with the same number they'd discovered the night before. A map of the twelfth arrondissement with the Bel-Air quartier circled, photos of a young woman and Gérard. A chauffeur service card, Réserve la Luxe, with a Deauville address.

René felt tingles in the soles of his feet. This had to be where the legionnaire's accomplice worked.

He called Aimée. *Busy.*

Saj answered on the office line.

"Can you manage the office this afternoon, Saj? Handle my scheduled meeting? The client file's on my desk."

"*Pas de problème.* What's up, René?"

"It looks like I'm going to Deauville."

"Hitting the casino? Or the beaches of Normandy?"

"I just found out the legionnaire's accomplice is a chauffeur. His company's based in Deauville."

"Nice work. Let me help. Give me what you've got."

René read out the information he had and heard Saj's clicking of keys.

"Not based in Deauville anymore." Saj whistled. "Réserve la Luxe opened a new branch on Avenue Daumesnil."

Not far.

"How many employees?" René asked.

More clicking. "According to the business records, just a Jean Moulin. Seventy-five Avenue Daumesnil, along the *viaduc.*" Saj paused. "Sounds like an alias. So tasteless to use the name of a famous Resistance hero. According to the record, there are several firms at this address. Probably a business front, nothing but a mailing address."

"So possibly a money laundering operation?"

"That's usually the case," said Saj.

"Any other addresses for him?"

"Let me check around."

Thursday, Early Afternoon

Aimée hopped on the crowded number 57 bus, wedging her way past women of a certain age with shopping bags or grandchildren in tow, holding her breath against the fug of damp wool and Guerlain L'Heure Bleue. She jumped off at the next stop and ran past the rear rehab wing of Hôpital Saint-Antoine. Would Morbier be in therapy then?

Why hadn't he come up with anything yet? He'd promised.

She punched in his number. The call rang through to voice mail. She left a message.

It turned out Yvon's brother's studio on Passage Brûlon was closer to the hospital than to the market. She hurried, threading through a narrow street, and spotted the Ivoirian resto — the one she'd called — in the middle of the block. *Stupid. Should have thought of this place first — GBH might know fellow Ivoirians here.* Or have passed by this way en route to Yvon's brother's, if in fact he had gone there after he was rumbled at the safe house.

Despite the CLOSED sign, the resto door was open. Soapy smells drifted from inside. Aimée peered into the interior, small and wood paneled, decorated with macrame wall hangings and plants, which gave it a greenhouse look. The specials were chalked on a board: *l'omiata maison,* a type of pepper water, and *poisson braisé.* Yellow cushions brightened up a window seat. The *télé* mounted on the wall showed a cable news service, Afrique News, with a news feed running at the bottom.

"Il y a quelqu'un?" she said.

A middle-aged woman looked up from mopping the floor. She had dark-honey skin and ample hips; a yellow scarf tied up her hair.

"We're closed," she said with an accent stretching her *r.* "Come back tonight."

"Excusez-moi, madame. May I take a moment, please?" said Aimée, stepping inside, trying to avoid the wet areas of the floor.

"Be careful. It's slippery . . . What do you want, *mademoiselle?"*

Smells of pine disinfectant drifted from a wash pail. Aimée pulled out Gérard's photo. "So sorry to bother you, *madame,* but have you seen him?"

The woman set her mop against the wall, took glasses from her smock pocket, and peered close. "This man? *Mais bien sûr.*"

At last. Aimée brightened. "You know him?"

She pointed to the *télé.* "There he is."

That would have been too easy. "I mean here in person."

The woman shook her head. "I see him on the *télé.* But if he were to eat here, I'd remember. Why?"

"I'm a journalist," she lied. Pulled out a press pass from her alias collection, flashed it. "Writing an article on Gérard Hlili's Paris connections, how the Ivoirian community thinks of him."

The woman tightened the knot on her scarf. Thought. "My nephew believes he's the best political leader for change in Côte d'Ivoire. So do many of our customers."

"A popular man, eh?" She smiled encouragingly. "And you, *madame,* what's your opinion?"

"*Moi?* My province floods every year. People die. Crops are destroyed," she said, gesturing again to the *télé.* Scenes of a storm, wind-lashed palm trees almost bent in half, debris strewn on streets, and flooded villages. "I support him, too; he's real. Hlili's mother died in the last cholera epidemic, as did many in my family. He's promised to fund a new water system. A purification plant." She made the sign of the cross. "I hope to God he'll help change our country."

Germaine had hoped so, too.

Aimée glanced at her Tintin watch. *"Merci, madame."*

Catching her breath a few blocks later, Aimée entered the building code from the kohled numbers on her wrist. The buzzing door let her into the courtyard of an old printing factory — still in operation, at least parts of it. The residual ink and chemical smells competed with whiffs of fresh paint. Painters were at work on the courtyard's wood-timbered exterior.

"A sin, to cover those ancient beams," said an older man pushing a trolley cart. "Doubt you think so, eh?" Clearly he was resentful of how the quartier, a victim of *boboïsation* by bourgeois *bohèmes,* was changing.

"Mais oui, I agree."

"But you're a new tenant. People like you think it's trendy to live in old factories and shoot prices into the sky for everyone else."

Monsieur Chip-on-he-Shoulder. Still, she could understand. His gnarled hands spoke of hard labor.

"Not me," she said. "I'm looking for Franck Triquet's studio."

"He's away."

So this codger kept his eyes open. "Right, but I'm looking for his brother's old school friend —"

"*Le noir?* Hightailed it out of here."

Racist. Whirs and pounds came from the nearby presses in a steady beat.

"And you know this how, *monsieur?*"

"My eyes don't lie."

Cryptic old coot. "When did he leave?"

"He climbed out the window into my bathroom at dawn. Scared the hell out of me."

She caught herself before she could stamp her foot in frustration. She'd missed Gérard again. An escape artist with self-preservation instincts.

"And you helped him out of the goodness of your heart?" she asked.

"A thousand francs covered it."

Her shoulders tightened. "So why tell me?"

"You asked. Have a soft spot for *les jolies femmes.*"

She doubted that. "Let me guess — two young *mecs,* one in a leather bomber jacket and the other in a hoodie, came here looking for him."

"*Pas du tout.* It was someone in a black Renault with smoked windows. They parked beneath my window by the island of trees. It's illegal to park on our pedestrian passage."

The legionnaire's accomplice, who'd chased her and René.

She didn't hold much hope as she climbed the stairs, found the key under the geraniums, and unlocked the door.

"*Il y a quelqu'un?*"

The only answer was the melody of wind chimes clinking on the metal hasp of the half-open window. The apartment was cold and held a faint trace of pine scent. The tousled duvet and greasy pan in the small sink indicated Gérard had stayed there. She checked for anything personal.

Nothing.

But that pine scent . . . why had it lingered? Had he really been wearing such a distinctive scent on the run?

In the bathroom she found a small snowball of stiff lather under the sink ledge. In the bin a few crinkly hairs.

He'd shaved off his beard, or his hair.

Disguised himself.

Outside, she returned the key to under the geranium pot. That was when it hit her.

She found the old man by the dumpster.

"You're very helpful, *monsieur*. Almost too much so. How could the man who escaped have put the key back under the geranium pot?"

"I did."

"He asked you to put the key back and . . . ?"

The man nodded. "Another thousand francs covered me threatening to call the traffic *flics* on the Renault driver if he didn't move his car."

She believed him.

"But wouldn't that put you in trouble with the driver?" she asked. "Or in danger for helping the young man escape?"

"A man my age? No one gives two eggs from the same hen about old people." He looked at her. "We're invisible."

Thursday, Early Afternoon

She tried to look on the bright side: still one step ahead of the DGSE. But several behind the legionnaire's accomplice.

Not good.

She speed-dialed René. "You all right, partner?"

"We've got things to catch up on."

René's code for a problem.

"I know." Vigilant, she looked around for a black car. Only women pushing strollers, a boy feeding the pigeons under the falling autumn leaves.

"Meet me at Marché d'Aligre," she said. "The corner café. You know the one. Ten minutes."

She'd get off the street, take a shortcut through a passage.

The oldest market in Paris sighed with a spent tiredness in the autumn light. Apart from the stallkeepers sweeping cauliflower leaves and the flattened persimmons squishing below her feet, it was mostly empty. Only the legal and illegal *brocante* did a brisk business. With a few minutes before she was supposed to meet René, she stopped in the Graineterie, a North African spice haven, for the lentils Chloé loved in her puree.

The outdoor café tables and the counter were full. So Aimée kept walking, stretching out a cramp in her leg, taking deep breaths to clear her mind. The wine bar, le Baron Rouge, was jammed as usual, patrons choosing oysters from the shucker on the street. A few leaned on car hoods, an oyster in one hand, *un verre de rouge* in the other.

Her eye caught on a man standing inside at the counter. So familiar. That corduroy jacket, those patched sleeves, his stance, his arm gestures. She saw his reflection in the dimly lit mirror — thick stone-white hair, those basset-hound eyes.

Morbier. So this was why he hadn't answered. Out drinking. Typical. But hadn't she encouraged him to get out and go to cafés, the market?

Before she could call out to him, her phone trilled.

"Where are you?" said René.

She looked up. "Outside the café, but I

see Morbier —"

"No time for that, Aimée. It's important. I've snagged a table; hurry."

When she looked back, a group had entered le Baron Rouge, and she couldn't see Morbier anymore.

THURSDAY, MIDAFTERNOON

She found René at a back table sipping a steamy herbal tisane.

"René, the car that chased us last night was seen at dawn outside Gérard's bolt-hole nearby. *Alors,* he escaped. He's got more lives than a cat."

"Where'd he go?"

"I'm working on it," she said, gesturing to the waiter. *"Un expresso, s'il vous plaît."*

"Work on this," said René.

He unzipped the roller bag as he began updating her on the pool hall, Nestor, the legionnaire's roommate at the hotel, and Réserve la Luxe, the chauffeur service with the new Paris address. He showed her the contents of the legionnaire's bag.

"Impressive, René." On a mission, he got things done all right.

"Saj checked," said René. "From what he could make out, this address is probably a front, just a mailing address. And it's Jean

Moulin's address, too."

"Jean Moulin? The Resistance hero?"

"*Mais non,* this Jean Moulin's the legionnaire's accomplice who doubles as a chauffeur," said René. "An alias? Anyway, the business address is part of the *viaduc,* with garages behind it."

Wine-fueled conversations and the whoosh of the milk steamer made a din.

"But how does that help us find Gérard?" she said. "How important can this be?" Aimée unwrapped the sugar cubes. Plopped them in and stirred. The sweet jolt woke her up.

"For one thing, he's after us, too, remember?" said René. "Takes out anyone in his way. Moulin and the legionnaire tracked Gérard down —"

"That's it," she interrupted. "Somehow, the accomplice knows where Gérard goes every time. So we follow him to find Gérard."

René raised his hand to stop her. "*Zut,* I want to bring him down. No one gets away with blowing up my car."

"How, then? Got an idea?"

"We use this burner phone," said René. "Draw him out."

Aimée downed the rest of her espresso. Put down five francs. "Let's go."

And then she froze as the truth finally hit her. What kind of an idiot was she?

Why hadn't she registered what she'd been seeing — what had been wrong with that picture?

Morbier was standing at the bar.

Thursday, Midafternoon

But Morbier was gone.

When she asked, the bartender shrugged. "Just came on shift."

She joined René on the pavement, where he stood with the roller bag.

"Aimée, I've got a taxi waiting." René looked at her, eyes blazing. "This guy murdered those homeless men and blew up my *classique*."

She'd never seen him like this.

They made a plan to flush out the legionnaire's accomplice as the taxi sped the few short blocks down rue de Charenton and turned onto Avenue Daumesnil, which paralleled the Promenade Plantée.

"Ici." René had pulled out the legionnaire's cell phone with its fading battery. The address was a vacant storefront in the rose brick with limestone lintels.

"Let's settle the tab, *monsieur,*" said the young taxi driver. "I've got to get my wife to *le dentiste.*"

Aimée pulled out a wad of francs. Got a receipt. "Business expense, René."

"Would be great if we had a paying client," said René, lips pouting in a *moue* of disgust.

With an eye on the Réserve la Luxe storefront, they waited out of the wind in an archway. Behind them was a tunneled street and a switchback of stairs that led to the walking path above.

"Look." René pointed to a narrow driveway near the storefront. A tight squeeze for a delivery truck or car. On the burner phone, he hit REDIAL on the only number it had ever called. Put the call on speaker.

It rang and rang. Finally a rasping voice: "I know where you are."

Who did the accomplice think was calling him?

René knew what he was supposed to say, but he stood frozen, his eyes wide. A choking sound came from his mouth instead of what they'd rehearsed. Their plans hung in the balance.

Aimée did the only thing she could think of — leaned down and tickled behind his knees. René sputtered and burst into surprised, nervous laughter.

She grabbed the phone and put her finger

to his lips. Shook her head.

"Think it's funny?" said the rasping voice. "You won't think so when I find you." He thought he was talking to Gérard Hlili. "Your pal, the old caretaker, he likes the bottle, *non*?" Pause. "I'll drop by."

The scene in the schoolyard came back to her: the caretaker's reticence, his flushed face and spider veins, the way he'd looked up at the pavilion.

Aimée hung up the phone.

I'll drop by.

They knew where to find Gérard Hlili. But they didn't have wheels.

"You know I hate you tickling me, Aimée."

"If you'd said the wrong thing, our lives might have been in danger, René."

He pointed to the white glow of lights reflecting off the rose brick. A black car. "They still might be."

Thursday, Late Afternoon

"He's getting away," said Aimée. The black Renault was backing out of the driveway they'd spotted earlier. She pulled out the spare outfit she'd packed in her bag. Slipped the dark blue cowl of a nun's robe over her head.

"Monsieur, monsieur?" she said, waving. The car kept reversing. She jumped aside and pounded on the trunk. But the Renault edged into the street — any minute, it would have space to nose out and shoot away.

Merde.

She ran around to the front of the car — couldn't see through the smoked windows. Reached for the handle and pulled the driver's door halfway open. The driver accelerated in reverse, the gear whining. With a loud dull crunk, the car crashed into a Mercedes behind it. The door whipped back, and she stumbled into the street and fell.

René was running. "*Mon Dieu,* Aimée, are you hurt?"

Stunned and embarrassed more than anything, she picked herself up. The driver, a wiry *mec* in a black suit, had squeezed out the passenger door and sprinted into the tunnel. The car's rear had crumpled into the Mercedes's engine grille.

Sirens wailed as a blue-and-white police car pulled up at the corner. Had René called the *flics?* Talk about quick. Then she realized the *commissariat* itself was at the corner of the street in front of them.

The accomplice was taking the stairs up two at a time. No way the *flics* would catch him. She took off, lifting her trailing robe as she followed up the metal stairs. "Which way did he go?" she yelled down at René when she reached the top.

"Wait for the *flics;* it's not safe. He's armed."

Cherry, linden, and hazelnut trees and lush bamboo lined the old rail line's Coulée verte, stretching along the *viaduc* from near the Bastille to Jardin de Reuilly and beyond. Above the bustle of the city, she was surrounded by green. No time to enjoy that.

Where the hell had he gone?

To her right, a couple sat smoking on a bench. A father and his laughing son zinged by her, kicking their *trotinettes.*

"Did you see a man in a black suit run by?" she called. But her words were lost in their wake.

Every second, the accomplice got farther away.

Which way to go?

Sunlight sparkled off the rustling leaves. Her gaze caught on a black-suited figure weaving among several white-haired men wearing matching red Bayern München windbreakers. She caught phrases of what sounded like German.

"Stop him!" she shouted. No one paid any attention to her. She took off again, nun's habit flying, every step accompanied by leg cramps. Tried to remember some German from school. *"Bitten sie halt!"*

To a person, they all turned. She blinked in surprise — she'd forgotten how these people obeyed orders. *"Können wir helfen?"*

"Ja," she panted, pointing at the man. *"Mein koffer."*

She'd meant to say "bag," but the closest word she knew was the one for "suitcase." Oh well.

Meanwhile, the man had pushed his way through the tourists and darted ahead

251

among the trees.

The German men sprinted to her aid, and one grabbed the accomplice's arm, managing to slow him down. The man shook him off, launching him against another helpful tourist, who tripped. Before her eyes, the German tour group fell like dominos.

Habit flying, she jumped over sprawled arms and legs. No time to help them, unfortunately. The accomplice dodged among planters, appearing and disappearing from her line of sight behind tall decorative grass. Ahead she saw another set of stairs down to the street. Lungs on fire, she pushed herself to catch up with him. She was so out of shape, and this heavy robe got in the way. She struggled out of the habit as she ran, pumping her legs. He was turning toward the stairs. Getting away.

With all her might, she spurted forward, whipped the nun's habit at him. It lassoed his head like a net. His arms shot out, trying to bat it off, grabbing the stair handrail. But in the nanoseconds he was blinded by the cloth, she tackled him. Landed on hard muscle, a wiry frame. Just as suddenly she was shoved away, flying through the air. Her thigh smacked into a wall. She tottered on the staircase, about to fall headfirst down the stairs. *Grab his arms, his ankle, some-*

thing. Shielding her head with one arm, she lashed out and caught the cuff of his pants just before he could kick her down the stairs and to another concussion.

"Waah . . . what the . . . ?" he yelled.

She heard a thunk. The crack of bone on the steps. The accomplice sprawled against a planter as René administered kicks to his head.

The man was out cold.

Catching her breath, she grabbed the railing and pulled herself up. "Good timing, partner." Too bad they'd get no information from him. White bone and gristle stuck out of a hole in his suit-jacket elbow. A nasty fracture — he'd be lucky if the doctors could get that bone back in. Not her concern. "Let's get him behind the bushes."

Together they dragged the unconscious man from view. René grunted, checking his pockets. "We need to find out his tricks."

"Doubt there's anything there but his wallet and keys," she said, catching her breath. "Whatever tricks he uses are probably in the car."

Aimée took the accomplice's keys as René rifled through the wallet, tossed it. "Let the *flics* chew on this."

"Good thinking." Then she noticed the

253

panting men in red jackets straggling toward her.

"Sind-sie polizei?"

She grabbed the habit. "Hurry, the Germans are coming."

She needed to end this. Find Gérard. Return the money.

Save her mother.

They backtracked a block to the corner where the accomplice's Renault stuck out like a sore thumb. The rear end was crinkled like an accordion. The owner of the Mercedes the accomplice had backed into was involved in a heated discussion with a tow-truck driver.

"What do we do now?" said René. "We've got to get into that car."

Aimée's lungs burned, and her sore legs protested her every step. "Stay here . . . *Non,* walk toward the *mairie.*"

"Look, Aimée, forget whatever you're thinking. That Mercedes owner's seen you."

"He's seen a nun. Do what I say, René." She stuck the nun's robe back in her bag, and smoothed down her catsuit.

Thursday, Late Afternoon

"What's going on, *monsieur?*" Aimée asked, her tone brisk.

"What's going on?" the Mercedes owner said, bristling. "I'm told the idiot who crashed into my new Mercedes is involved in a police investigation."

Aimée thought quick. "Correct."

"What's it to you?"

She flashed her faux police ID. "My orders are to take this vehicle to police impound," she said, gesturing toward the Renault.

"*Quoi?* Wait a minute wasn't that you . . . a nun?"

"Undercover operation." She pulled out the car keys from the pocket in her catsuit.

"But, er . . . Officer, you can't do that . . . I need details for my insurance."

"*Bien sûr,* meet me at the impound lot."

"I insist we do this now."

"It's a safety issue, *monsieur.* This vehicle's

255

blocking traffic." She nodded to the tow-truck driver. "Meet you there."

"I thought Traffic handled this?" Not stupid, the tow-truck driver squinted in suspicion.

"Not when there's an ongoing police investigation," she said.

"Where did the *flics* go?" the Mercedes owner asked. "They were here one minute—"

"It's a manhunt, *monsieur*."

He blinked.

"I'd suggest taking cover."

With that, she opened the driver's-side door. Inserted the key into the ignition and prayed the damn car would drive. An answering hum from the engine. Good. She pressed her foot on the clutch pedal, shifted into first, her nerves taut as wire.

The car responded.

She turned left, keeping an eye on the Mercedes owner and the tow-truck operator in the rearview mirror. Half a block down, she pulled over.

René got in, hiking himself up onto the seat. Pulled on his seat belt.

"How many lies did you tell just now?" he asked.

"Enough to get you in here so you can

find the tracer or whatever he's been using."

"I hate this car. The bumper's about to fall off."

"If that's all that happens, we're lucky. At least it's running."

René searched the glove compartment while she circled the Place Félix Eboué roundabout three times. Convinced no one had followed them, she entered rue de Reuilly for the second time that day.

Her phone buzzed. Keeping her eyes on the road, she reached into her bag by the gearshift. The screen was blank.

"It's your other phone, Aimée."

Merde. The DGSE burner phone.

"Going to answer it?" René asked.

"Not yet." Her hands trembled on the steering wheel. "Find anything, René?"

"Spare car keys . . . hold on." He held up a dark grey metal widget. "Sophisticated tracker. But the batteries are dead. He turned off the GPS."

"Can you activate the thing to see his trail?"

"I'll try." René took a cord from the glove compartment, plugged the tracker into the lighter socket. Fiddled with buttons, muttering as the tracker charged.

"They work for someone, René."

"*Evidemment,* but you don't think the DGSE staged this, do you?"

She shook her head. "The DGSE are even more in the dark than I am. This *mec* has an employer."

René tugged his goatee as he played with the tracker. "*Bien sûr,* doubt the accomplice is the brains behind a two-man operation. Any ideas?"

"It smells like a contract job."

She recalled Yvon's recounting of his conversation with Gérard, how the man on the run had felt he couldn't trust anyone.

A minute later a music ringtone trilled from the tracker in René's hand.

"Crocodile Rock," she said. The third crocodile reference that day.

"My favorite Elton John," said René.

"Why's music coming from the tracker?"

"*Je ne sais pas!* The song is set up as the ringtone for the only contact."

"Can you geolocate this person? By responding?"

"He disabled those functions." But René grinned and held up the tracker. "This contact is called 'The Crocodile.' Any idea why?"

"We're about to find out."

THURSDAY, EARLY EVENING

The peach-pink band of a fading sunset settled on the zinc rooftops and pepper-pot chimneys. As dusk descended on rue Montgallet, people scurried from the Métro, shoppers clogged the boulangerie and *épicerie,* parents pushed strollers from the *crêche.* At the corner on rue de Reuilly bike riders competed with cars.

"A light's on upstairs," said René. They'd parked, keeping the Renault's motor running and the heat on, in front of the pavilion at Sainte Clotilde's gate. "You really think Gérard's hiding there?"

"He's on the run and out of options."

She'd caught René up on her earlier visit and suspicions that Sainte Clotilde's caretaker was hiding Gérard.

René shook his head. "In Gérard's shoes, I'd get the hell out of Paris. Hop it to Côte d'Ivoire."

"Not until he has what Germaine wanted

to give him — money for his coup, map to some kind of valuable cargo. He must desperately need it — otherwise, what's he risking his life for? He knows it's here. We wait."

"What's to say the caretaker even gave him your card?"

Her nerves tingled. "Nothing. You're right."

Saj answered on the first ring.

"What can you find out about a Baptiste who works as the caretaker at Sainte Clotilde's school?" Aimée asked. "I need to get him out of his loge."

"*Namaste* to you, too, Aimée."

She heard the clicking of Saj's keyboard. She put speakerphone on so René could hear.

"Need me to flush him out?" Saj said as he searched. "Fire alarm, bomb scare, burst water main? An evacuation?"

"I like how you think, Saj, but we'll go low-key." *For now.*

More clicking.

"*Et voilà*, Baptiste Cornu, born in Paris, fifty-three years old, employed twenty years as caretaker at Sainte Clotilde, lives on the grounds in the pavilion. Served as a lieutenant in the French military in Côte d'Ivoire, volunteer at l'Armée du salut, head parishioner at Saint Éloi church. A veteran with connections to Côte d'Ivoire and a religious man."

"Any family?" Aimée asked.

"Widowed."

Lonely. That gave her ammunition. But how to fire?

"*Merci,* Saj." She hung up.

A postal truck pulled up on the street, blocking her view of the pavilion fronting the school.

"Come on, René. Can you run interference, deflect the caretaker? Say you're interested in volunteering at the school's chapel; think of something."

"What about you?"

"I need to get inside that pavilion."

Snapping her black leather jacket closed and looping her flea-market vintage Hermès scarf around her neck, she joined René on the pavement behind the postal truck. The postman was coming out of Sainte Clotilde's gate. A woman — a teacher, judging by the notebooks poking out of her bag — hurried out behind him.

"Now, René."

Just before the gate closed, Aimée slid inside and held it open for René. Not even a backward glance from the postman or the teacher, who'd crossed the street toward the Métro. So far, so good.

Across the grass the caretaker, Baptiste, stood in conversation with the school receptionist. Aimée motioned toward him, and René took the hint. Aimée tried to melt into the ivy on the pavilion's wall as René trotted forward and interrupted their conversation, pointed toward the chapel, drawing Baptiste's attention. A minute later the two men were walking toward the chapel, the receptionist turning toward the office.

This was Aimée's chance.

THURSDAY, EARLY EVENING

At the pavilion's side service door under hanging ivy, she got to work with her lockpick set from her LeClerc compact. Thank God there was more than one entry. A minute later, she was in a faded yellow pantry with an ancient laundry press.

Stepping into the kitchen was like stepping into the past — beveled glass cabinets, a cracked porcelain sink, a half-drunk bowl of café au lait with a brown skin on top. A rock-hard baguette sat on the stained red-checked tablecloth. The air held an odor of grease.

She took advantage of the dim light in the foyer with its cracked marble tiles to stop and listen. A faint voice . . . a radio or someone on the phone?

She took the staircase, cringing at every creak. No one stopping her so far. Her hand closed around the DGSE burner phone in her bag, ready to dial Lacenaire.

A door opened on the landing, and she squinted in the bright light. She stuck the phone in her catsuit's back pocket.

All of a sudden a hand clamped over her mouth. She stumbled and tried to resist. A strong arm pushed her into a room, and the door slammed shut behind her. Perspiration broke out on her neck.

The hand released her. She whirled around to stare into a probing pair of deep black eyes. She recognized Gérard from the photo, despite his shaven head and cap. This was the charismatic young Ivoirian who'd rallied so many to his cause. Relieved she'd found him, she caught her breath. "Gérard Hlili, I'm Aimée Leduc."

"Should I know you?" he said in a deep rolling accent. Those watchful eyes were set under thick knit brows. He had a muscular, tall frame encased in jeans and a T-shirt under a work coat.

"You're a difficult man to find."

"I like to keep it that way," he said, sizing her up. "Who sent you?"

"*Desolée,* but didn't Baptiste tell you to contact me?" It could have been easy; instead she'd had to hunt him down.

"You broke in here," he said. "Why should I believe you spoke with him?"

Understandable that he'd be suspicious.

264

She had to gain his trust. Finish this.

"Germaine's documents are safe," she said.

"Then show me."

"No way I'd carry them on me."

"Use gifts for good, not evil, or . . ." His words hung in the air. A test.

"Suffer their curse," she said, finishing the saying from the page torn from the book.

"Apologies, I realize this is no way to get acquainted," he said. "But I have to be careful." Then Gérard smiled, a radiant smile deep in his eyes, emanating a magnetic force. Even knowing this warm, personal smile was a politician's cultivated tool, she felt special, felt her pulse speed up.

"What does that saying mean?"

"Mean?" Gérard parted the curtains, glanced out the window, and shook his head. "Do right or suffer — that old saying paralyzes our people." Now his dark eyes burned. "We need clean water, decent roads. Schools that are part of a modern educational system. French companies suck us dry by convincing us our duties lie with them. Abidjan teems with the Parisian educated elite, like I was once," he said. "Spoiled, full of attitude, wearing Hugo Boss suits, and blind to the struggle around me." He shrugged and shook his head again.

"I heard you lost your mother to a cholera epidemic. I'm sorry."

His eyes closed a moment. When he reopened them, she saw deep hurt. "It's called the blue death. Your skin turns blue from severe dehydration. My case wasn't severe because when we got sick, my mother insisted I drink all the bottled water. She thought she'd be able to survive with the water from her own village. But she died in my arms."

He stopped and turned his face away to stare at his hands. Long fingers, palms calloused.

"Just a simple thing for the government to provide clean water, sanitation, and hygiene. Basic, right? My father and I contacted the World Health Organization to organize a clean water project and combat the epidemic. Corruption prevented that. It forced me to wake up. But I'm a realist; I know that to make meaningful change, we need to heal political and ethnic conflicts. Many of us want the same thing — a system that works for everyone."

He crackled with intensity. She was drawn in by his passion, could see how people followed him.

"Côte d'Ivoire was France's pet," he was saying. "A tool of their colonialist policy until we gained independence in 1960. We became one of the most stable countries in Africa. But today, we can't control the price of the cocoa bean, our national crop, because of corrupt politicians and the Paris elite. Recently, the IMF, World Bank, and European Union have suspended all our aid. We're in crisis."

It wasn't her fight, but she understood.

"But what is it that brings you here? Where's Germaine?"

He hadn't heard.

"*Desolée,* but she didn't make it," she said.

Gérard's hand went to his forehead, and he turned to the window. She gave him space to grieve, looked around. The room had a high ceiling, curlicue wood *boiserie,* and faded floral wallpaper. Stained-glass windows were covered by dingy lace curtains. A bed bore a crumpled sleeping bag and was strewn with political pamphlets; the whole room gave off a musty smell.

When he turned back, his face was creased with worry. "Terrible. They want to ruin everything we're trying to achieve for our country . . . Germaine, her brother — they killed him, too, covered it up as an accident. So what do you have for me?"

"Documents," she said, keeping it vague.

"Names, lists, diagrams, a kind of map. Nothing made sense to me. I'm just carrying out Germaine's promise to get them to you, Gérard. Look, the legionnaire who was chasing you is dead. You knew he was coming. That's why you escaped from the safe house, right?"

"How do you know about that?" He was suspicious again.

She looked at her Tintin watch. "I've got a car waiting for us outside." She held out the grey tracker. "Who's the Crocodile?"

"Maybe you're one of his thugs."

He moved and stood in front of the door.

"Why doubt me, Gérard?" She didn't like his edgy reaction. Her heart pounded; her brain was on high alert.

"Who are you, really?"

"Someone who didn't want to get involved."

"So why did you?"

"Does it matter?" She was tired of having to prove herself. Wasn't she there to help him? Aimée had taken on Germaine's mission because her mother's safety was at stake, but she wasn't even sure her mother was alive. She had no choice but to work with the DGSE. Would explaining that to Gérard help anything, though? "Let's go. We need to leave now." She wished she could see out through the dingy lace curtain.

"You still haven't explained who you are or why I should trust you."

"Talk to your friends at the DGSE."

"Those clowns? They'll sell me out to the highest bidder. Or try to buy me to continue French influence. You think I trust the generals competing for power, forces like the CIA?"

Did her mother? A vision of Sydney sitting with Chloé, drinking *chocolat chaud* . . . from cocoa, his national crop.

"Gérard. I'm trying to get you the documents — and the money — you need. For your cause. To get you out of here, out of danger. Do you even have anyone besides Baptiste in your corner?"

"I trust him. I still don't get what's in it for you."

She bit her lip. "I'll explain later. Let's go get the documents from my office."

A double knock on the door. Gérard opened it, and Baptiste, the caretaker, stared at her.

"That's the one," he said.

Where had René gone?

The caretaker shook his head. "Don't believe anything she says, Gérard."

"What?" Aimée blinked. "I'm trying to help you. Can't you understand?"

"I do," Gérard said. "But you're a wild card. We didn't expect you, and I still don't know that I can trust you."

The caretaker nodded. "She sent someone to distract me."

Her heart jumped. She didn't like how the two men were blocking the door. "Where's my business partner?"

"The little guy you're in cahoots with? He's wrapped up in the chapel. Literally." The caretaker smiled. "He pretended to be interested in volunteering. Saw through him right away."

Her heart thudded as guilt filled her. She'd sent René into danger.

What the hell were these two up to?

None of this had gone the way she'd thought it would. She should've called the DGSE as soon as she'd discovered Gérard's whereabouts and let them take over. She could've gotten her mother back, if they'd made good on their promise. She felt as if all she was doing was treading water between massive waves hitting her.

"Please let him go," she said. "I'll take you to my office right now."

In response, Gérard grabbed her bag. "Get the keys, Baptiste. Go yourself."

Terror filled her. "Look, why can't you trust me?"

Gérard's arms folded in a defensive position. "If I trusted others, I wouldn't be alive right now."

"You say you're a leader for peace and change for your people. Germaine died trying to get this to you, and I'm only trying to help."

The caretaker's eyes burned. "Lies. She murdered Germaine, Gérard. She's their agent."

Gérard's dark eyes flickered in hesitation.

The caretaker took Gérard's arm. "What if she's planning to hand you over?"

"I'm on your side, Gérard," she said desperately. "I've put my life on the line for this. The Crocodile's men have tried to kill me twice. They blew up my friend's car." She'd taken a guess about the Crocodile, didn't know for sure. "Who is he? Why is he trying to stop you?"

"I think you're CIA," said Baptiste. "I saw enough agents in l'Afrique to recognize you. You're the new generation."

"Moi?" She almost laughed. "No way."

"See? She thinks she's smart," said Baptiste.

"I'm telling the truth. Why listen to him?"

Gérard was gripping her shoulder. Tight. "Baptiste knows Côte d'Ivoire."

"And how does that help you here and

now? How does that get you the information in my office, which is protected by an alarm? Why won't you trust me?" Perspiration dampened her collar.

"I trusted the DGSE, and look where that landed me."

"I thought you were working with them."

"I did, too, until . . . I realized they were using me."

"So use them back, Gérard. Play their game."

He smiled. He was still holding her bag. "Right now, Baptiste and your partner, who will disable the alarm, will go to your office and pick up the documents. If they're there, that is."

THURSDAY EVENING

Before she could react, the caretaker had grabbed her hands and tied her securely to a chair with her own cashmere scarf. So fast — the old codger moved like lightning.

"Your partner will drive Baptiste." Gérard hung her vintage Vuitton bag on a hook on the door, high out of her reach. "If your partner doesn't cooperate, things will go badly for you."

Mon Dieu. René was in even more danger now. All her fault.

The door slammed behind the two men, and her bag bounced against it. She heard the lock click from the other side.

She'd walked into this like an idiot. Wanted to kick herself. What had happened to Gérard the charismatic good-guy patriot? If he'd acted that part with Germaine and her brother, he was sure displaying other colors now.

Never assume, her father had always said.

She thought back to the documents. Remembered Saj hitting a major firewall blocking access to a cargo manifest. What if what the cargo plane carried wasn't meant to get into Hlili's hands? Contraband? Arms?

She struggled in the chair. Wished she could get at the Swiss Army knife in her bag. Fat chance. The scarf was cutting into her wrists, causing her hands to go numb. Somehow she had to break these ties and reach the DGSE phone. Get the hell out and alert the DGSE to everything that had happened.

Gérard could return at any moment.

Perspiring in this hot, high-ceilinged room, she scanned for something sharp to saw apart the scarf. *Nothing.*

Hurry, she had to hurry.

She pushed with her feet, rocking the chair until it fell over. A loud thump.

Great.

Pain sliced up a rib. Still tied to the chair, she scooted in her heels over the parquet to the bed. Dust balls caught on her favorite last-season find, the agnès b. catsuit.

With her head, she pushed up the not-so-fragrant mattress. Thank God it was the thin cheap kind. She twisted her back, angling around and lifting her aching arms behind her to try to catch the scarf on a spring. After the third try, one of her bound wrists finally made contact with a sharp, rusty-feeling spring.

Back and forth she sawed, her neck aching from holding up the mattress. Not a tear or a rip. Damn Hermès scarf held up under duress.

She tried to uncoil the spring, use the sharp edge to pick at the double knot. But the wire stuck in a tight coil behind her. No luck.

The clanging of metal, a low voice, came through the floorboards from downstairs.

That was when she saw the rusted loose nail poking out of a warped floorboard where it met the window.

She'd had a tetanus shot, hadn't she? Or was that Chloé?

Wincing, she leaned, made her aching legs push her toward the window. With the chair on its side, her tied wrists caught on the rusted nail. She yanked and pulled, up and down, back and forth, until the cashmere caught. Layer by layer, she fought her way through the thick double knot that bit into her skin.

She hated ruining vintage Hermès.

Strand by strand, it ripped. Breaking free, she shook her numb hands and rubbed them to get the circulation going. She undid the window latch. Pushed up.

The window was bolted shut.

Now what?

She went to the next window, a grimy fantasy in violet and blue glass, unlatched it. Not a budge.

Nothing for it if she wanted to get out of there.

She took off her jacket, wrapped it and her tattered scarf around her fist, and punched. Colored shards and lead-framing pieces fell tinkling to the ground.

Steps pounded on the stairs.

Again she punched the glass. And again, until she had a big enough hole to crawl out. Got one leg out. Then she remembered her bag.

Merde.

The steps were outside the door.

She shoved the metal bed frame as hard as she could, jamming it under the door handle at an angle diagonal to the ground. Someone pounded on the other side of the door until it shuddered. She snatched her bag off the door hook, put the handles between her teeth, and squeezed through the window, grabbing at the creeping vines on the pavilion's stone façade. Prayed they held her. The vines moaned, tearing away from the wall under her weight. She swayed a flight above the stone walkway. Then a loud crash as she landed on her derriere in a bush, her arms tangling in the brown and yellow branches.

She heard a crack in her back pocket. The phone. *Merde!*

Somehow she extracted herself, got to her feet, strapped the bag across her chest, and ran. As she pressed the buzzer on the gate and ran out into the street, she grappled with the phone, hoping it would work despite the cracked screen. The car sat parked where she'd left it.

She crouched down behind it and punched in the office number on her phone.

"Saj, is René there?"

"He's at the door, saying he forgot the code." Saj was whispering. "Like René would forget."

René wouldn't have been able to drive without accommodations for his height. Baptiste must have insisted they take a taxi.

"Never," she said. "Do what I say, Saj."

"What's wrong, Aimée?"

"Just listen. Take everything down from the whiteboard and put it back in the envelope. Now. When you let René in, grab the old man with him, and tie him up. He's tough."

She hung up. From behind the car, she peered up through the darkness at the pavilion. The lit window.

She hit the number programmed in the DGSE phone.

"Oui?" a voice answered.

"One-oh-three rue de Reuilly. You better hurry."

"We're here."

"Already?"

"You turned on the phone."

They'd been tracking her with GPS.

"Now your part of the deal," she said. "Where's Sydney?"

A car had pulled up. Doors slammed. "We'll be in touch."

She hunched, shaking, behind the car, hoping she'd done the right thing.

What was "the right thing"? Her father had always told her the right thing made your gut clench so tight it gave you cramps.

Gérard had made her gut clench — in the wrong way.

Any minute, she expected the DGSE to haul him off. Could she trust them to protect her mother? So far, she'd accomplished little besides playing into their hands.

She rang Babette. "Heard from Sydney?" Aimée asked.

"No news, like they say, can mean good news."

So her mother wasn't free. She would've called right away.

"How's Chloé?" Aimée asked.

"Loved her aubergines. Just fell asleep. Martine says hi."

Relief filled her. She missed her little Chloé. Those rose-pink cheeks, those pearly toes.

"Martine's got a new door code."

Aimée heard footsteps approaching. Voices. "Leave it on my voice mail, okay?"

She hung up and peered over the hood. Laughter erupted as Gérard gave a playful punch to the man walking next to him — the DGSE agent still in the same hoodie he'd been wearing when he'd given Aimée the burner phone earlier. With another laugh, Gérard got in the passenger seat.

Furious, she wanted to throw something. She watched the red taillights get smaller until they turned the corner.

THURSDAY EVENING

"Under control, Aimée," said Saj over the phone. "Package secured. René declared code four. You okay?"

"Fine. I'll grab a taxi."

"We'll meet you out back. *Un moment.*" She heard Saj put his hand over the phone. "René says take the car. Spare keys are behind the back driver's-side wheel."

Her gaze caught metal glinting in the streetlight. "So he does like this car."

She popped the hood and checked for a tracer, which she should have done before. Found it under the grille. *Merde.*

She looked around. No one watching. No one she could see, at least. She dropped the tracer into the gutter.

She got in, switched on the ignition, and shifted into first, looking for a tail. She didn't have to wait long. In the rearview mirror, a brown camionette pulled out and followed at a set distance down rue de Reuilly.

She turned right onto the first street she came to, accelerating past the Diaconesses hospital; shot onto rue Jaucourt; and joined the outer ring of Place de la Nation's roundabout. Ran a yellow light and swung into the next street. By the time she made it to the inner roundabout, she didn't see her tail.

She circled twice more, changing lanes, and at the last minute shot onto Boulevard Diderot.

She'd lost him. She kept to narrow streets, weaving through Bastille and into the Marais, her eye on the rearview mirror. Drove up rue de Rivoli, then took a right before the Louvre. By the time she turned onto the street behind their office, her damp palms were slipping on the steering wheel.

She flicked the headlights at the corner. René stepped out of the doorway of the boulangerie, Saj behind him, supporting the dead weight of caretaker, Baptiste.

"Code four, René?" she asked once they all were in the car, Saj in the back seat with the caretaker, René in front with her.

"Laptops, burner phones, in my bag, per our procedure."

"What procedure?"

"You'd know if you'd read Saj's new manual. I wired up the office alarm for remote check-ins." René eased his briefcase and satchel to the car floor.

She turned. Scanned behind her. *No one.* Took off down rue du Louvre.

"What happened to Baptiste, Saj?" she asked.

"I've applied arnica to prevent bruising. I wanted to administer melatonin to calm him, but he'd passed out."

"Before or after you tied him up?"

"Hard to say."

"I need him to talk."

Aimée pulled into a parking spot by the vacant Bourse de Commerce, Marie de Médicis's astrological column silhouetted behind it. Kept the engine running.

Saj pulled a rose-colored bottle from his madras cloth bag. Unstoppered it and wafted the bottle under the caretaker's nose. Baptiste stirred, and his heavy-lidded eyes opened. Closed. Opened again, and he mumbled something.

"What's that, Baptiste?" Aimée turned and lifted his chin. "The Crocodile? That what you said?"

"*Non,* that's not . . . Where am I?"

"But the Crocodile is what I want to hear about, Baptiste," she said.

"Let me out."

"Who is he? Why's he after Gérard?"

"That's . . . He's . . ." His eyes closed.

After a nod from Aimée, Saj again passed the bottle under his nose.

"The Crocodile's after Gérard," she said. "Why?"

He blinked. "Gérard needs the cargo."

"Why's this cargo important? What is it?"

"Only way for the country . . ." His voice trailed off.

Condensation from their breath fogged the car's windows.

"You're saying the Crocodile wants the cargo, too, Baptiste?" she asked.

No response.

Saj again passed the bottle under his nose.

His eyes opened, half-lidded.

"Why are you involved with Gérard, Baptiste?" she asked.

"Knew his father . . . Côte d'Ivoire . . . a good boy, like a son."

Talk about the odd couple.

She turned up the defroster, which gave off hardly a whiff of air. Light-headed, she rolled down the window. "Who's the Crocodile?"

"Gérard's afraid . . ." he said.

"Afraid of the Crocodile?"

"Afraid . . . a big shot, I don't know."

After five minutes, that was the most she'd gotten out of him. She didn't think he knew any more than he'd told her.

"Let's get rid of this old coot," said René.

"Dump a religious old veteran who has dedicated his life to caretaking?" she said.

"I know the perfect place."

René had Aimée make a stop at a corner shop blaring Arab music. A minute later he emerged with a bag. "Avenue Frochot, Minou's place," he said.

In front of the transvestite club in Pigalle, Saj lifted Baptiste out of the car. He propped the caretaker in the doorway, and René sprinkled cheap brandy all over him.

Minou, in platforms and with a boa over his broad shoulders, appeared and lit a cigarette.

"I know you don't care for garbage at your door, Minou," said René.

Minou waved to Aimée and clucked at Baptiste. "A disgrace."

René handed Minou the hundred-franc note Aimée had slipped him. "Drunk and disorderly, too. Better call it in."

"Civic duty, *c'est moi,*" Minou said, flouncing with his boa back into the *boîte de nuit.*

Exhausted, Aimée pulled the blanket over

Chloé in the makeshift crib in Martine's apartment. Felt Chloé's cheeks — cool, no fever. Aimée always worried about fevers. Worried she didn't pay close enough attention to the admonitions of Dr. Dolto, the pediatric-psychologist guru.

A grin erupted on Chloé's sleeping face. Thank God her little one had sweet dreams.

She couldn't deal with filling the ancient claw-footed bathtub and instead gave herself a sponge bath with Martine's Florentine lemon-verbena soap. She slipped on a soft linen teddy, climbed under the duvet with Martine, her best friend since lycée.

"You've got cold feet," said Martine.

But Aimée had passed out.

FRIDAY MORNING

Aimée held Chloé on her hip in the morning, sunshine streaming through the tall window overlooking the Italian Cultural Institute's garden. Chloé squealed in glee at a hummingbird, a colorful helicopter of wings, at the outside feeder. Situated in Talleyrand's former *hôtel particulier,* where Napoleon had visited him, the Italian Cultural Institute's grounds occupied a back lane of the chic seventh arrondissement, a world away from everything that had happened the previous night.

Putting her espresso down, Aimée leaned over and powered on her laptop.

"You sure it's okay if I work here this morning?" she asked.

"As long as I can babysit my goddaughter," Martine said. "Gianni's in Rome until tomorrow."

Martine, who was at the stove cooking up something fragrant with apricots, positively glowed. She wore her blonde hair clipped up in a tousled knot, Gianni's silk pajamas, and a smile as she stirred. A seasoned journalist, she'd taken the Italian kitchen-mama thing to heart and was determined to master culinary skills. Blame Gianni, the Italian cultural liaison Aimée wanted to distrust. She'd never seen Martine so happy. A giant rock on her left ring finger sparkled in the sunlight.

"I'm worried," said Aimée.

"About what?"

"That any minute you'll break out into an Italian aria and insist I cook with you."

"That's next. First, read the email attachments I sent you."

Aimée clicked open her email. " 'Ripe for coup d'etat in Côte d'Ivoire.' That one?"

"For a start. Remember you asked me about the ongoing situation this morning?"

"I did?" She remembered mumbling to Martine at dawn when Chloé woke up the first time.

Martine set a bowl of warm apricots garnished with mint and out-of-season raspberries on the table. Opened her arms to Chloé. "Come to your *marraine,* gorgeous."

Martine took her godmother duties seriously.

287

Chloé wriggled and kicked her strong legs.

"Voilà, ma puce," said Aimée, setting her in Martine's lap. She opened the attachments. "So these news releases explain what's going on in Côte d'Ivoire?"

"It's a start," said Martine, spooning apricot into Chloé's open mouth. "You need more espresso."

"Tell me about it." Aimée wanted to sleep for a week.

By the time Babette arrived with Gabrielle and bundled up Chloé for the playground in Jardin du Luxembourg, Aimée had read the releases and had a grasp of the ongoing situation. The predictions of an imminent coup and power struggle mirrored what the DGSE told her. But what did it mean in relation to Gérard Hlili and the documents Germaine had been murdered for? Aimée heaved an exhausted sigh.

Martine looked up from the stove. "What's this to you?"

"Sydney's disappeared."

"Quoi? She promised me an interview. Exclusive."

"Vraiment?"

"My editor will shoot me if she doesn't show up."

"But she's back in the shadow world."

Maybe she'd never left it.

"That makes Sydney a real scoop," Martine said. "And me with an inside story. I like it."

"No, you don't. It's twisted."

Aimée poured another espresso and told Martine everything. As she had since lycée.

"So. Sydney ditches Chloé at playgroup," said Martine, lighting a cigarette and then resuming stirring a bubbling tomato sauce. "A woman's murdered in the convent after hiding documents at a mausoleum in the Picpus Cemetery; a legionnaire threatens you; then a rebel Ivoirian escapes from the DGSE's safe house; the legionnaire accidentally bites a bullet after shooting at you; his cohort blows up René's car and shoots a bunch of winos for a cell phone; you track down the rebel Ivoirian, who believes you're CIA; and you get held hostage until you escape and fall out a window. Oh, and you think the Crocodile's still after you." Martine exhaled a plume of smoke. "Did I forget anything?"

"Sydney needs to redo her CT scan."

The spoon Martine was using to stir paused. "Redo? Then there's a problem."

Aimée nodded. Sipped her espresso. "I can't believe I trusted the DGSE just because they said they'd protect her."

"Those clowns?"

289

The second time she'd heard that.

"But it's not like I had a choice, Martine."

"*Le militaire,* that's who you need to talk to. Whatever happens in l'Afrique, the military's behind it. Not saying in a good way, but they run the show. Too bad you don't have any contacts."

Hadn't Syndey said she trusted only Aimée?

Martine sprinkled in basil leaves.

"Let me talk to your uncle, Martine."

"*Oncle Robert?* He's from the colonial era. You know, cocoa plantations, floral tea dresses, everyone sleeping with everyone else. He's out to lunch mentally with his cronies at the rest home."

Wait. Aimée had her own military connection. Stupid. Why hadn't she thought of him?

Faulty memory?

"I do know someone. Colonel Max." While investigating a fugitive Serbian war criminal, an assassin hired by a renegade high-ranking military officer, she'd rooted out the betrayal, saved face for the army. And let them take credit.

"You saved his prosciutto, Aimée. He owes you big-time."

True. Though calling in an owed favor from a man like him could come with an obligation, one she'd vowed never to incur.

But his office was only a few blocks away.

She'd switched off the burner phone the night before to avoid the DGSE tracking her down. Now she needed to check in. Why not make a call from a pay phone en route?

"Got that Lacroix I can borrow?" she called on her way to the shower.

"So last season. My sister has *le smoking* from YSL — now *that's* timeless."

Coordinated with black stovepipe trousers and one of Gianni's white shirts, *le smoking* was *parfait,* she thought.

She toweled off, dabbed Chanel No. 5 on her pulse points, and ran her fingers through her red-streaked shag. Tousled it dry. She stroked mascara through her lashes, smudged her lids with kohl, and swiftly applied Chanel red to her lips.

Thank God she and Martine wore the same size shoe. Martine's low-heeled Louboutin ankle boots with red leather soles called out to her.

Martine looked up from her laptop and grinned. "I don't know how you do it."

"Do what?"

"That thrown-together look. So effortlessly chic."

Aimée shrugged. Grabbed her leather biker jacket for warmth. "But you're glowing — radiant."

Martine smiled. *"Amour."* A pause. "Sydney needs you, you know."

And Aimée hadn't needed her mother all those years?

"I know."

FRIDAY MORNING

Dried salamis hung from strings in the café across the passage from the Italian Cultural Institute. Aimée eyed the creamy white *burrata* and pickled capers on the counter as she headed toward the pay phone in the rear. She dialed the number she'd called the night before.

Three rings, then a recording saying that the voice-mail box was full. Her gut knotted. She remembered the way Gérard had laughed with that DGSE agent the previous night. Who was playing whom?

Was she caught in a setup?

But why?

Gérard could have had Germaine's documents and money in his hands by then. Instead, both were zipped into the bottom lining of Aimée's bag.

Outside, she walked to the narrow rue de Martignac and stopped midblock across from a church. *Better the devil you know than the one you don't,* her father had always said.

She pressed the buzzer under a shiny, innocuous bronze plaque.

"Oui?" came a voice over an intercom.

"Aimée Leduc, to see Colonel Maximilian."

"You have an appointment?"

"You could say that."

"*Mademoiselle,* you either have an appointment, or you don't. I don't see your name on the agenda. He's in meetings all day."

And she was tired of standing on the cold street talking into an intercom while the wind whipped her scarf.

"I'm the appointment you don't find on the agenda, *comprenez?*"

"Un moment."

Five chilly minutes later, the door in a gate clicked open.

She crossed the cobbled courtyard as she had several months before, wanting to never do it again, and walked into the den of military intelligence, a seventeenth-century townhouse with the tricolor flag waving from its gabled roof.

"A welcome surprise, *mademoiselle.*"

She doubted that.

Colonel Maximilian, known as Mad Max, wore a crisp army uniform, a silver crew cut, and a neutral expression in his granite eyes. He sat behind a *directoire*'s desk that bore only a single pad of paper, a pen, a telephone, and a fat leather-bound diary. The office was sparse and elegant and offered no hint of what went on there.

"You've got something for me, I take it," he said.

She sat down, startled, on a Louis XV chair. "The other way around, I think."

His thick silver brows furrowed. He consulted the diary, ran his finger down a page. "*Ah, quel dommage,* I thought we'd recruited you. Tried, didn't we?"

"I'm too expensive for that."

He beamed. "How might I change your mind?"

"Do me a favor before there's any negotiating." *Fat chance.* "As you may remember, Colonel, I once saved your derriere."

"*Mademoiselle,* I remember the newspaper front page that day and the paparazzi photo of you in an army uniform with your décolletage showing."

As if she needed reminding.

"A trail of journalists hounded me for weeks to get that story," she said. "Still, I kept quiet."

He shot back, "We also encouraged them to abandon the story, if they wanted to keep valid press credentials." Pause. "There are rotten apples in every barrel. But the military's a good calling, and you served the *république.*"

The only acknowledgment she'd ever get.

"I need to know about the important players in Côte d'Ivoire," she said.

He closed the diary. Drummed his fingers on it. "That's not my part of the world." He ran the Balkan operations. "You already know that, *mademoiselle.* Why ask me?"

"Long story." She sat back, crossed her legs. "Put me in touch with your counterpart in l'Afrique."

"Why would I do that?"

She had to tell him part of the truth. "The DGSE made me an offer, difficult to refuse."

"Ah, they tend to do that."

"But I trust you more than I do them."
Something about the uniform.

He smiled. "A wise choice."

Huge antagonism existed between the military and foreign intelligence.

She continued. "Given what I did for you, I'd like a return favor."

"I'd like to think serving your country is a reward in itself, *mademoiselle.*"

She wouldn't let him get away with that. "There's someone who goes by the moniker

Crocodile. He thinks I have something he wants. Something others want, too."

His eyes lasered in on hers. "Do you?"

"I could get my hands on it. But if I did, it would cost."

He tore a sheet off the pristine pad. Wrote a number on it. Folded it, then slit it in two with a paper knife emblazoned with a military symbol. He slid the half sheet across the polished mahogany desk. *Frugal, this Mad Max.*

"Call this number in fifteen minutes." He showed her to the door. "Let's keep in touch. I'm much better at changing minds than the DGSE."

FRIDAY MORNING

Aimée stood in the leaf-swept square behind the church to make the call.

"Oui?" a voice answered.

"I was told to call this number."

"Who referred you?"

What should she say?

"Someone from rue de Martignac."

"Two rue de l'Élysée. Fifteen minutes."

She ran and hailed a taxi at the corner of rue de Grenelle. Gave the driver the address.

"Ah, and you want to arrive in fifteen minutes, *n'est-ce pas?*" the driver asked.

Some code? Or did these people do everything by the quarter hour?

"Exactement," she said.

Fifteen minutes later the taxi pulled up the side street around the corner from the Élysée presidential palace. The driver waved away the francs in her hand.

"I don't understand," she said.

"We have an arrangement."

She dropped the francs on the front seat. "Consider this a tip."

He grinned. *"Merci."*

The side door opened at her first buzz.

"Rue de Martignac?" asked the Garde républicaine, a distinctive red pompom topping his *képi.*

Aimée nodded.

"Entrez."

Beyond the glass marquise overhangs and treetops loomed the Elysée Palace roof, the flying flags indicating that *le Président* was staying *chez lui.* She stood so close she could have strolled into the garden.

Doubted the Uzi-toting blue-uniformed gendarme on guard ahead would let her.

"This way," said the Garde républicaine.

She swallowed hard, following the shined black boots to an anteroom.

The Garde républicaine gestured for her to sit on the only chair, a gilt affair with maroon velvet cushions. Then he disappeared.

What had she gotten into?

One half of a carved double door opened. The Garde républicaine reappeared and beckoned her from inside. She walked into a light-filled white salon with woodwork carved as lightly as if it were swirls of meringue and a Gobelins hunting tapestry on the wall.

The salon contained a desk and a round table surrounded by spindle back chairs. She recognized Jean-Christophe, the son of the former president, by his distinctive mustache and dark aviators, which she had seen often in the newspapers. He was wearing a long-sleeved safari shirt. Next to him sat a smiling older man in an ill-fitting suit. Pink faced and bald, with a self-effacing manner. He pulled out a chair.

"Join the round table, as we call it," he said.

She couldn't believe Michel Delorme, the shadow man, a diplomatic power broker who'd run French Africa since de Gaulle's time, was serving her chilled water from a carafe. "So dry in here." Delorme indicated a portable humidifier going at full blast. "We do what we can."

"Merci."

Jean-Christophe, the former president's son, had been a journalist, head of the French secretariat *en Afrique* under his father. He was known as a ladies' man. He watched her, expressionless. Whether he was bored or eyeing her as a piece of meat would have been good to know.

"How can I help you, *mademoiselle*?" Delorme asked in a gentle voice.

Delorme was called the *tonton,* uncle, of African presidents and leaders because of his close relationships with each of them. He nurtured an unsurpassed web of contacts. A close confidant of de Gaulle, he had served successive presidents in the *africain* secretariat, run French operations on that continent for more than thirty years. As she gulped down the water, he smiled at her again, benign and warm. Underneath was a sleeping spider.

She'd heard he'd retired. Heard wrong. Once the house was built, it may have changed owners over years, but its wiring remained the same.

She gathered her thoughts, afraid her dry tongue would stick in her mouth. Why couldn't she get the words out?

Delorme broke the ice. "I had dinner with your grandfather Claude years ago. Such a gourmand. And that little dog, he fed it filet mignon from the table, spoiled it. Did he spoil his granddaughter, too? Of course, that's what grandparents do."

She couldn't help but grin. "He took me to piano lessons and read me stories, baked wonderful tarte tatin."

"He helped us here once," he said. "A friend of the *république,* your grandfather, in many ways. I'm sure you learned much from him."

Grand-père? The things she didn't know about the old rascal. She found her tongue. "Enough, *monsieur,* to know when to ask for help."

"We help each other in our world."

It sounded like Christmas. But she doubted things were so simple. The former president's son sat impassive, like a lizard in the sun.

"Who's the Crocodile?" she asked.

"The only crocodiles I know much about are the famous crocodiles of Yamoussoukro," said Delorme. "The political capital of Côte d'Ivoire, as you know, birthplace of the founding fathers. The crocodiles are still regarded as sacred today."

Baiting her with a reference to Côte d'Ivoire? She shook her head. He hadn't answered her question. "I mean referred to as '*the* Crocodile.' "

"*Bon,* there's Mgwanga, an Ivoirian general," he said, "with suspected ties to Liberian death squads, but he's called the Water Snake."

A guarded tip, she figured, if he'd bothered to mention this Mgwanga.

"That's to say you're not in negotiations with him?" she asked.

"The United Nations is always in negotiations," Delorme said. "As are we."

Typical diplomat's response. "Would you or the UN be in talks with Gérard Hlili?"

"The region's moderately stable. There are several players."

Evasion. There had to be a reason he'd mentioned General Mgwanga. She'd follow up on a hunch.

"You wouldn't know about anyone playing Hlili and, say, this Mgwanga against each other, or supporting a coup d'etat?" she asked.

She'd put it out there.

"We're a neutral country, *mademoiselle,*" Delorme said. "We happen to have ground troops across parts of l'Afrique at the request of host countries."

More like on hand to support French companies.

"However, I've heard you might have access to something interested parties would like," Delorme said. "Did I hear correctly?"

Obviously Mad Max had communicated this to him; otherwise she wouldn't have gotten this interview. She had to give him something. "I might."

"I'm sure we'd be interested."

So Delorme wanted in on this, too.

"It's getting crowded with the DGSE and

the Crocodile's mercenaries," she said.

He gave her a knowing look. "That can be handled."

For him, a snap of the fingers. Her nerves jangled. "There's a price."

"Bien sûr, I'm listening, *mademoiselle."*

"Sydney Leduc's freedom."

He thought for a moment. Stared at the former president's son. "Is this on your radar? Know anything about her?"

Jean-Christophe took off his sunglasses. Polished them with his sleeve. When he looked up, his small brown eyes surveyed her from under hooded lids. His lifestyle had taken its toll. He appeared fifty going on seventy. She suddenly remembered *Le Parisien*'s infamous photo of him in a pink Rolls-Royce with the son of an African president.

"I'll talk to someone," he said. A gravelly voice. Too many cigarettes.

Talk to someone? How reassuring. Or did that mean more than she thought?

She shivered in the hot, dry room. Things didn't go any higher than this. Every part of it smelled.

She'd have to figure this out on her own.

She stood. "*Merci* for your time."

"We'll be in touch," said Delorme.

Again that phrase — why not something

304

more original? They'd all read the same intelligence manual.

FRIDAY MORNING

Out on rue de l'Élysée, Aimée sucked in the brittle air. She'd shuddered as they'd scrutinized her as if she were a butterfly specimen pinned in a frame.

A car with diplomat's plates pulled up, and a chocolate-skinned man in sunglasses and overcoat alighted. Without glancing left or right, he entered through the door she'd come from. Just in case, she memorized the plate number.

She hated being a pawn in whatever political game was playing out beneath the surface. That's how they saw her — a pawn to move around a chessboard she couldn't see in full.

Her hands trembled. She had to get answers. Time for an unannounced visit to the DGSE.

She caught the Métro under the Champs-Élysées roundabout. Changed at Reuilly-Diderot and took the 8 line two stops to

Daumesnil.

On the corner, a man was roasting chestnuts. Next to him, a fruit stall with dusky persimmons that made her mouth water. She paused, opened her LeClerc compact, and pretended to check her makeup in the mirror, searching behind her for a tail. Only shoppers.

Ten francs poorer and several persimmons richer, she turned off onto a smaller street. The quartier was still full of countrified names such as rue de la Brèche aux Loups, the name of the former thirteenth-century valley path where in winters, centuries ago, hungry wolves had passed en route to the les Halles market. Nearby, an intricate scrolled metal gate was the only remnant of a once-booming nineteenth-century cigar factory. To her right, a small cobbled impasse was dotted by geraniums on the balconies. She remembered the faded Dubonnet sign on the building she was looking for.

She pressed the bell to the right of the wood gate. Heard a resounding echo. She pulled out the burner phone and hit the programmed number.

A recording that the voice-mail box was full.

She listened, quiet.

The cul-de-sac lay deserted.

She climbed onto the ground-floor windowsill opposite the foundry. Couldn't see over the fence. On the building next to it, she noticed an exterior flight of stairs, like a fire escape.

She climbed those stairs until she was high enough for a vantage point from which she could look into the foundry courtyard. It was empty of cars.

Craning her neck, she could just see into the old assembly-line floor. No busy hive of computers. It was as empty as the courtyard.

How did that make sense?

"Get off my property."

The voice startled her, and she jumped. Grabbed the rickety railing.

Behind her at the door on the stair landing, a *mec* in black leathers brandished a crowbar. His long straggly hair was tied under a stained bandanna. He looked as if he'd just woken up.

"Desolée." She started down the stairs. "I was here the other day, and they invited me back, but I can't find anyone." A lie she hoped wasn't too transparent. "What happened to the people who were working there?"

"Get lost," he said.

Like she wasn't already. "Where did they go?"

He raised the crowbar threateningly. "I said leave, nosy *salope.*"

She descended to the street and looked back up. He hadn't moved. "They own the whole block, don't they?"

"You're smoking something better than me."

"Did they pay you off?"

He snorted. "You mean the little green men in flying saucers?" He slammed the door.

A white-haired woman with a full shopping bag over her arm stooped, struggling with her keys at the next building, a stuccoed two-story *maisonette* with shutters in need of paint.

"May I help you, *madame*?" Aimée asked.

"Non, merci."

"When did the people in the foundry leave?"

"Leave? It's vacant. Has been for several years."

Aimée tried to think of an explanation for this. "Haven't you heard noises, maybe seen trucks at night recently?"

"I wear earplugs, *mademoiselle.* Ever since the war." She closed her eyes and mimed sleep. *"Comme un bébé."*

That old chestnut? Too bad Chloé hadn't gotten the memo.

"Did they pay you to say that?" Aimée's voice rose, and the old woman looked at her in alarm. "Are you part of the act, too? Do you even live here?"

"I was born here."

The woman turned into her house, and the door slammed in Aimée's face.

What the hell was going on?

Where was her mother?

Friday Morning

So many dead ends. She needed to understand what these documents in the lining of her bag meant. Saj and René were both working from home. Time to recruit them to help her get to the bottom of it.

René answered on the first ring. "We're caught up, Aimée. You've got meetings scheduled into the afternoon."

Right. She still had a business to run. Brought back to her usual world, she checked her Moleskine. Three appointments and deals to close.

"*Bon.* For now, Saj handles the day to day." She walked to the Métro, explaining to René that Saj had hit a major firewall delving into the last cargo manifest. "I told him we had too much on our plate, but now I need you to figure out what the cargo might have been."

"Worth a shot," said René.

She told him about her morning.

"Impressive," he said. "The halls of power work in mysterious ways. But if the DGSE has shut up shop and no one is following you anymore, could be a moot point."

She hadn't thought about that. "You mean the operation's . . . ?"

"Bungled, cancelled, or done and dusted, Aimée. The DGSE got Hlili, right?"

She paused before the Métro, rooted in her bag for her pass. "I did my part of the deal and found Hlili. Now they've gone silent. Nothing explains where my mother is."

Or whether she was even alive. Had someone gotten to her after she'd left that message for Aimée?

She took a deep breath. "René, I have to know what those docs mean, or meant. Delorme, the power broker at the African secretariat, is interested in them. The DGSE claimed they wanted GBH to influence the coup d'etat without their fingerprints on it. And then there's the Crocodile, identity still unknown, who was willing to kill for these documents." She took a few steps down into the Métro. Stopped. An island in the crowd, an endless stream jostling around her. "I can't rule out that GBH and the DGSE were colluding on something. What if my 'mission' was a cover?"

"Let me ask my source at Air France."

Since when did René have a source at Air France? "While you're at it, can you check out these diplomatic plates?" She gave him the number. "I'm heading to the Prosper meetings right now," she said, consulting her notebook. "Fax the agenda ahead, okay? I need to impress them."

"Done. By the way, Marc from Securadex left several messages for you. I don't trust him."

"Neither do I."

Pause. "I think he likes you."

Doubtful. What he liked was to come out on top. "What's he proposing now?"

"Dinner."

She smiled. "Tell him I'll be in touch."

Three meetings back to back. One thankfully over a baguette dripping with melted cheese — a *casse-croûte* that René called the workers' fast food. Three contracts signed. Success. But a hollow feeling dogged her as she headed toward the Métro.

Morbier owed her information — and an explanation. Why hadn't he answered her calls? As she took out her phone, about to call him again, it rang in her hand.

An unknown number. *The DGSE?*

She debated. Answered.

313

"Mademoiselle Leduc?" A woman's voice. She pronounced the word "mademwazelle," with a flat intonation. Hard to tell the accent, but it wasn't French.

"Who's this?"

"You see the café in the square? I'm on the terrace at the back table. Let's meet."

Aimée froze. How foolish to have assumed she'd escaped surveillance. "Why?"

"About Séverine Lafont."

Sydney.

FRIDAY, 2 P.M.

Aimée sipped a double espresso next to a woman one would have never noticed in a crowd. She was mouselike in a brown wool coat, matching Monoprix scarf, and worn tan boots. As she introduced herself, Aimée understood why.

"I'm part of the liaison team at the American embassy," the woman said.

CIA. And a horrific American accent with barely passable grammar.

"You have a name?" Aimée asked.

"Nancie Clare."

"Nice alias." Aimée didn't wait for a reply. "Why track me, Nancie?"

"Nancie's my real name. I'm from Ohio."

Aimée glanced at her Tintin watch. Reached for her bag. "I don't have time for someone who's not being straight with me."

"I'm telling the truth. Besides liaising for the embassy, my job includes other, more specific responsibilities."

"Like following me?"

Nancie Clare looked around. "I haven't been the only one."

"Still?"

A small shake of the head, which made the tip of her thin brown ponytail quiver. "I'm sorry. But this year's Prosper conference list showed you'd be attending a seminar." She gestured to the Haussmann building across the square. "It's right on the website. So I took advantage."

Great. This trained spy had found Aimée with a simple Internet search. She had to remind René to stop posting her name on those seminar lists.

"You seem young for this job," Aimée said, balling up her sugar wrapper.

"I'm thirty-two, but I look about twenty-four right?" she said, matter-of-fact. "A student type. It's why I'm assigned these kinds of jobs."

Did she mean surveillance and tracking targets? She certainly blended in.

"Fascinating," Aimée said. "But what does that have to do with Séverine Lafont?"

"Lafont is an occasional field agent for us," Nancie Clare said, drinking her mint tea. "She recently reached out."

Aimée almost choked on her espresso. Somehow managed to swallow. Attempted a bored look. *"Et alors?"*

"Lafont requested funds authorization to procure an asset. After approval, with the bank deposit processed, she went dark."

"What's it to me?"

"Séverine Lafont's in the French medical system. She receives mail at your place of business."

Was that all they knew? She doubted it. She'd gone from military intelligence to the African secretariat and now was talking to the CIA — all in a day. But feeding the CIA tidbits did seem like her mother's style. Maybe this meant Sydney wasn't the big player she'd allowed Aimée to believe she was. Just did the occasional job to keep her hand in and stay safe.

Was the new Portuguese concierge in on this, too?

"You said this Séverine Lafont's an occasional field agent," Aimée said. "What does that mean? A freelancer?"

"I can't tell you."

"What *can* you tell me?"

"That I need to contact her. I'd like your help. Do you know how to reach her?"

Aimée could play this game, too. She'd stay as close to the truth as possible. Keep it simple.

"I wish I did." True. "Yesterday was the

first I heard about this, when I picked up mail addressed to her from my building concierge. It bothered me." Also true. "There's a scam using legal addresses to obtain false residence permits, so I worried."

"Do you know her?"

"Never met a Séverine Lafont." True, under that name. "Don't know why she'd use my work address." Aimée downed the rest of her espresso. "You could have just telephoned the office. Way easier than tracking me."

"But we're not the only ones interested in her, or in your connection to her."

"You're mistaken about a connection. Whatever fraud this woman's perpetrating —"

"It's not fraud. It's saving someone's life."

But Genelle was dead.

"What do you mean?" Aimée asked.

Nancie took a Chap Stick from her bag. Ran it over her lips. Clear. Too bad, this woman needed some color. "We can only operate assuming Lafont's at risk," she said. "Or . . . that it's too late."

Fear sparked up and snaked through Aimée's veins. "What can I do?"

For the first time, Nancie smiled. "Check your mail; keep your eyes open." She slid a card across the café table. Stood. "Keep in touch."

Couldn't these spooks be a little more original? At least with their wording?

Queasiness rose in Aimée's stomach as Nancie Clare evaporated into the crowd entering the Métro. Aimée ordered a Badoit. Sat back, closing her eyes. She pictured herself lying in her darkened bedroom, Chloé's gurgles coming from the salon, where Sydney Leduc delighted her granddaughter with finger puppets. Melac cooking in the kitchen. That sliver of a dream of what it might be like — to be a family.

Aimée thought of her grandfather, who had spent so much time with her when she was a child. If only he were there beside her, in that café. In her head, she heard his voice on his lecture tapes. The man had written the damn undercover manual they all quoted from. He'd worked with the old African hand, Delorme, the diplomatic fixer. What would her grandfather tell her to do?

By the time she'd drunk her Badoit and paid, and her stomach had settled, she'd figured it out.

FRIDAY, 3 P.M.

She reached Yvon Triquet's mother on the sixth attempt as she ticked her way through the Triquets listed in *les pages blanches.*

"Yvon, *mais oui,* my son's at his atelier. Not here. Do you need his number?"

"So kind of you," she said, writing down Madame Triquet's address instead. "Excuse my call."

Aimée hung up before the woman could ask why she hadn't looked the number up herself in the phone book.

She caught the number 29 bus toward Saint-Mandé. En route she got a call from Martine, who'd taken over for Babette. "Chloé's *une petite ange.* Out like a light after the park." Aimée heard the flick of a lighter. An inhale. "So what happened with the military?"

"He referred me to Delorme at *le secrétariat de l'Afrique.*"

"Delorme, de Gaulle's former right hand

— that old spider?"

Aimée gave her the play by play.

"I'm impressed. Branches of two ministries and approached by a foreign intelligence service, and it's what? Not even *apéro* hour."

And she'd signed three contracts.

"It's serious, Martine," she said, trying to keep the irritation from her voice. "The DGSE, or whoever they were, pulled up stakes. It's like they never existed."

"Deep ops, Aimée."

"Sounds like a movie."

"The dark layer. Unofficial. The ones who do wet work."

"Great. That makes me feel better." Aimée clutched the rail as the bus juddered to a stop. "Please ask your friend on the Afrique desk about anything going on on the Côte d'Ivoire border with Liberia."

"If you'll come for dinner with Gianni's cousin tomorrow. And bring prosecco."

Martine, the eternal matchmaker.

Aimée hadn't heard a peep from Benoît since their recent sleepover.

"I'll get back to you, Martine. Talk to your contact."

Getting off the jerky bus, she walked under the old metal bridge of the Petite Ceinture.

The rails had been abandoned to weeds, graffiti artists, and the occasional vegetable garden. Up a sloping side street stood Villa du Belir, a curious cobbled lane overlooking the neglected line. A plaque, circa 1895, proclaimed these were residences for young ladies.

Madame Triquet's half-timbered, Norman-style house was on the corner of Sentier des Merisiers and, tall with pointy gables, could have come out of a medieval fairy tale. Aimée's shoulders brushed the passage walls on both sides. This had to be the narrowest path in the city, a remnant of Saint-Mandé village before Paris had swallowed most of it.

Snapping sounds, the crackle of a fire, and the smell of burning leaves came from the open door in the wall of number 18.

"*Bonjour,* Madame Triquet?"

A lithe woman raked crinkling cinnamon leaves into piles in a large walled garden. She wore a pink-and-red wool cap, blue rubber boots, and a fleece vest. A cell phone on an embroidered lanyard thumped on her chest. Her cheeks were flushed, and she gave Aimée an inquisitive look.

"You can leave the package on the doorstep," Madame Triquet said. "I'll sign . . ."

She thought Aimée was there to deliver

something. Should she go along with it?

Too late — Madame Triquet had noticed Aimée had nothing in her arms. "Who are you?"

She wondered that, too, sometimes.

"I believe you know Séverine Lafont," Aimée said.

It was a shot in the dark. Yet Yvon Triquet had pointed out Aimée's resemblance to Lafont, a friend of his mother. Now, with the CIA on her heels, Aimée was even more afraid of what danger her mother was in.

If she was even still alive.

"I might." Madame Triquet scooped up an armful of leaves and dumped them on an already burning pile. A whoosh and crackling as licks of flames shot up. "Didn't you call looking for my son, Yvon?"

Aimée nodded. Of course — the woman recognized her voice. "*Desolée,* but I needed to speak with you in person."

"So speak." Madame Triquet continued raking leaves.

"It's important, *madame.* In private, please."

Madame Triquet gathered up another pile of leaves and tossed them on the fire. Wiped off her hands. "We'll talk inside."

The decor inside the medieval fairy house

didn't disappoint. The dark wood paneling was hung with carved statues, gourd bowls, paintings showing different views of the port at Abidjan. There were African rugs and colorful throw blankets everywhere. Madame Triquet shook her long, frizzy but lustrous grey-flecked hair free from her cap. A middle-aged hippie in her own commune.

She sat down cross-legged on a woven sisal mat. Indicated for Aimée to do the same. She was makeup-free, with clear hazel eyes, sharp cheekbones, and a ruddy complexion — a striking older woman comfortable with herself. Not the type to worry about expression lines or crow's-feet.

"How do you know Séverine?" Aimée asked.

"Guests first," she said.

Aimée took a breath. "She's my . . . We're related."

"Funny, she never talked about any family."

That stung. "Yvon said I looked like a friend of yours, so I thought . . ."

"Turn your head." Aimée did. "Now to the light." Madame Triquet nodded. "I see a resemblance."

"She's disappeared. I think she's in danger."

"Your hands, the way you clench your

324

knuckles — it so reminds me of her."

Startled, Aimée looked at her knuckles. White with nerves.

"When did you last see her?" Aimée asked.

"Ah, a few weeks ago, maybe? I've known Séverine since Abidjan." Madame Triquet stood and contemplated a picture on the wall. Took it down and showed Aimée — Sydney, six or seven years younger, looked back.

Aimée sucked in a sharp breath. "How did you two meet?"

Madame Triquet sighed. Sat back down. "Years ago, when Yvon was in school here, my husband worked in training overseas managerial staff at EDF. We lived near Place de la Nation, a wonderful place not far from here. This was my parents' house. Anyway, my husband took a post in Côte d'Ivoire. I loved it there. Still do. We met at a friend's birthday party. Séverine's so committed."

"In what way?"

"She joined our foundation for educating children working on the cacao plantations . . . made it a priority. She worked in export, traveled all the time, but still found time to raise funds for the foundation. Then our post ended, and we returned." Another sigh. "Yvon had been accepted into an art restoration program here and left Abidjan much earlier. My daughter has missed all the good friends she made. They still come to visit."

Madame Triquet paused, as if tiredness had caught up with her. Her eyes wandered.

"You were saying . . ." Aimée prodded.

"My husband passed two years ago, and I moved here. Thank God Yvon found his path, learned his métier. I couldn't be happier for him. Now, Florence, his wife — *maintenant,* dealing with her is another bowl of *pistou,* as they say."

Aimée had no trouble imagining that.

"Getting back to Séverine . . ." she said.

"Recently, we reconnected in Paris. Exhibitions, walks, you know. She came for lunch. That was the day Germaine, my daughter's best friend, was visiting, too. Such a talented girl."

"GermaineTillion?"

"You know everyone, it seems." Madame Triquet pulled out an album and flipped to a picture of her daughter and Germaine, laughing on a beach of endless white sand.

Go on, Aimée wanted to say, excited to hear the story. But she stopped herself. The woman must not have heard the news.

"Germaine was in a state. Fired up about something, but scared."

Aimée leaned forward. "How do you mean?"

"She's gotten political. I've never seen her like that. She played tapes of her friend Gérard's speeches. I remembered him from their student days, and now he's leading a peaceful change movement in Côte d'Ivoire."

"You remembered him from when your husband trained the EDF managerial staff here?"

"Maybe so," she said, thinking. Seemed confused for a moment. "But he would have been much younger, *non?* Anyway, he's full of passion, one who can lead the young, the old; speak to the uneducated and the elite . . . He's got a gift. Germaine's convinced his party will win."

A price placed on his head by rivals? Was that why suspicion had gotten the better of him the night before? Aimée kept her thoughts about him to herself.

"What did Germaine want to do?" Aimée asked.

"Germaine kept saying it wasn't safe; she didn't want to put us in danger. Séverine offered to help her."

"How?"

"People she knew. Friends? I'm not sure. My daughter got so upset when Germaine

327

left. I haven't seen Germaine or Séverine since." She wistfully observed the photo of Sydney. "You know, people fly into my life and out. My philosophy's to treasure them while they're here."

Aimée had to keep the woman on track. "What was Germaine so upset about? Did she say?"

Madame Triquet looked away. "*Les maudits* — the curse never stops haunting them."

"What do you mean?"

"Germaine's whole family. Bad juju."

The woman actually believed that?

Aimée took out the copy she'd made of the saying she had found in Germaine's stashed baggie. "Can you tell me why this would have been important to her?"

Use gifts for good, not evil, or suffer their curse.

"A curse followed that family," Madame Triquet said.

"Curse? Why do you say that?"

"*Allez,* look what happened. Everyone's dead now, *non?* Germaine's mother married a Frenchman, and rumors were an uncle had a shaman put the hex on her. Her whole family. He got the plantation."

"That wasn't a hex, or bad juju, *madame.* Those were political murders."

"They died in a car accident." Madame Triquet shrugged. "You can believe what you want. I spent enough time in that country to think it's possible. Many Ivoirians wear protection amulets."

Aimée tried to piece together what she knew. "How did you keep in touch with Séverine?"

"You're scared, too. Why?"

"Séverine tried to help Germaine. Now she's in danger."

The woman's eyes were far away. "I thought she had a husband. Why isn't he trying to find her?"

A husband? Another life Aimée had no clue about? She put that aside for the moment. Had to get something useful out of this rambling, superstitious woman. "Were you the one who told her about the playgroup in Picpus?"

"Playgroup? The one Florence takes my grandson to?"

Aimée nodded.

"That's right; Séverine did ask about a playgroup for her grandchild." Aimée heard a beeping from the lanyard around the woman's neck. "Time for my pills." She stood in a too-swift movement and stumbled. Aimée caught her before she fell. Handed her a plastic medication holder

329

from the table — it was labeled MORNING, AFTERNOON, and EVENING.

"I'll get you a glass of water."

In the small kitchen, Aimée turned on the tap. Noticed the pill bottles on the windowsill. Donepezil. Wasn't that Alzheimer's medication?

When she returned with the water, Madame Triquet was speaking on the phone. "*Oui,* Yvon, I'm taking my pills. There's a nice woman bringing me water. Who? I'm not sure. I was working in the yard, and then . . . I'm not sure."

On the refrigerator Aimée had seen a pamphlet about a school in Côte d'Ivoire. After watching Madame Triquet take her pills, she went back to the kitchen to return the glass and stopped to read it. *Donations left at our office will help our school program in Abidjan, which is run entirely by volunteers.*

If her mother had gotten involved with Germaine through Madame Triquet and the organization that ran this school, Aimée would chase down every detail. No stone unturned. Aimée copied down the address.

She pulled a colorful blanket over the woman, who'd fallen asleep on the couch.

FRIDAY, 4 P.M.

A short bus ride on the number 56 took Aimée past Place de la Nation's massive stone pavilions, octroi, once toll gates and part of the eighteenth-century city wall. A block later she arrived at Empress Eugénie's foundation on the corner of rue du Faubourg Saint-Antoine. The building was designed in the shape of a necklace. Empress Eugénie had refused her wedding gift, a diamond necklace, insisting a charity for poor young girls be built with the money. Today, it housed a vocational school, *école maternelle,* offices, and student housing. It was also the address of the nonprofit that ran the school Aimée had found the pamphlet for on Madame Triquet's refrigerator.

She followed behind a student, hurrying through the security gate and into a burst of color — a circular autumn garden of purple hydrangeas, orange dahlias, marigolds, and red and purple anemones.

331

After making her way down long corridors, mounting multiple staircases into different wings, and taking several wrong turns, she found the organization's name on an office door.

Knocked.

No response.

Knocked again.

"Donation?" asked a young woman's voice.

"May I come in?"

"No one's here. I just accept donations for them."

"*D'accord.* But I've got a donation question."

"The requirements are on the flyer."

Irritating. Why wouldn't she open the door?

"But Séverine Lafont told me I could ask her —"

"She's not here. No one's here. I'm not allowed to let people in."

"Can I leave a message for her?"

"Suit yourself. Write it down."

"Any idea when she'll return?"

"Like I said, no one's here. There's no set schedule for office hours. I'm the cleaner."

Aimée believed her. She tore a page from her Moleskine. She was conflicted over what to say: *Are you okay? Where are you?*

Wrote: *Assembled donation package, un-*

332

sure of recipient's bkgd — then crossed it out.

Ended up with: *The right thing seems the wrong thing — call me.*

Lame. But she hoped her mother would understand what she meant.

Knocked again.

"Slide it under the door," the woman said.

"Okay. Has Séverine Lafont been in the office recently?"

"No idea."

FRIDAY, 4:30 P.M.

Aimée found her way back to the garden, a tight knot of dread between her shoulders. Morbier hadn't returned her calls. The DGSE had disappeared along with GBH. The Crocodile was still on the loose. And no word from her mother, fate unknown.

Or help from Delorme. Nor anything from Martine's contact on the African desk. Too many pieces were missing. How could Aimée make sense of what had happened? Her mind scrambled for the meaning of it all.

The purples and oranges blurred and faded in and out. Her depth perception was wavering.

Not now. She couldn't let this happen now. Couldn't lose control.

Panicked, she remembered the doctor's dictum: *You have no control. Rest,* dé-stressez, *and it will pass. Fighting the symptoms won't work.* She found a bench. Sat

334

and closed her eyes. Breathed in. Let it go.

The sunlight warmed her legs as she inhaled the drifting scents of the flowers. The bark of a dog came from the distance.

Breathe; inhale and exhale. Her mind slowed.

She sat for she didn't know how long.

Her phone bleeped. Her eyes popped open. Shards of sunlight made diamond patterns on the gravel path.

"Saj and I think you should look at something." René's voice sounded tight.

Right now? "René, what's up?"

"Meet us at my go-to motherboard *mec*'s."

He thought someone was listening in on her phone.

She knew the place, by Montgallet. She was close.

"En route," she said.

FRIDAY, 5 P.M.

Store after store on rue Montgallet special-
ized in computer sales, parts, and repairs,
prices negotiable. In the seventeenth century, the narrow street had been a country
road named rue des Six-Chandelles, street
of the six candles. René liked to joke the
place had always been tech minded.

Upstairs at René's friend Ming's shop,
computer skeletons and wire boards filled
the benches. The air smelled of metal solder.

The documents she'd found in the mausoleum were spread out over a long table on
top of a flight route map of the African
continent. Tacked on to a wall were flight
routes between the former Soviet Union
and the Gulf States.

"My source at Air France came through,"
said René.

"Et alors?" Aimée said.

"It's simple if you know what you're looking for," said Saj.

"Care to explain?" she asked.

"We retraced the plane's route via refueling receipts and bills of lading, which are on file at every airport stopover," Saj said. "This flight originated in Belarus. Stopped in Tehran, with Bouaké in the central part of Côte d'Ivoire as the final destination. Cargo items are listed as farm equipment."

"We knew all that already, Saj," she said.

She sat on a rickety stool by René. He looked up from a computer screen. "I've been serving our paying clients."

Touché, René.

The cash register's ting drifted from Ming's shop below.

"But we didn't know the plane, a Soviet-era workhorse identifiable by its registration, crashed somewhere in the border area of the two countries," said Saj, "Côte d'Ivoire and Liberia."

"On purpose?" Aimée asked.

"We don't think so. This was a well-oiled operation. Similar planes flew this same route each month for a year."

"Similar planes?"

"Interchangeable, from the old Soviet fleet. Warlords hire Belarusians and ex–Soviet Air Force pilots and Ukrainian crews who know the planes. If one crashes in the jungle or the desert, they salvage parts and tool up another one."

"Germaine's brother, Armand, died in a shootout in Bouaké," said Aimée. "He supported GBH's revolutionary movement . . ."

"Say instead of farming equipment, the plane contained arms and contraband destined for whoever could pay the price," Saj suggested.

She'd wondered about that, too. "Any evidence?"

"I found UN reports in Genelle's documents that mention arms and contraband carried in similar flights earlier this year." Saj leafed through a report. "Try this for a working theory. Armand heard about the crash and wanted whatever the cargo was. He went out to collect the contraband."

"How's that legal?" said René, always the straight arrow.

"Who says any of it's legal?" Aimée said.

"Then he got shot by rivals," Saj went on. "But let's say before that, Armand had managed to give these documents to his sister. Telling Germaine this and showing her the contraband location at the crash site. Say Germaine knew this would essentially mean giving GBH the keys to the castle. Or in this case, arming his takeover. Funding the coup d'etat without the French."

René looked at the maps. "Why wouldn't

Germaine furnish all this to the group herself?"

"Maybe she couldn't?" said Aimée, poring
over the report. "Or she'd promised her
brother she'd flee the country. A good friend
of hers lives here, and she thought she could
come hide out for a while, but after realizing
she'd been tracked, she didn't want to put
her friend's family in danger. Kept looking
for GBH, who was hidden in a safe house
by the DGSE. So she asked my mother for
help — she'd met her at Madame Triquet's
house."

"Who?" René and Saj said in perfect uni-
son.

Aimée told them. "She's in early-stages
Alzheimer's and got cloudier the more she
spoke."

"Did I miss something?" said René.
"How's your mother involved?"

"Does her working with the CIA help to
explain?" Aimée said.

Both René's and Saj's eyes popped. Ming,
who'd just reached the top of the stairs,
zipped his fingers across his mouth and
returned the way he'd come.

"You're kidding, right?" said René. "If not,
count me out of this."

"All I know is what Nancie, a liaison from
the US embassy, told me."

Saj stood and stretched. "You know what liaisons do, Aimée?"

"She trailed me from the Prosper seminar, thanks to the fact that René emblazoned my name on their website."

"Now it's my fault?" said René.

"*Non,* she's a plodder," said Aimée, realizing that had come out wrong. "She would have found me anyway."

"We're about getting Leduc's name out there for business," René said. "I always do that."

No time to argue over that. She needed his help. "The CIA okayed a payment for an asset, presumably GBH, and has heard nothing else since."

"Blood money," said René. "The CIA funds his coup. They stay in control."

Aimée sucked in her breath. "That would make sense," she said. "GBH could wait for the sweetest bidder for the contraband. Still doesn't explain why the DGSE enlisted me, implying my finding GBH was the only way to keep my mother safe." What detail was she missing? "Any luck on the diplomatic plates I saw at the African secretariat?"

René nodded. "Embassy of Côte d'Ivoire."

She looked back over the flight plan, the list of names, the reports. Again, that nagging feeling of a missing puzzle piece. "Something's wrong."

FRIDAY, 5:30 P.M.

FRIDAY, 5:30 P.M.

"Wrong how?" asked Saj.

She pointed to a report. "Why would someone carry this UN report on an illegal flight?"

"They wouldn't," said Saj.

"So did Germaine or her brother add this to the packet?"

"Looks like it."

"*Attends,* look at this," said René, pointing to a document he'd pulled up on his screen. "It's the same one here on the UN website, a report on a sanction on Liberia's arms import."

"That's right," said Saj. "Germaine's docs include this part of the UN report. There's a clause here saying arms shipments to Côte d'Ivoire need an exemption."

"Arms shipments to Côte d'Ivoire need an exemption?" said René. "Yet there's no exemption included and no actual proof of arms. Not a lot of help if it's a continent away."

"Whoever holds the cargo's contents holds the balance of power in the upcoming coup d'etat," she said. "I don't know how, but that's the only way it makes sense."

"The CIA, DGSE, and Delorme at the secretariat all want to back the winning horse," said René. "Feed it sugar to keep it sweet."

"So they're all in on this," said Saj.

"Don't forget an Ivoirian with diplomatic plates had an audience after me with His Highness the grand meddler of l'Afrique." Her phone vibrated on the table. She checked the display. "Speak of the devil," she said, then answered, "*Oui,* Monsieur Delorme?"

"I think we should talk, *mademoiselle.*"

"Concerning?"

"I'll explain. Fifteen minutes?"

FRIDAY, 6 P.M.

Delorme sat alone at the round table in the dry air of the salon. No former president's son this time. He offered her a chair, and she took it.

"You said we should talk," she said. "What do you have to tell me?"

"*Mademoiselle,* there are two things you need to know." Delorme's pained smile, meant to garner sympathy, she imagined, left her cold. "Our French special forces in Côte d'Ivoire live by the motto that every mission only works if it's accomplished by, with, and through the local population. We prize our elite units for their ingenuity, adaptability, language skills, and because they know who to finance and how."

Her ears pricked up. *The money.* What was he really saying?

"The units partner with local forces and broker strategic alliances with local leaders. That's how success in l'Afrique works."

344

Aimée crossed her legs. *"Et alors?"*

She wasn't there for a geopolitical lesson.

"The second point: it's like chess," he said. "We play the long game."

"Meaning?"

"We plot several moves ahead for the country's stability. Take into account all possibilities. Plan countermoves for every scenario."

"Sounds like manipulation to me." *Diabolical.*

"It's called diplomacy." Delorme opened a photo album. "Here are some examples." He flipped the pages. Photos of him with Bokassa, de Gaulle, Mitterrand, and several African leaders Aimée didn't recognize. In each photo, Delorme stood on the periphery, easy to spot with his distinctive glasses and baby face. The shadow puppeteer. Among the photos of African dignitaries, she noticed several of the former president's son, Jean-Christophe, in a safari suit. "I call these men friends. Relationships built over decades. I've attended their sons' baptisms and then their weddings."

What had he called her in to tell her? "How does this relate to Sydney Leduc, Monsieur Delorme?"

"A Côte d'Ivoire coup d'etat is imminent."

"Nothing to do with me."

"Hear me out, please. It doesn't suit our interests, or anyone's, that General Mgwanga's acting up. He arrived after your visit, full of demands."

No doubt the man she'd seen alighting from the car with the Ivorian diplomatic license plates. The one Delorme had mentioned with ties to Liberia.

"He was poorly raised, that one. Thinks he's entitled to always get his way. His father never listened when I told him spare the rod, spoil the child." He sighed. "I'll get around Mgwanga. With your help."

"By help you mean furnishing information to this Mgwanga, who, in your words, supports Liberian death squads, while there are UN arms sanctions against the country? Sounds like offering matches to a pyromaniac."

And getting no closer to finding her mother.

"Mgwanga's easily appeased. He likes to feel he's in control. He's not. However, he causes too much collateral damage with his Liberian connections, using mercenaries, kidnapping women for female soldiers. He needs to be kept in check."

Her gut twisted. Delorme had appeased and played world leaders against one another for years — moving pieces on the chessboard. Any cooperation felt dirty.

"But the DGSE indicated Gérard Bjedje Hlili's the contender carrying huge popular support."

"My contacts tell me he's out for himself."

Meaning Delorme couldn't control him like he had Mgwanga?

She shifted in the gilt-back chair. "What's to say the information's still valid?"

"Recent reports indicate a plane crash occurred in a remote site in the highlands. If you trusted me with the maps and coordinates, which I assume you have," said Delorme, "we could have a ground unit liaise with paratroopers."

So he knew. How? She stared at him but said nothing.

"If it's difficult to get in, it's ten times more difficult to get out alive and with equipment. You need our special forces. It's what they do."

"And you want to give it to a spoiled Ivoirian general with Liberian sympathies?"

"Mgwanga could get to it before we can. Time's running out. Our focus is on maintaining stability in the country. Keeping it conflict-free in a time of transition."

Right.

Getting out five hundred kilos of arms and ammunition, a.k.a. farm equipment, might prove tough for even him. And she had the map.

She pretended to think about it. "We have nothing to talk about unless Sydney Leduc's freed."

"*Tant pis.* Mgwanga doesn't know her whereabouts. Neither does the DGSE."

She almost snorted. "Then we're done here."

Delorme took off his black-framed glasses. Pinched the bridge of his nose. Emitted a world-weary sigh. "My conversations with both parties were conditional on her release. If either lied to me, they'd lose my protection. As I said, neither the DGSE nor the Ivoirian general knows of her whereabouts. I believe them."

Frustrated, she stood and shouldered her bag. "I can't believe my grandfather worked with the secretariat. He would have never trusted someone like you."

She walked toward the door.

"There was a bond, like it or not, *mademoiselle*," he said. "Your grandfather and I fought together in the *libération de Paris*."

She stopped. Turned around, surprised.

Delorme put his glasses back on and adjusted one of the earpieces. "You didn't know? A small part of it, but we liberated the Mairie of Batignolles. Captured the

Boches, found their hidden stash in the cellar, and met de Gaulle with vintage champagne. I respected Jean-Claude."

Despite everything he'd done, she believed him.

"It's time for you to do your duty."

Her mother had told her to do the right thing.

"I won't do anything dirty," she said.

"That's the DGSE. They lie and manipulate."

"What you're doing isn't the same?"

He watched her. Sensing her hesitation. "Your mother's smart. She's calling the shots. Probably holds the ace."

"What do you mean?" she asked.

"Otherwise you wouldn't be here at the table. Or walking around freely."

He made her skin crawl. Was she merely bait to hook her mother?

And was her mother playing everyone, Aimée included?

"Let's say I've got a weakness for fascinating women," he said. "Remember my help is valuable right now."

She cringed internally. Didn't want to think about what his help might entail or cost.

"Sounds like a threat," she said.

"Did I say that?"

No way would this fossil control her.

"You didn't have to," she said.

She slammed the door behind her. *Childish.* But she was angry and scared. And she had no idea what to do.

FRIDAY, 7 P.M.

Outside in the fresh chill, the sun's last gasp fired a tangerine glow over the Grand Palais's glass-tiled dome. Her phone vibrated in her pocket. A number she didn't recognize.

"I'm Michel, on the African desk at Agence France-Presse," said a man's voice. "Martine told me you're need to know on the situation in Côte d'Ivoire."

Need to know? "Exactement."

"It's unfolding."

"How?"

"Our correspondent is embedded in the northern Nimba Highlands of Côte d'Ivoire," said Michel. "A few weeks ago, he reported on a plane crash. Followed up by trekking to the site. Today, several sources led him to believe the plane's cargo contained chemical weapons, including sarin. Reliable intel. However, he hasn't been able to confirm this."

Mon Dieu. And she'd told Saj to hold off on trying to crack that firewall. So stupid.

"Who else knows about this?" she asked.

"I just hung up with him. So far, it's just us three."

"You're serious?"

"I'm typing the release as we speak."

"Where's the French military, the special forces?"

"Six hours away from the site, according to his source."

"Who is . . . ?"

"Can't reveal. But put it together, eh?"

"So . . . the rebels who found the plane," she said, guessing, "stripped it and took the cargo?"

She heard him typing. He didn't negate it.

"Any reports of illness?"

"He thinks so. Local doctors more active than usual."

"Where's the cargo?"

"Good question. But signs are it's not far from the crash site. Tell Martine we're even now."

The phone went dead.

Back upstairs in Ming's shop, René was making marks on the topographical map. "We'll use these as satellite coordinates."

"Don't satellites constantly orbit?" said Aimée.

"Nature of the beast," said Saj. "It can take up to four days to get a specific visual."

"Then how does that help?"

She'd filled in René and Saj on the latest.

"The good thing is, we know the coordinates indicate a point in the nature reserve," René said. "Here."

She compared the topographical map to the more detailed atlas map of the Nimba Highlands. Used Saj's metal compass and drew a circle.

René pulled at his goatee. Something he did when concentrating. "What do you see within five kilometers?"

"Mountains, ravines, crevasses, water erosion, deep-pitted areas." She scanned the legend. "Caves. Right here. Perfect hiding places."

"What we need is a satellite view of this five-kilometer radius." René lifted the map and showed Saj.

"On it, René," said Saj. "See if Ming can get us another computer to hook up, and we'll talk to my pal at SUNSAT. He's in Johannesburg and loves to show off."

"You've got a friend in South Africa's satellite system?" asked Aimée.

"Lars used to run the imaging systems,

CT and MRI technology in nuclear medicine, at Val-de-Grâce."

Saj knew the most incredible geeks all over the world.

"CT" — her brain stuck on the abbreviation. Doctors used CT scans to diagnose conditions from torn ligaments to tumors. What was it Sydney needed a scan for originally?

Saj handed her a memory card not much bigger than her thumbnail. The kind used in handheld PDAs, not that she could afford one. "I scanned the data, inputted everything on this. Less bulky."

"Brilliant." She unstrapped her Tintin watch and taped the card to the back of the face. "Got a backup?"

Saj pointed to his man bun.

"Work this remotely okay, Saj?" she said. He nodded. "Scrub these hard drives. Burn the paper."

She grabbed her reserve scarf, a vintage Gucci, from her bag. "Gotta run."

René looked up from hooking up a cable. "Something wrong? Is Chloé okay?"

"Fine. Martine's teaching her Italian," she called over her shoulder as she clattered down the stairs.

FRIDAY, 7:30 P.M.

She jumped on line 8 and two stops later was running up the Métro stairs and into Hôpital Saint-Antoine. Ten minutes of searching took her to the oldest building, Bâtiment de l'Horloge — and down into its cavern-like bowels to PORTE 19 — 1ER SOUS SOL.

Why were all places like this underground?

She consulted the letter and smiled at the receptionist. "May I speak with Dr. Celine Pradel?"

"You have an appointment for the evening clinic?"

"*Mais non,* but my mother missed hers. I'm worried. May I speak with her doctor, just for a moment —"

"*Attends,*" the receptionist said, cutting her off. "You want to reschedule for her?"

"I'm not sure. Her doctor may have a different recommendation."

"Let me see if the doctor's doing a consul-

355

tation. She's on evening-clinic rounds."

Several phone calls later, the receptionist waved her through. "Five minutes, eh. Squeezing you in. You'll be quick, *non*? She's got another appointment."

"Merci."

Dr. Celine Pradel, Aimée's height, thin, and with a no-nonsense gaze behind her wire glasses frames, was reviewing a chart at a nursing station.

"Doctor, my mother got a letter saying the machine malfunctioned during her CT scan. I had no idea she was scheduled for one, and I'm worried." Aimée showed her the letter.

"No problem. Check with her and reschedule."

"It's not that, Doctor; I want to know why she needs a CT scan. Would you have that information?"

"Ask your mother."

"I would. But she's disappeared."

"Ah, that's why you're concerned." Dr. Pradel clicked her pen. "Let me consult her chart."

For once, Aimée felt someone was listening to her.

The doctor reached for a pile of files. Went through the *L*s. "At this stage in her condition, the CT's advisable."

356

"What condition?"

"Patient confidentiality forbids me from discussing medical issues."

"You mean it's serious." The world seemed to go into slow motion, the scuffed green tiles swimming up at her, the fluorescent lighting pressing down. From the corridor she heard the rubber squeak of a gurney's wheels as it whooshed by. "She's dying?"

"I didn't say that." The doctor took her arm. "Don't worry."

Aimée wanted to grab the file. Read it. But the doctor had stacked it with others in a pneumatic chute, pressed a handle. It winged out of sight.

"All those terrible things I said." Aimée chewed her lip. "Those things I can't undo. Can't even say goodbye."

"I want to help, but I'm forbidden from telling you more. You understand, *non*?"

"What if she's too sick to take care of herself?"

"You're not making it easy, *mademoiselle.*"

"*Desolée,*" she said, her eyes brimming with tears. "But what if it was your mother?"

Aimée read and reread the name Dr. Pradel had written down. *I referred her to a private*

clinique, she'd said. *Have no idea if she followed up. And I never did this, comprenez?*

FRIDAY, 8 P.M.

The bland seventies building that housed *le polyclinique* on rue Taine gave no hint of the sleek, efficient institution inside, all calm ambient music and subtle pastel furnishings and a business-like nursing staff. As Aimée stood in front of the reception desk, two women in wheelchairs, chattering away, were pushed past her. One of their attendants nodded to the nurse. "*Apéro* time."

"*C'est privé ici,*" the nurse said when she turned back to Aimée. "We don't release information on patients."

"*D'accord.* Can you just tell me if Séverine Lafont is a patient?"

"And you are?"

"Her daughter."

"I'll need ID."

Aimée showed her.

"That's a different last name, *mademoiselle.*"

Great. "That shouldn't matter."

The nurse eyed the security guard who was emerging from the elevator. "I can't help you, *mademoiselle*. The security guard will escort you out."

Time to improvise, worm out information, and find out where her mother was.

She spotted the café on the corner across the street from the *polyclinique*. Traditional, with a glassed-in terrasse. At the outdoor tables squeezed up against a bike rack, those ladies in wheelchairs were enjoying a mild evening under the rising moon.

Apéro time, all right.

There was a third woman, also in a wheelchair, who seemed to have been waiting for them there. All three were laughing and smoking cigarettes on the lit *terrasse*. No attendants in sight.

They reminded her of when she and Martine used to sneak behind the lycée to smoke.

She sat down at a table next to the ladies. Ordered *un diabolo menthe*.

"Naughty girls," she said to the ladies with mock severity when the waitress was gone.

"Pwah, they're candy cigarettes," said the one in a red scarf. "Don't spoil the fun."

The crescent fingernail of an autumn moon hung above the *grisaille* rooftops.

"Never." Aimée grinned. "Teasing you,

c'est tout."

The third woman, who was wearing a black hat and designer sunglasses, was watching Aimée. She noticed the woman's clenched hands on her teacup, knuckles white. The clubbed fingertips. The thin face caught in the streetlight glow. Aimée became aware of a faint drifting scent. Muguet. Lilies of the valley, the scent of the perfume her mother always wore.

A little smile appeared on the woman's face. She gave a slight shake of her head as Aimée's mouth opened.

Keep quiet.

She did. Trying to remain patient while the two old biddies sipped tisanes, gossiping about the doctors, complaining about the food. Aimée tapped her heels, her *diabolo menthe* long gone.

Finally, the attendants reappeared, one flicking a thread of tobacco from his lip. The two women finished their candy cigarettes and complained of the chill. A minute later, the attendants wheeled them back across the street.

"Not here." Aimée's mother clenched her knuckles.

"Why didn't you tell me —" Aimée began.

"Were you followed?"

Impatient, Aimée ran her chipped onyx-lacquered nails over the marble-top café table. "Not recently." She thought back to the doctor's office, meeting René and Saj, before that at the ministry office with Delorme. Hadn't spotted a tail.

"Who has been tailing you?"

"Who hasn't? The DGSE, the CIA, the Crocodile's mercenaries . . . Tell me what's going on."

Another little smile. "I'm handling it."

Aimée noticed the wool blanket over her mother's lap. Why was she wearing sunglasses at night?

"Just like that?" Aimée said. "You're ill. I can tell."

"Right now, you need to tell me what you found."

"Clubbed fingertips are a sign of serious lung disease — emphysema," Aimée said, pointing to Sydney's fingers. Her voice quavered. "There's an oxygen tank behind your wheelchair. I assume your CT scan was to follow up on a questionable chest X-ray."

Sydney Leduc expelled air. "One year of premed and you know everything, eh?"

She blinked in surprise. Were they going to get into a fight? "You've been here this whole time of your own will?"

"Basically."

"Why did you just vanish without telling me?"

Sydney shook her head. "Not now, Amy." Only Aimée's mother used that American name for her.

"You worried me to death, and you say, 'Not *now*'?" Then it dawned on her. "Did you want me to believe you were in danger because you knew that was the only way to get me involved? Did you plot this with Lacenaire? He gave me a note from you."

"Lacenaire's a liar and a lackey. I never gave him a note for you."

And she'd fallen for it. *What a chump.* Yet she couldn't afford not to at the time. "And I believed him."

Sydney lowered her large sunglasses and scanned the street. "It wasn't meant to go this way. But you're the only one I trust."

Aimée took a breath. The streetlight caught the hollow cheekbones in her mother's pale face. "Trust?" Anger vibrated in her voice. "You put this on my plate, led me into danger on a wild-goose chase. What do you even know about these people?"

"Germaine was desperate. I have connections, and I thought I could help her."

"But what's Gérard Hlili's cause to you?"

"Professional. I hated that they'd involved you already."

363

Involved her? "Who? I don't understand."

"Never mind who. The bastards broke our agreement. They were watching you. You needed tools." She lowered her glasses and surveyed the street again. "Look, tell me what happened with Germaine. We do that first, okay?"

Aimée nodded. Why did she feel like a little girl again? She pushed that aside. Related how she'd traced the key to the mausoleum in the cemetery, what Germaine had stashed there, how GBH had held her captive.

"I knew you'd find him."

"I wanted to do the right thing. But I don't trust him."

"Why?"

"After badmouthing the DGSE, he joked and backslapped them as he got into their car freely. But Germaine gave her life to get him those documents."

A muffled cough. "I know. She underestimated this job."

She did? "Then why didn't . . . Were you too sick?"

A brief nod. "Go on; what was on that plane?"

"Chemical weapons, it seems like," she said, keeping her voice low with effort. "Sarin, or something like it. Local rebels hid it — probably in caves in the mountainous highland reserve by the Liberian border. They're getting sick."

Her mother took off the glasses. Those eyes looked tired. "What else?"

"Delorme will have heard by now. The French military's six hours away from the site. It's on the AFP wire, out there."

"You know what chemical weapons mean?" But she didn't wait for Aimée to answer.

"Assemble enough of them, and you've got a very dirty kind of bomb. You could wipe out an entire neighborhood or city."

"Assemble enough . . . ? Who's doing this?"

"That's not important right now." Sydney pulled out a business card. "Most important is to call this number from a pay phone in the Gare de Lyon. Let it ring once. Hang up. When someone calls back, answer. Give the name on the card and then repeat everything you've told me. But first, say, 'Use Dany at Ouagadougou' — that's important."

"Why?"

"This number reaches the US military unit attached to the closest airport. That's in Burkina Faso."

"Burkina Faso? That's an entirely different country."

"The US maintains a hub there for airborne intelligence operations. Turboprops disguised as private planes, full of surveillance equipment. It's only three hours from the crash site. They'll handle it from there."

Now it made sense. "Look, we need to talk —"

"Severe emphysema. Good guess. Don't contact me. Or come here again. It's difficult to arrange this kind of anonymity."

"I can hide you —"

"We do this my way, please. It's for your safety. And Chloé's. That's it. Go."

"That's it?" Her mother dismissing her after putting her at risk, sending her on a hunt for days? Her knuckles clenched. "You abandon Chloé at playgroup — which she's been kicked out of, by the way — and then justify this as part of some perverted line of duty?"

"I left Chloé safe. You're a good mother; I knew you'd get her. And you did."

Of course she did. Aimée almost started yelling, she was so angry. "Don't you even regret —"

"Regret's a luxury in this work. Brutal, but true."

"But you jeopardized my work and my colleagues." She caught her breath. "And you're still not going to tell me why the DGSE grilled me, told me someone was holding you hostage, but you expect me to believe things are *safe*?"

"Did the DGSE take you to that fake office on Impasse Tourneux?"

Aimée's jaw dropped. They shared a laugh. If they could still laugh together, then maybe everything would be okay.

"I'll be in touch." Her voice rasped. She stabbed out the brittle candy cigarette. Grinned as it crinkled into white sugar shards. "Force of habit."

She grabbed her mother's warm, slim fingers.

"Not now, Amy. We'll talk later."

"Not until I know why you did this."

"I gave my word to Germaine. It was simple, at first. She counted on me."

And Aimée didn't?

"When I take a job, I don't let people down." Pause. "But my lung collapsed, and the next thing I knew I was under the knife."

Aimée's shoulders stiffened. "So an operation put you out of commission?"

"It happens. I needed a chest tube."

Aimée noticed how Sydney leaned and favored her right side. *A painful incision?*

"What's going on now is too important, Amy. It's bigger than us." A squeeze. "Grab that taxi at the corner." Sydney pulled her hand away. "For Germaine — do the right thing."

FRIDAY, 8:30 P.M.

Running, Aimée flagged down the taxi. At the Gare de Lyon, after trying three out-of-commission pay phones, she found a working one by the northern entrance off the Cour Châlon.

She called, as her mother had instructed. Let the phone ring once. Hung up. She jumped when the pay phone chimed to life a second later.

She picked up the greasy receiver. "Le Sports Shop," she said, reading what was printed on the card.

Heard several clicks. Then a voice: "Go ahead."

She looked around. No one watching that she could pinpoint.

She related the information: the cargo's contents, her guess that it was hidden in caves, the rebels' illness, and the coordinates she'd written down.

"You're not our usual sports shop," the

voice said, sounding suspicious.

She knew she should hang up soon. But first, as her mother had told her to, she said, "Use Dany at Ouagadougou."

"That bad?" said another voice with what sounded like a Texan drawl. *A three-way call?*

"I'm just the messenger," Aimée said.

She hung up. Breathed in slowly. Head down, she mingled with a group headed toward a train, hikers wearing large back-packs. On the platform, she broke away from them and joined a family dragging rolling designer suitcases, blending in with them until she transitioned to another group, following the advice for losing sur-veillance in a public place that her grand-father had given on his tape. In this man-ner, she worked her way through the crowd to the front of the train. A regional train to Sens, thank God. She'd ride to the first stop, then catch a train returning.

Twenty-seven minutes later, she alighted at Melun. Strolled up the platform, looking in the reflective kiosk glass for a follower. None.

She crossed the platform and got into a train bound for Paris as the doors were clos-ing.

Her phone trilled. *René.* She took a seat and watched the dark patches of countryside around Melun under the night sky.

"Where are you, Aimée?" he asked.

"On the train. I'll be at the Gare de Lyon in twenty-six minutes. Tell me you and Saj got lucky with the SUNSAT satellite. We need all the proof we can get."

"Working on it. I just read tonight's *Le Soir.* Typical."

"What do you mean?"

"Sensational headlines but scant details about what's going on in Côte d'Ivoire. They're trying to sell newspapers without facts."

So the story was out.

"Didn't you and Saj notice the flights to Côte d'Ivoire every month on those old Soviet planes? I don't know who or why, but someone's assembling a dirty bomb of chemical weapons."

She let out a breath. "It's out of our hands now."

"And — let me guess — in the hands of Delorme, the old African spider?"

"A stars-and-stripes spider that's three hours away."

"*Merde,* not the CIA? Why get the Americans involved?"

"Thank Sydney. Turns out they've had a dog in this fight since she agreed to help Germaine and furnish funds to GBH's movement."

"You mean the Americans are playing behind the scenes, a third-party investor in GBH for the coup d'etat?"

"Got it in one, René. But do you think a spoiled dictator's son's better? This Ivoirian general Mgwanga with ties to Liberian death squads. That's who Delorme would appease now, to keep him and Côte d'Ivoire under his thumb later on."

The train sped past a series of lights; dimmed by fog, they blurred together into a charcoal snake.

"See you soon," said Aimée.

FRIDAY, 10 P.M.

On arriving back at the Gare de Lyon, Aimée bought a wool cap from the Cama-ïeu shop downstairs in the station, took the stairs to the Métro. Got off at the next stop and walked a few short blocks, then down rue Montgallet. Black leather jacket collar up and head down, she joined the late evening crowd. Buttery smells emanated from a closed boulangerie-pâtisserie doorway framed by nineteenth-century painted panels of wheat sheaves and a mill. The baker in a flour dusted apron, smoked outside. Starving, she smiled offering him ten francs and took a warm *pain au chocolat.*

At the shadowy corner across from Ming's shop, she licked the dark chocolate that had oozed between her fingers. Punched in René's number. The call rang through to voice mail. She tried Saj. Voice mail again.

Always glued to their computer screens,

those two.

Ming's shop shared a rear courtyard with the limestone-façaded apartments on the side passage. She went around to the back delivery entrance, hoping the code still worked.

But the tall blue doors were open. She wondered if he'd just taken a delivery. She slipped inside the courtyard and past the cars to Ming's back door. Unlocked.

Something was off. She knew Ming was security conscious with his stock.

The shop hummed with customers. Unseen, she climbed the back stairs.

Papers everywhere. Two open laptops. Computer parts filled the shelves.

Muffled knocking sounds came from the back of the storeroom. She kept to the walls alongside the shelves of equipment and pulled out her Swiss Army knife. René sat on the floor, ankles tied, arms flex-cuffed behind him. Her wide eyes fluttered over the computer paper stuffed in his mouth. She pulled the paper from his mouth and put her hand up in a *wait* sign before cutting the flexi-cuffs off him.

"Anyone else here?" she whispered.

René nodded rubbing his wrists. "Saj."

Behind cardboard boxes in the corner, she found Saj trussed to a file cabinet. Quickly,

374

she cut him loose and hurried back over to René.

"Who did this to you?" she asked.

"I didn't hear them with all the noise from the shop," said René, spitting and rubbing his mouth.

"Are you all right?"

He looked sheepish. "Fine. Before I knew it, I was bound and gagged from behind."

"They were wearing black balaclavas," said Saj. "Asked me where the maps were. I pointed to the laptops. Then they tied me up. Took them two minutes, tops."

René nodded again. "They copied the hard drives onto a memory card. Not a scratch on us. In and out. Professionals."

That bothered her.

"Sounds like the DGSE," she said. "Late to the party, as usual."

"*Bien sûr,* I'd already scrubbed the hard drives." Saj grinned. "And thrown a virus in for good measure."

"Nice touch," she said, returning his grin.

"*Alors,* since you called in *les cow-boys,* doubt you'll need this."

"Need what?"

Saj pulled a photo from a hidden pocket in his yoga pants. It was still sticky with printer ink.

"Courtesy of Lars at SUNSAT," he said.

"I, meaning you, owe him big-time."

In the satellite photo of a rocky outcrop in front of a dark cave opening, she recognized the distinctive shape of wood pallets covered by tarpaulins. The photo was time stamped earlier that day.

"By now they've moved the pallets into the cave," she said.

He pulled out another photo. "And this one."

A broken line of what appeared to be trucks.

"Who's this?" she asked.

"Not sure about specifics, but SUNSAT captured the view this morning. It's on the Liberian side, about forty Ks from the border."

Aimée rubbed her temple. Tried to think. "Could this mean the Ivoirian general Mgwanga somehow got the crash site's location and alerted a Liberian militia to it?"

Saj peered closer. "Anything's possible. Or maybe GBH's rebel group couldn't wait any longer and started hiding the cache for him. Or prepared to transport the pallets. Do any of them even know about the toxic contents?"

"Good question."

This put a new spin on everything. But to what end?

"The French military is six hours away from this crash site, the Americans three," said Aimée. "Nobody's clean. Nobody really knows what's happened — the Liberians or the Ivorians. Let's just hope it's not too late."

On the first photo, Saj pointed to a cluster of low buildings bordering scrub and forest. "Another place to hide the cache?"

René had stood, dusting off his trousers and jacket. "Haven't the rebels had the cargo for several weeks?"

She nodded. "But who knows if they could transport it across the border?"

The truck convoy could have been Liberian freedom fighters — something she doubted. Or the female soldiers pressed into gritty and dangerous work.

Mon Dieu. Her colleagues had been trussed up like pigs and the place sacked. And she felt more in the dark than ever. "We need to leave."

"True. We're already burned, no point in staying," said René, heading to the stairs. "I'll drive back and pick you up. I fitted out the Renault."

He'd already customized the car with controls for his height? Aimée tried not to smile. "So you do like the accomplice's car."

"It's wheels for now. Nothing replaces the DS."

Saj winked. "Not even the *classique* Mercedes you swooned over in that car mag last week?"

René made a face. "Come and help me with the equipment, Saj. I'm parked two blocks away."

Her phone bleeped. *Morbier.*

"Okay, I've got to take this," she said. "Meet you at the corner."

FRIDAY, 10:30 P.M.

In the courtyard, she looked around before she took the call. Dark shadows and parked cars, as before.

"Leduc, you've cracked open a hornet's nest." Morbier was fuming.

"Long time, stranger," she said. "Apparently, I'm my mother's daughter."

A brief pause. "Do you know what you've stepped into, Leduc?"

"What else could I do?" Upset, she paced in the courtyard.

"Eh? What do you mean?"

"Try returning my calls sometime, Morbier," she said, the cork off her pent-up anger. He'd lied to her, played on her sympathy. "You promised to help, remember?"

"*Tant pis,* Leduc, Lacenaire's team got reassigned before I could find out —"

She couldn't stop. "Why didn't you tell me you could walk?" She remembered those files at his place. Was he on some mission? "I saw you standing at the bar at le Baron Rouge. What's going on? Don't you trust me?"

"It's complicated —"

"But you said you'd retired — that you were paralyzed!" she interrupted. "All the time you've been lying to me?"

Only the thupt of a match lighting, an inhale and long drag on what she imagined was an unfiltered Gauloise.

"Smoking again, too." She felt the sting of betrayal.

"*Ça suffit, Leduc.* Don't blow my cover."

Her jaw dropped. "An undercover operation? At your age?"

"Like I said, Leduc, it's complicated," he said, irritated. "I'm old, but not in the grave."

Yet.

She wanted to kick him.

"Undercover for what?" she said, unable to contain her curiosity.

Another lengthy inhale. She wished it didn't make her long for a drag. *Just one.*

Worried, she tramped over the cobblestones to the courtyard entrance, one eye on the road watching for René in the Renault. Started walking on the glistening pavement toward the corner.

"High-up strings yanked the DGSE and Lacenaire off that case. Now I'm a peripheral part of it assisting in a sting operation, code name Crocodile."

She felt a sharp sting in her thigh. Grabbed her leg. Gasped and almost stumbled into the *mec* with an umbrella passing ahead of her.

The boulangerie's lights blurred, twirled. Noises blared. Her phone tumbled onto the cobbles. Her throat constricted. She panicked, sucking for air. Tried to breathe. Stupid, stupid, why hadn't she paid attention? The sensation of someone lifting her, the sliding of a truck door. Then everything went black.

FRIDAY, LATE EVENING

Humid air. Darkness. Her head pounded.

She gulped in air. At least she could breathe.

Recognized the smell of wet cardboard boxes. And a sooty, dusty odor.

The back of a warehouse? An attic?

A strong vibration shook her. She reached out and felt only air. She was tumbling, bumping into metal; everything was vibrating. Shaking, stronger and stronger, her body slamming against something cold. Pain shot through her chest, her ribs. Her head. She cried out.

Things went black again.

FRIDAY, LATE EVENING

She grew aware of voices. Her throat was as dry as sandpaper. *So thirsty.*

The voices were raised — an argument. But they came from somewhere else, distorted, as if coming through an air vent.

"She's got it. Then I'll get rid of . . ." A blurring echo.

Clanging. She strained to make out the words. "An Aladdin's cave." Booming echo. "Money for the taking . . ."

Metallic screeching that hurt her ears.

"Idiot. Everything's there." This sounded like another voice. "It's how you read the map."

It's how you read the map.

What did it mean?

"Lining up already. I'm taking orders . . ."

It was like listening in a wind tunnel.

"Do it my way." The short, staccato phrase bounced and echoed.

"Mine in the first place."

That voice. She knew that voice. Gérard Bjedje Hlili.

But could she be sure?

"I pay you . . . Take care of this."

Blasts of wind. "Liar. Where's my money?"

"Deal with her." Metallic whining. "Payment on completion, as we agreed."

An hour, two, more . . . how long had she been out?

Her hands scrabbled over the cold metal she was sprawled on. What felt like wire-mesh grating around her. Darkness.

Was she in a cage?

Her heart thudded.

She felt the mesh for a hole or a space. No door or entrance. Was this some shaft, a chute?

She tried to stand. Stumbled. Tried again. This time, cold air hit her face as she pulled herself up. Her hands explored in the darkness. The only light was a dim glow somewhere above her. Her fingers found a piece of rough metal about waist high that curved around the chute. She rubbed her fingers, smelled them — flakes of rust. And soot. Greasy soot.

Every so often, her seeking hands caught knoblike protrusions — rivets? Maybe she could use those to climb out.

Somehow.

She wedged her leg against the mesh, her back against the metal chute, and hoisted herself up. Then fell, scraping her ankle.

She'd have to leverage herself up the side bit by bit, starting with the lowest rivet, then using Martine's Louboutin heels to push herself up. Not that she could see anything. She closed her eyes. Concentrated, taking deep breaths. She could do this, couldn't she? She had to.

She hoisted herself up again, wedged one leg against the grating and swung the other, finding the first rivet with her heel. Quickly pushed off, straining her burning legs. She made it a few centimeters higher.

Keep going. She had to keep going. Focus.

And ignore the stabbing pain in her ribs; her scraped, burning ankle; the fear she'd fall back down. The dread of being stuck in that tiny space.

The cold air dried the perspiration on her temples and her upper lip as she pushed and worked her elbows and legs up the rusty chute. Slow progress. If only there were handles to grab, a way to pull herself up.

Her heel slipped. She jammed it back in place before she could plummet, elbow slamming against a rivet for purchase. She had to make it out.

The air got colder. Her elbow hit a metal

rung. Large enough that she could wrap her arm around it. There had to be more. Fighting the pain, her exhaustion, she hoisted herself up until she felt another rung and grabbed it.

Thank God.

Not over yet. She stuck her foot on the rusted rung and climbed, praying it would hold.

A band of light glowed under a black saucer. She stopped before she hit her head on the metal disk capping the chute. The cap was held up by struts, leaving an open space below it half the length of her arm. She peered through and saw lights below her. The Seine. Dark trees in a park ahead, rail lines on the right. She was above Bercy. The tunnels, warehouses, and loading docks.

Hunched, head down, she pushed up on the cap with her shoulder with every ounce of strength she had left. It was rusted tight. Now what? Could she fit through one of the openings?

Perched on the rung, she took off her leather jacket, pushed it to the outside, and tied the sleeves around one of the struts supporting the cap. If she could wiggle through the space under the cap, she could use the jacket sleeves to help steady her on her way down.

She hiked her hips up and got stuck. With all that damned bed rest, she'd gained a kilo.

More.

Merde.

Jostling and twisting her hips got her a few centimeters further. More twisting and her right hip scraped through. Painful brush burns from the metal stung her wrists. An updraft blew rust flakes into her eyes. *Don't stop.* Too much was at stake. Wiggling and scraping, somehow she got her left hip through the space. Climbed onto the metal cap.

Congratulations, Aimée. You've just climbed out of a furnace.

The city's lights spread below her, the Tour Eiffel a shimmering needle. It was a huge drop to a concrete lot. The fall would kill her. Going back down into the furnace would guarantee the same result.

What had she done? Thrown herself into danger, left her little daughter helpless. If she got herself killed, Chloé would be left without a mother.

Hadn't Aimée vowed she'd never leave her daughter as her own mother had left her? She couldn't let that happen. Wouldn't.

Think.

There was a building abutting the one she

387

was on, its broken-tiled roof only about two stories down. If she could slide down the outside of the old furnace stack she'd climbed out of, she had a chance of being able to get across the gap to the lower roof without falling to the ground.

Not a huge chance. But what else was there?

Then she saw the rungs along the outside of the furnace stack alongside a pipe. Of course, if they had them on the inside, they'd be on the exterior, too. She untied her jacket and slipped it back on.

The wind whipped painfully at her eyes. With one leg on the cap's roof, she stretched the other down along the stack, feeling for the top rung. Too bad her fear of heights was making her legs shake. Her arms tingled. *Don't look down.*

She felt for the highest rung with her foot. Got it. She held the pipe, hoping it wouldn't break, and lowered herself feet first, rung by rusty rung.

Halfway down, her vision blurred. The rungs wavered, and she felt a burning sensation behind her eyes. Those warning signs coming on. *Oh, God, not now.* She couldn't sit down, breathe, and *déstresser* while she was clinging for dear life to a pipe.

Dizzy, everything spinning, she lost her grip.

Where was she? Eyes closed, she shook as the wind went through her, her legs touching something jagged and cold. Then she remembered.

One deep breath after another. She slowly opened her eyes to the blurred edges of the furnace stack right above her. She'd landed in a declivity in the slanted tiled warehouse roof.

She stretched her arms and legs out . . . nothing broken. Closed her eyes and took more deep breaths. No more burning sensation. And when she opened her eyes this time, she saw a raised walkway with broken metal rails leading to the building's far side. And a door. Whether the walkway would hold under her weight, she would have to find out.

She got on her hands and knees and began progressing over the slippery walkway while trying to ignore the pain in her side. She reached the door that had a sign that indicated it was a staircase entrance and breathed in relief. She tried the handle. *Locked.*

No lockpick, no phone. Nothing. Just the memory card taped to the back of her Tintin watch.

Her heart skittered.

It was only a matter of time until they discovered she'd escaped. Started searching for her. Maybe they already had?

FRIDAY NIGHT

She crawled down the jagged tiled roof, her hands feeling the way as she kept low. In the yard below, she saw a Mercedes parked near an Eco-Emballages truck. Next to the truck was a dark-green crushing machine on a raised platform. A conveyer belt connected to the machine led to a dumpster loaded with truck tires. Part of Eco-Emballages' industrial rubber recycling operation in the old Bercy wine-depot warehouses. The yard was a long drop from the roof — easily two stories.

The yard was lit, and she could see figures moving. The crushing machine had started. Blades spun in the gaping open space of the top loader, fed with tires by the whirring conveyer belt. Grinding, metallic whines — the same sound she had heard in the furnace.

The crusher machine was probably meant to have been her next — and last — stop.

She shivered.

No time to think about that.

Only how to get down.

She watched two men in overalls check the conveyer-belt feed, then walk away to another building. Squatting at the edge of the roof, she calculated how far she'd need to jump to land straight on top of the semi's cab. She'd break an arm or a leg — if she was lucky. She didn't see any other choice. After stuffing the ankle boots into the pockets of *le smoking,* she slung her biker jacket sleeves around the iron post of an old billboard sign. Let them dangle in the wind.

She made herself stand on the broken tiles. Clinging to the jacket's sleeves, she backed up, step by step, as far as she could, then gave herself a small running start and leapt, swinging her body forward.

Her body slammed hard against the semi's roof. She was slipping and tried to grab the ridge of what she realized was the top of the cab. She couldn't help it — she screamed. Caught hold of a windshield wiper. As she held on desperately, it began to bend, then broke off in her hand.

MIDNIGHT

Aimée found herself splayed like an eagle on the semi's warm hood.

"What the . . . ?"

Gérard Hlili was standing with Jean-Christophe, the former president's son, on a loading dock under the old warehouse eaves. Then they were running toward the semi. Was Jean-Christophe's voice the other one she'd heard in the furnace?

Her mind struggled to make sense of this. Germaine had died to help Hlili, and Aimée's mother had urged her to do the right thing and get him the documents. But unless she was mistaken about what she'd heard in the furnace . . .

"It's her," Hlili said.

The gun in Hlili's raised hand decided for her. She scrambled off the hood and dropped onto the running board of the rumbling semi. The engine was on. She pulled open the passenger door, got in, and climbed over the gearbox, rushing to hit the lock on the driver door.

She had to do something — couldn't let herself be trapped in there. In front of her was a lit-up control panel with buttons and levers. *Merde.* She'd never driven a freight truck.

She hit one button, then another, and heard grinding. The cab tilted. She pressed more buttons, pulled a handle. Thunks and whines . . .

A shot splintered the side mirror. She threw herself down across the seat as shots peppered the driver's-side window and door. Shaking, she scooted down into the well by the pedals and pushed down the clutch with one hand, reaching for the gearshift with the other. Strained to push the gear into first, keeping pressure on the clutch pedal.

The truck jolted and sputtered. The engine died.

The damn emergency brake was on.

As she reached for the brake, strong hands gripped her arm, and she was yanked up and across the seat. Someone had reached in through the shattered driver's side door window. She kicked, trying to free herself as she was hauled straight up. But then her feet were in the air, her body scraping through the broken window out into the night air and deafening noise.

"Where is it?" Hlili yelled in her ear. They stood on the crusher's vibrating platform adjacent to the truck. He'd hooked his arm around part of the framework holding the conveyer belt to maintain his balance. Pointed the gun at her head.

"The plane's cargo's toxic, Gérard. Chemical weapons. It's going to kill your people."

If she'd expected surprise, it didn't show on his face.

"It's sarin." She gasped, catching her breath. "Don't you understand? You're supposed to be fighting for them, but it's ordinary people who will die."

"It's a tool for our revolution!" he shouted over the metallic grinding whine. "It's only a small part of a bigger picture."

He knew. Didn't care if innocent people died hideous deaths. They were only a means to an end.

"Call yourself a visionary, a change maker?" she said. "You're a terrorist."

He shoved her, shaking, still trying to keep balanced on the platform. The blades of the crusher below chomped like angry teeth in the glow of the warehouse yard lights. "Give everything to me now. Including the money."

The conveyer belt's steady whirr moved the tires and dropped them into the crusher with ear-blasting crunches.

Sickened, she reached for her watch. Unbuckled the leather strap, drenched in sweat. *Worthless to him now.*

He cocked the pistol. "Trying something?"

"I don't think so." She pulled the memory card off her wrist. "Here it is."

He looked at the small piece of plastic and scoffed.

"Gérard, I do computer security. What do I need with old papers? I've got chips and bytes."

"Liar."

"Anyway, it's all useless to you now!" she yelled above the noise. "Surveillance planes have already found the sites."

"Not all of them," said Jean-Christophe, who'd climbed onto the platform. He was still in his safari outfit. "Let me handle her."

"You? What haven't you screwed up?" Hlili was yelling. "It was simple. So simple until you hired the legionnaire, that idiot."

Her heart thumped. Jean-Christophe was in cahoots with GBH. They'd kidnapped her together.

"Why are you working with him?" She had to yell to be heard above the relentless grinding. "Those stockpiled chemical weapons in the caves mean disaster."

"Silly girl," said Jean-Christophe, gravelly voice yelling back over the chomping.

"Silly?" she replied. "By now, the CIA's taken over the stash with the French military hot on their heels. You've lost your assets."

"Don't be so sure of that," said Jean-Christophe.

Hlili pointed the gun at him. "You tried to double-cross me all along!" he screamed. "You're only in this for the money."

"And you're not, Hlili?" Jean-Christophe asked.

"My people, the operation, the planning, the work . . . I did it all. You jumped in when you smelled the money."

"You needed me, Hlili!" Jean-Christophe shouted, his eyes on Hlili's gun. "Never would've gotten anything off the ground without me and my connections."

"If you're hiding anything, my rebels will tear you apart."

Co-conspirators no more, it seemed. *Think fast. Keep them talking.*

"Shut up," Jean-Christophe said to Hlili. Then he turned to her. "Hand it over," he said, his eyes flicking from the memory card in her hand to the pistol.

"Why?" she asked. "Everything's already been found."

"Let me worry about that," said Jean-Christophe.

Did he plan to slide away with the help of that spider, Delorme? Or the Liberians?

She extended her shaking hand — and drew it back. "Wait. Who's the Crocodile?"

"Who do you think?" With a swipe of his arm, Jean-Christophe whacked Hlili aside. A scream as Hlili slipped and his arm came loose from the framework pole. He was dumped onto the churning blades in the crusher along with the tires. She heard what seemed like minutes of screaming amid the grinding and cracking bone. Saw a cloud of bloody mist. The pistol had clattered to the platform. Jean-Christophe grabbed it.

She backed up. But there was nowhere to go. Terror and bile rose in her throat.

"Want to end up like him?" Jean-Christophe's slitted eyes bore into hers.

No honor, as the cliché went, among thieves.

"You really want this?" she said, holding out the memory card. "Still?"

His hand grabbed at it, and she threw it into the crusher.

"Go get it," she said.

His eyes followed the card. In that brief second of inattention, she batted the pistol out of his hand into the crusher.

"You idiot!" he shouted.

He lunged at her. But she ducked, clutching the framework for support, and kicked out. He tripped and struggled up, his right arm swinging. With her last bit of strength, she shoved him off the platform. A yell as he flew headfirst onto the concrete.

She had never wanted to get involved. But somehow, she'd ended up attacking one man and watching another ground alive. All because her mother's cloudy morals had encouraged her to do the right thing. But had she done right by Germaine?

SATURDAY, 12:30 A.M.

With wobbling legs, she climbed down and found an unconscious Jean-Christophe lying on the cracked concrete, a leg at the wrong angle, arms akimbo. Felt for a pulse in his carotid artery. *Faint, but beating.*

Made herself rifle through his pockets. Found his car keys and cell phone. The entire time, the roar and churning of the crusher pounded in her ears.

She became aware of a man by the dumpster, recognized him. Baptiste, the caretaker. She took a few steps toward him and saw tears streaming down his cheeks.

"You?" she said. "I thought you were a religious man. You were going to let all those people suffer and die. But why? The money?"

"Don't be stupid. Gérard had a vision for Côte d'Ivoire," said Baptiste, his lip quivering. "His plans for education, a water system, a modern infrastructure were bril-

400

liant. Forward thinking. He couldn't do it alone."

Hlili had brainwashed the old fool with his charisma, his grand plans, as he had Germaine and her brother, the DGSE, and the CIA. Once Hlili had gotten control, the cause he'd touted wouldn't have mattered.

Baptiste's shoulders slumped. "Do you know what you've done?"

She stood up to him. "The right thing." Locked eyes with him. "You should try it yourself."

He roared, raising an Eco-Emballages shovel smeared with garbage and swinging it at her. She dodged the swing easily, and the old man fell to his knees, sobbing.

Leaving the old man on the ground near Jean-Christophe's prone body, she climbed into the Mercedes, switched on the ignition, and got the hell out of there.

She drove to Port de Bercy and got out, leaving the car door open. Let her ears accustom themselves to the almost quiet of the Seine. She breathed in the fresh air, the algae scents, the damp, until her nerves steadied.

Barefoot, she walked down a deserted ramp. Sat down, letting her legs dangle over the water. A dark moored boat bobbed in the wake of a blue-lit *bateau mouche*.

Laughter and conversation drifted over the water.

Hollowness filled her. *All these lives, this mess, and for what?*

But regret was a luxury, as her mother had said. No time for that. Time for the surviving instigators to pay.

She slipped on her boots and pulled out Jean-Christophe's cell phone. Hit the number for SAMU — emergency — gave the Bercy warehouse location, and hung up.

Next, she punched in Morbier's number.

"*Allô,* who's this?" he said.

"By Crocodile, did you mean Jean-Christophe?"

"Leduc? Whose number is this? You all right?"

"He's not."

Pause. "Alive?"

"For now. You'd better alert whoever you trust to get over to the Bercy wine-depot warehouses." Wavelets lapped, whisper-like, against the quai. "Later, you're going to tell me about your undercover job. You owe me, Morbier."

She hung up.

Looked down at the third-to-last number called on Jean-Christophe's speed dial. Hit call.

"All taken care of, Jean-Christophe?"

answered a familiar voice.

So the spider was in on this, too.

SATURDAY, 1 A.M.

"Almost taken care of, Delorme," she said. "But call me disappointed."

A nanosecond elapsed. A clearing of the throat before he responded. "Why, *mademoiselle*?"

He was quick, the spider.

"Jean-Christophe will turn himself in, if he plays it smart. That's after he recovers consciousness, if he gets to the hospital in time. Admits he was behind this" — she took a deep breath — "and made a mess of things."

A long silence.

"Ah, Aimée, he's spoiled, like all the sons of great men. Now he's failed. *Tant pis.* We were only doing what was needed to ensure a stable country."

"Deadly toxic gas isn't what I call stability."

Not in General Mgwanga's hands, or those of GBH or Jean-Christophe, the

404

Crocodile. It was a weapon. Power.

"Remember my offer? You have a skill set I admire, Aimée. I'm open to negotiation," said Delorme. "Your grandfather was."

Was it true? Her lip trembled.

"I found everything myself," she said. "No help from you."

"Keep the money," he said. "We'll work it out. There's a post in my office perfect for someone with your skills."

The spider certainly knew how to survive.

"Work it out?" She thought for a moment. "You'll be getting a call, Delorme. Give the caller all the details of what happened; answer everything they ask you. Then, if I hear back from them, we'll do business."

"*Bien sûr.* Good to know that you, like your grandfather, understand how things work."

She hung up.

She didn't think so.

She punched in Martine's number next.

"*Oui?*"

"It's Aimée."

"Lost your phone?"

And her bag, and everything in it.

"Is Chloé okay?" Aimée asked.

"Fine. She loved my pesto linguine. Honestly, you've got to expand her palate."

Relief flooded her. "Listen, write this

down. I'll give you a phone number, and you have to do exactly as I tell you, okay? Please."

"So mysterious. Why? Aren't you coming home? I've got extra bowls of linguine."

"Please, make this call first. Record the conversation. Then you'll know what to do."

"I don't like this."

"You like a scoop, don't you?"

"Hold on." Scuffling noises. "Okay."

"See if you can get your friend at the Africa desk of Agence France-Presse on the line beforehand, too. He'll owe you big-time. Ready?"

SATURDAY, 1:30 A.M.

Jean-Christophe's Mercedes responded with a powerful velvet purr as she accelerated, gliding along the quai. She could get used to this. Maybe René could, too.

"Where are you, René?" she asked when he picked up his phone.

"Aimée? I could ask you the same thing. I've been calling. What happened? We pulled up at the store, and —"

"Long story. Tell me where you are. I'll pick you up."

René and Saj sat outside a crowded bar on rue du Faubourg Saint-Antoine. She honked. Blinked the headlights until she had René's attention.

She powered down the window as he approached the car. "Care for a lift?"

"Nice ride. Government plates, too. You going to tell us about it?"

"Get in."

"I parked the Renault —"

"Leave it. *Desolée,* this isn't a *classique* Mercedes, but I hope you'll like it better than that Renault."

René blinked. "A Mercedes E-Class?"

"For you, René, the best or nothing."

"Now you're stealing cars?" His voice cracked.

"I'm hungry. Let's go have some linguine."

She took off down rue du Faubourg Saint-Antoine as soon as Saj had shut the door. He pulled a clump of sage from his Madras bag and lit it. "I feel like we could use a cleansing here. A purification."

For once, she agreed.

SATURDAY, NOON

The darkness moved and woke her. There was something wet all over her face. She shuddered. Was she back in the furnace? Trapped?

A bright light hit her eyes. She sat up in terror.

Chloé had crawled on top of her, drooling mouth and all. Martine had opened the curtains on to the garden. Aimée hugged a sweet-smelling Chloé, smothered her with kisses, and fell back in relief.

Newspapers were spread across the duvet. Martine pointed to a steaming demitasse of espresso by the bed. "Might want to fortify yourself."

"Merci." She reached for the espresso, her eyes catching on the headline in a special edition of *Libération:* MINISTRY DENIES LINKS TO CÔTE D'IVOIRE SCANDAL. Under it: AMERICAN RECONNAISSANCE PLANES RECOVER CHEMICAL WEAPONS CACHE AL-

LEGEDLY INVOLVING FORMER PRESIDENT'S SON. Big, juicy articles with Delorme's and Jean-Christophe's names front and center.

"Brilliant, Martine." Aimée grinned. "So Delorme admitted it?"

"*Pas du tout.* Denied everything." Martine grinned back. "But with your info, my article raises enough allegations, hints at deep corruption, blah, blah, blah, et cetera, that the rumor mill's predicting he'll retire to avoid serious and embarrassing charges."

Another day at the office. Case closed. And yet, poor Germaine. Aimée sighed and pushed the thought aside.

"Sydney called and I said you'd call back," said Martine.

Finally.

"You're late," Martine said. "René's waiting downstairs to give you a ride. In a nice car, for once."

"A ride where?"

"The biggest weekend tech conference this side of the Seine. Remember?"

Another one?

"Seems you're the keynote speaker this afternoon."

Merde. She hadn't prepared. What would she wear?

"Oh, and someone is here to see you."

"Who?"

"Quite awkward. Too much testosterone."

She could hear raised voices coming from the kitchen. Gianni and Melac.

What was he still doing there? It was just supposed to be a quick pickup, a day with his daughter.

The door opened, bringing a woody fragrance of roses followed by Melac's musky scent.

Melac swooped up a gurgling Chloé and sat down by Aimée on the bed. His brow furrowed in concern above those grey-blue eyes so much like his daughter's. Martine snatched the roses off the bed before Chloé could fist the petals into her mouth.

"Are you all right, Aimée?" said Melac.

"Ask me after I finish this espresso." She yawned and reached for a robe that was lying on the pillow. "I need to get dressed."

"Why didn't you tell me?" He sounded hurt. Rare for Melac.

"It got complicated. Look, I did try . . ."

Melac leaned closer. His hand gripping her shoulder. That warm hand.

"You put Chloé in danger, disappeared." His voice lowered, as if he was struggling with anger. Or was it something else? "You're just like your mother."

Not this again. "This happened *because* of my mother. And I'm sorry; I never meant

411

Chloé to be involved. That's why we're hiding at Martine's."

"I'm her father."

Then act like one, she almost said. But she was running late. It wasn't the time to be hard on him or to fight. Chloé's diaper smelled less than fragrant.

Martine stood back at the door, wiggling her finger with the diamond ring and pointing to Melac. Taking a last sip of espresso, Aimée glanced down at Melac's other hand. The hand stroking Chloé's cheek.

"You need to decide, Aimée," Melac was saying, his right hand still resting on her shoulder.

Then it registered. No rose-gold serpent ring on his fourth finger.

"About us," he said.

She choked on her espresso. "Raising Chloé, you mean?"

"Us as a family. Us, as in you and me."

Her jaw dropped. Her heart pounded so hard she thought it would jump out of her chest. For a moment, all she wanted was for his arms to enfold her, to get lost in his smell.

But he'd stood, Chloé on his hip, and walked to the door by Martine. "Think about it, Aimée."

Gone. He was good at that. The master of

quick exits. Returns, not so much.

Aimée jumped out of bed. Grabbed a silk blouse from a hanger in Martine's armoire.

"Where did that come from?" Aimée said. "You think he's changed?"

Martine shrugged. "You're asking me?"

"What do I do, Martine?"

Martine pointed to her heart. "Ask this."

ACKNOWLEDGMENTS

A big two-decades-long thanks to the booksellers at independent bookstores who have supported Aimée and this series. To the libraries and savvy librarians across the country, thank you. In writing this story, I owe so many for sharing their expertise, their help, and their generosity. Above and beyond to indefatigable Terri Haddix MD, Senior Forensic Pathologist Technical Director Forensic Analytical Crime Lab; Elise Munoz; Carla Chemouni-Bach; Cathy Etile; toujours Anne-Françoise; Madame Gerbault, for showing me her Bel-Air and hospitality again and again; Isabelle and Andi Wajda; Benoît Pastisson, historian; Commissaire Rocher, *chef du* SAIP, head of the tenth district investigation unit in Paris; Commandant Department de Police Judiciare Michel Villefaux. Immense gratitude to Raymond Debelle, former investigator for the UN Security Council Sanctions

Committee on the Cote d'Ivoire; Nicolas Sebire of UNICEF; idea man Arnaud Baleste; former Brigade Criminelle Marie Pierre at *la Cours de cassation;* Jean-Claude Mulés, former Brigade Criminelle; always Docteur Christian de Briere, *expert agréé par la Cour de cassation;* Naftali Skrobek *et* Lidia; Gilles Thomas; and Gilles Fouqué. Big *merci*s to Aurelie; Ingrid; Jean Satzer, my alpha and beta; Libby Fischer Hellmann, cohort in crime; Katie Herman; James N. Frey, the *plotmeister;* dear Katherine Fausset and the Curtis Brown team; my Soho family who make this all come together: Rachel; Amara; Janine; Rudy; Paul; Bronwen, our amazing publisher; and my patient, brilliant editor, Juliet. Nothing would happen without Jun or my son, Tate.

ABOUT THE AUTHOR

Cara Black was born in Chicago, Illinois, on November 14, 1951. She was educated at Cañada College in California, Sophia University in Yotsuya, Tokyo, in Japan, and finished her degree at San Francisco State University with a BA and an MA in education. She has worked as a preschool teacher and as director of a preschool.

Black is a bestselling American mystery writer. She is best known for her Aimée Leduc mystery novels featuring a female Paris-based private investigator.